About the Author

Martin Morton lives mostly in the Adriatic on a boat.

The Water's Edge

Martin Morton

The Water's Edge

Chimera

CHIMERA PAPERBACK

© Copyright 2019
Martin Morton

A CIP catalogue record for this title is available from the
British Library.

ISBN: 978 1 903136 65 2

Chimera is an imprint of Pegasus Elliot MacKenzie
Publishers Ltd.
www.pegasuspublishers.com

First Published in 2019

Chimera
Sheraton House Castle Park
Cambridge England

Printed & Bound in Great Britain

1

'Not what I was expecting.'

'What were you expecting?'

'Something dramatic, but not this. I thought you might be leaving, going somewhere else.'

'Leaving? Me? Giving all this up?'

She waited, it felt like he was leaving a pause.

'Why would I do that?'

'It was just an impression I had.' There was another pause.

'I get spooked sometimes when you seem to know what I'm thinking better than I do. It had been on my mind. I didn't know what was coming next and I couldn't see a way forward – but now they've come up with this. What do you think?'

'Well, it's always excited you, hasn't it? You seem to like being out there. You've been there enough. Where would you live?'

'I haven't said yes yet. And if I do, I can think about that when I talk to them. I have said no once before. But nowadays you're allowed to talk to family and think about things.'

'And what does the family think?'

Claudia knew he wouldn't answer but she expected evasion, not another, longer silence.

'I don't know, I haven't said anything yet. You're the first person I've spoken to – and obviously you won't say anything about it.'

She could picture him smiling as he was saying that. Of course, she wouldn't. She never did, and she knew he trusted her completely. After all, there had been many late-night, for him, conversations from the Far East where the most scandalous things were said by a man who had clearly been enjoying his evening and the saké. And she sometimes wondered if he had been enjoying more than that. There were stories – but not from people who would really have known.

'Of course, I won't.'

'Listen, I'd like to talk more about it. I'm back in tomorrow afternoon, could you stop a bit late?'

She stopped herself asking if he wouldn't want to get home and talk. She'd guessed enough about how he would put that off.

'Yes, I've nothing planned.'

'Good, I won't keep you that long. Thinking about it, it wouldn't be a bad idea to meet offsite. Can we do that discreetly?'

She laughed. 'Not really, even I'm known by too many people – and too many recognize you that you're not even aware of. Let me think about it.'

'OK, gotta go. Talk tomorrow.'

She emailed him an idea. Should she book a meeting room in the local hotel they often used? Being seen anywhere informal would have provoked gossip and speculation over and above what would arise when rumours began to circulate about his moving.

Next morning one of the VPs asked, 'Where's he going then?'

'Who?'

He smiled 'Jack, of course.' She was on her guard already. Maybe the story was leaking out.

He had emailed back: *maybe we'll just stay in the office, it's not exactly unusual.* She felt a twinge of disappointment – that they couldn't speak so freely? Or that they wouldn't meet elsewhere?

He had said hello when he came in but then lost himself in phone calls and meetings, even wandering off around the office for an hour for a series of apparently random conversations. It was his way.

It was Friday, and the office was emptying early but she had plenty to catch up on. She was almost shocked when the cup of coffee appeared beside her – with earphones on she had heard nothing as he approached. She stopped and pulled the phones out.

He smiled. 'When you're ready.'

'I'm ready.' She followed him to the glass office behind his desk.

'Have you made up your mind?' she asked before they even sat down.

'I haven't said yes.'

'But you're going to.'

'I'm tempted. I like it out there and it solves some problems.'

They looked in each other's eyes.

'And home? Have you talked it through?'

'If you can call 'I suppose you'll do what you want' talking it through, then yes. We had a brief phone call.'

'She's not going with you?'

'I maybe should have said more to you before. You know I've been at the flat more often lately, well, I've been there on my own. She stays in the house. The boys know.'

'About the job, the move?'

'No, no, not that. They know we find it easier to live apart and just get together for family things. Had you guessed?'

'There's been talk.'

'Well, there's always that, isn't there? Your coven meets round its cauldron.'

He smiled. She knew he was joking. There were circles of gossip, but she was always very careful. She knew a lot but would only let out what didn't really matter, just to keep her place in the ring. The others sometimes found out interesting things and it was important to be aware of what was going on, she told herself.

'I sometimes wonder where they get these stories from. My life isn't that interesting.'

'Maybe it will be now.'

'Hah. You think I travel too much already. This is going to be all over Asia and ten weeks in the US. That doesn't leave much time for interesting.'

'You need to be careful. The last two years weren't easy. You said so yourself.'

He'd said many things in the phone calls, never whingeing but letting her know where some of the stresses lay, serious and outrageous by turns. And she'd guessed at other stresses he hadn't discussed, one of which he had just confirmed.

'And where will you base yourself?'

'Probably Singapore, I think. I'll make my mind up after I've been around and met the people. China's most important but I don't want to sit on the guy's shoulder there, he's doing a good job and it might look like a demotion if I get too close.'

'Would you go back to Tokyo?'

'I'd be tempted but it's a bit on the edge of things. I'll mull it over.'

'I shall miss you.' It slipped out. She hoped it had sounded light-hearted.

He was silent, looking at her.

'Not as much as you think.'

She looked quizzically at him.

'I have told you sometimes, don't say I haven't, how much the phone calls have meant to me.'

She smiled slowly. 'Yes, you've mentioned it.'

He paused again, clearly thinking about how much to say. 'Many times, you've been the only one I could really talk to, to laugh and let off steam and to be wildly indiscreet. The VPs and staff all have their own agendas and it's not always the common good.'

She'd guessed this was true, but it felt good to hear him say it.

'It's always fun to listen.'

'Even when I'm pissed?

'Especially when you're pissed.'

'Well, you've saved me many times there. That's why I'm saying you won't miss me so much. I hope you won't mind if I keep calling. You're a wonderful sounding-board, you get things, other people seem quite stupid.'

'But I don't know the business, or the region.'

'It's just the business, it's pretty similar everywhere, and people are people. OK you won't know many of them, but I'll have fun describing them to you.'

'I'm sure I'll have fun listening,' she said smiling.

'Listen' – he looked suddenly awkward – 'I'll probably plan a trip for the week after next. Could we do dinner together next week? I'd like to chat more about it and say thank you properly.'

'Of course, we could,' she said, 'I don't need to check my diary. But you don't want to meet round here, do you?'

'No, definitely not, could you come into town?'

'I could manage that.'

'I'll fix it,' he said decisively then stood up. Typical, meeting ended, she thought. But, as she stood up, he hugged her. Rather too long for an office hug, but she was relieved to see when she left the room that the place was empty.

2

She took the car, she told herself, because it meant she wouldn't drink much.

She took the car, she told herself, because she wouldn't have to catch a train. Late night trains have drunks on them. And the last was at eleven thirty. She took the car because she could be as late as she wanted. She knew she wasn't being honest with herself, she would have to 'explain' herself anyway if Dave wasn't comatose, but she didn't know what the truth was anyway.

She had a unique relationship with this man, and he'd said as much – the only one he could talk to. But she guessed she knew him well enough to know him capable of saying as much to others. So, this would be a dinner and a chat and a thank you – that was nice, he wasn't often that thoughtful.

She was fairly punctual, even though the traffic wasn't easy to judge, and he'd organized a parking space at his flat.

She'd researched the flat, she was nosey, slightly small but good location, but the view when she arrived was still stunning: the river going north between parliament and the Eye. High enough to see the city, not so high as to lose the river. He let her take it in while he brought drinks.

'Quite impressive,' she said, staying as cool as she could.

'I like it a lot. It wasn't meant to be a bachelor pad, but it serves very well.'

'And have you been being a bachelor?'

He laughed. 'I've told you about those stories. This is a well-appointed monastic cell.'

She smiled. 'And I'm supposed to believe you.'

He looked serious suddenly as he handed her the champagne. 'Actually, you should. I'm pretty sure I'm more honest with you than I am with anyone. I haven't had to hide anything from you and I'm not going to start now.'

'So, I know everything?'

He smiled. 'No, of course not, but you know everything you've asked about.'

'So, if I'd asked about a relationship inside the business?'

'Are you asking me? I don't think I would have said while it was going on, but you and I weren't that close then and I'd have worried about why you wanted to know and how much I could trust you.'

'That's fair. And no, I'm not asking you now, it's not my business.'

And then they talked about the flat. He showed her round. Only two bedrooms, one converted to a TV room with a sofa bed, the main bedroom well-proportioned and traditionally decorated.

They were looking out at the river, drinks in hand. 'It's lovely. Kind of elegant but cosy.'

'I think that's well put, that's what I was striving for anyway,' he said. 'Are you ready?'

She'd read about Square. It was part of her job to stay in touch. She knew it was priced for only special occasions, so she was surprised and very pleased when he told her where they were going.

She wondered whether the large open room would permit a conversation which she expected to be quite personal but the corner table with empty tables either side, at least this early in the evening, helped her relax.

'You've made your mind up, haven't you?'

He laughed gently. 'Yes, I'm going.'

'I'm glad.'

'Oh. Not necessarily what I was expecting. Why?'

'I think you've done enough where you are and, I don't know, things seemed to be getting to you. You still seem to have plenty of energy but maybe you need a different challenge? Sorry, awful cliché. I know you don't like them.'

'Amen to the above. Shall I talk about it?'

'I wish you would. If we're going to carry on

talking, the more I understand, the better.'

'We are going to carry on talking, please.' And he talked. The food came, it was exquisite, beautifully presented and every course rich in distinctive flavours and textures. The tables beside them filled, one party included two beautiful young women who he scarcely seemed to notice. The other party included two loud Americans which, while irritating, helped mask their own conversation which was captivating her.

She had guessed much: home had been difficult for a long time; he hadn't always been a faithful husband; work had been stressful but intensely rewarding and he loved the businesses but was maybe running out of inspiration. But he was franker than she'd expected: a work relationship had complicated things, it had been ill-judged, professionally and personally and, although he now had some distance from it, this move would clear that more completely.

'And I'm excited by it. You know I love being out there. You can do business, people engage with the idea that you're going to do things. There's so much defensiveness and even antagonism about ideas and change in the West. I'm slowly feeling energised.'

The dessert came. 'My God, have I been talking that long?'

'Well, I kept asking you questions to keep you going.'

'Ah, so it is your fault.' They laughed. 'But I never talk about myself like that.'

She thought a moment. That was true. Even in the Far East phone calls there had been lots of self-deprecation but little real revelation.

'And anyway, I wanted to find out more about you.'

There was a pause.

'I'm sorry, that was totally fucking unsubtle. I got carried away with myself, it's wrong to treat you as a captive audience. And I am intrigued. You're much too good for what you do. You're so good we can't place you properly. Every year someone from HR comes to talk to me, it's someone different each year, and I tell them you're wonderful and you could do so much more, and they nod and make notes, and nothing happens. And I am, disgracefully, totally grateful that nothing does. But lots of what you do must bore you, doesn't it?'

'It serves a purpose. It's good hours and regular money and bits of it are very entertaining.' She smiled and raised her glass to him – and then realized they were into their second bottle. He had become his garrulous, social self but she had been drinking too. She put her glass down without drinking.

'I've thought of that.'

'Thought of what?' she asked, somewhat agitated.

'You obviously have to be driven home.'

'I'm listening.'

'Well, your car won't start. You called RAC and, when they finally come, they can't fix it, so you have to leave it with them and get a car home.'

'But I'll have to come back for it.'

'Ah, the plan unfolds.'

'What plan?'

'There is no plan.' He stopped. 'Well, strictly speaking that's true, it's not a plan but I am plotting to get you for myself for a while. Stay and talk, I've learned nothing more than I knew before. You're a brilliant listener but I want to know more about you.'

'Why?' That was a little provocative – she had been drinking.

'Am I going to have to say it? You've become very important to me. But that's not what keeps you where you are. What are you doing? What's next?'

Now she took a drink. Did that mean, she thought, that she would be staying longer?

'I guess I have no happier a marriage than you do.' She caught his small nod.

'I'd heard.'

'You'd heard?'

'Come on, I believe in gossip and you know I'm nosey. And my only word of complaint about you, ever, is that you're not indiscreet enough.' He smiled.

And she talked. About the kids, about him at home, about the job.

'And that's been enough for you?'

'There's been no time for anything else – even if I had felt inclined.'

'You've been asked?'

Her shoulders slumped. 'Of course. Yours is not a noble gender. And it's nothing like as tempting as it imagines itself to be. I've seen too many consequences and it so seldom turns out right.'

He looked glum and nodded.

'Did you think it was going to turn out right? Your affair at work?'

'It sort of has. We didn't have big expectations. We needed something and I think we got it. But it would have been better to have been clear about that at the start.'

'And what did you need? What did you expect?' She realized she'd put this a little aggressively, even before she sensed his reaction.

'I'd like to talk to you more about that, honestly I would. But I can't help thinking before I respond that you're asking the question at least as much about your life as you are about mine.'

There was silence. Coffee came.

'Do you want to get the bill?' He was right. Had she gone too far?

'I do, but only if you're going to sit and listen to my answer back at the flat.' He took her hand and squeezed it gently.

'OK,' she said without looking at him.

They sat on the sofa looking at the river and the lights of the city. He put his arm around her shoulder and pulled her gently to him. She snuggled in but stopped herself putting her arms around his waist.

'You were going to talk to me about relationships at work and their dangers.'

'I was. I am. It wasn't my first.' She stiffened slightly but, in truth, she was not surprised. 'Are you going to tell me about yours?'

'That's easy. There aren't any.'

'Are you going to tell me about how and when you met your current man?'

She bristled and made to pull away, but he held her firmly. 'That wasn't the same thing.' Although she had still been married when that started.

'It never is, is it? You watch all these other people doing something that's always unique for them in that moment, in that situation.'

'And was it unique for you?' She knew she'd put that rather pointedly.

'I will answer, but I'll preface it by saying that you're asking the question partly for yourself and how you might be in that situation.' This was true. She relaxed into him.

'You have two people living difficult lives,

unappreciated at home, together alone in a foreign place looking for…'

'Sex,' she said, partly meaning to tease but partly to pose the question to herself. She had been aware for a long time how attracted she was to this man, but she'd never tried flirting with him. But he wasn't yet ready to abandon the serious tone.

'Well, I honestly think there's more, but maybe that's just it.'

She sat up. 'I'm sorry. That was wrong of me. Please go on.'

'You're not wrong, obviously, but I don't think that was the main thought. You just connect and think you can do things for each other. But, staying honest, it helps if sex is a possibility.'

He pulled her to him again. This time she put her arm around his waist.

'Does that say anything about us?'

He rubbed her arm tenderly. 'I think it might do.' He kissed her forehead. 'But we don't have to rush anything.'

'You're leaving next week for the other side of the world and I'll hardly see you again and we don't have to rush?'

'I'd like nothing more than to take you to the bedroom and make love to you right now but, fortunately, your car is about to arrive, and you can think about things for a couple of days.'

'What happens then?'

'You come here on Saturday to pick your car up – and spend the day in bed with me.'

She was somehow shocked but not at all surprised and she was very aware that her body was already impatient.

'I'll-I'll have to check at home. I don't know what everyone is doing.'

They were standing. He put his arms around her. He kissed her. She knew he wanted her.

'I'll be here. You have some thinking to do. Just know that I want you.'

That thought stayed with her all the way home.

3

And it stayed with her through the next two days. She saw him in the office in between many meetings. She tried not to think about dinner and even less about Saturday, but her body kept reminding her. Occasionally she would lie to herself and tell herself she would take her son with her but in every quiet moment she knew she wanted him, whatever would happen next. And she was almost proud of herself for not thinking beyond Saturday.

How she looked was never commented on at home so how she dressed that morning was only about how she would appear to him. It was rare to give so much thought to underwear – or to study herself in it as she did that morning.

The grunt caught her by surprise: 'Thought you were going to pick up a car.'

'It's in town, I might as well go shopping while I'm there.'

'That's your shopping dress?'

'It is for London.'

The exchange, and the typical pall that such exchanges always left – always trivial, always painful –

left her that morning very quickly. She sat in a sunny window in the train. It would be sunny on the river. The city would look wonderful from the flat. Would he get lunch, or would they go out? Would he think about lunch? She smiled. He was only a man. He was probably thinking much more about what she was avoiding thinking about. But her body was thinking, she was aware of that.

The concierge guided her to the lift. 'He's expecting you, ma'am.' And pressed 4 for her.

He was waiting at the open door when she came out of the lift.

He smiled. 'Wow, you look gorgeous.'

Had she overdone it? Was she being obvious? He of course was casually dressed but in a smart shirt and chinos, as much as you could expect for at home.

He closed the door and wrapped his arms around her. 'Thank you for coming.'

'I had to get my car,' she said defensively.

'Of course, you did.' He stepped back, turned her round by her shoulders and guided her to the living room.

The table was laid, she noticed.

'We're eating in?'

'Yes, I've got some stuff together but there's no rush is there? It's barely twelve. Just about time for bubbles.'

'Oh, I should be careful. I don't think the excuse will work twice. Do you often come up with excuses like that?'

'I'm afraid excuses is my only area of creativity. I don't have your brain, always buzzing with fresh ideas.'

'I'm not.'

'You most certainly are, madam. It's one of the many attributes that fascinates me.'

'Other attributes?' She took the glass from him.

'Well you've caught me looking at your cleavage.'

'True, but you look at everybody's cleavage.' This was true but not unique to him, she admitted to herself.

'I suppose I deserve that, but I was trying to steer myself away from giving you an appraisal. Anyway, cheers and welcome' – they clinked glasses – 'come sit down.'

They settled at opposite ends of the sofa and sipped the champagne.

'You know I want you,' he said, looking intently at her, 'I feel I've spent two years courting you.'

'Always with the idea of having me?' She thought she could afford to be coquettish.

'No, I'll admit that's much more recent. But something's been developing while we've been talking and laughing. Haven't you felt that?'

'Yes,' she answered slowly.

He stood up and held out his hand. She put down

her glass, knowing exactly where they were going. The thought had been pushing into her mind for the past two days and she'd had trouble suppressing it.

She stood up and he put his arms around her. She was slow to raise her lips but was desperate to kiss him. He kissed tenderly, letting his lips melt on to hers. His arms were round her waist, but one hand slowly slid down over her arse to pull her closer to him, letting her know how ready he was.

He leaned back, still with his arms around her, and smiled. 'Come on. I want to know if these breasts are as beautiful as I've been imagining.'

He took her hand and led her to the bedroom, where he pulled her to him and kissed her again.

'Are you going to be a big girl and take your dress off for me? Or will you make me fumble like a schoolboy.'

'I don't imagine you would fumble like a schoolboy.' But she was already unzipping herself. She turned away to drape the dress on the chair, and to let him appreciate the underwear.

'Sorry, but I have to say: Wow! Maybe I'm being a schoolboy – but you look fabulous.'

'Thank you,' she said and turned slowly, slightly surprised to see him already lying on the bed, propped on one elbow, wearing only pants with an obvious bulge.

'Come here, just as you are.'

Good, she wasn't quite ready to undress yet.

He pulled her to him and kissed her again, his hand sliding gently over her skin. She barely noticed her bra release and, as his hand moved to her hips, she moved to help him remove the flimsy and exquisitely chosen knickers which flew somewhere in the room.

Should she touch him, she wondered, but he had already released himself and she felt him place his cock-head gently but firmly on her clit while he continued to alternately kiss her and look into her eyes. She relaxed back, her pussy was making it extremely clear that she was not only ready but almost desperate to feel him inside her.

And she took him very easily. Their arms locked themselves to each other tightly as she felt him push deep and fill her. They moved rhythmically, kissing gently but pushing each other firmly. She lifted her knees to take him as deeply as she could.

'Oh,' he groaned, 'not so fast, my dear, please.' He eased out slightly, lifting his head to look into her eyes. 'This is beautiful but if I'm not careful it will be also brief.' He straightened his arms and pushed deeper again. They smiled at each other and it felt warm and joyous. They were lovers now. They could take their time. But now he surprised her. He slid down quickly, before she could protest, and his mouth covered her petals completely. His hand gripped her elbows, she was pinioned. His shoulders kept her wide open. She had to submit. She wanted nothing else. She felt his tongue slide inside her, then circle and press on her clit.

'Oh, be careful, now you'll make me come too quick.'

He looked up and smiled. 'I'll try to judge that. Let me try to keep you on the edge for a while.'

And he did. She loved being pinned as she was. His mouth moved, his tongue was on her skin, inside her and then around her clit again, sliding away just before she came to a peak.

He released her arms. She held his head tenderly, pressing him against her when she wanted more. She felt wanton, she never been kissed this way before, never so deeply, never so intimately. She had never felt so wet before, it was glorious. She became aware of fingers exploring her, and then surprising her, exploring her everywhere. It was new, it tingled, it was extraordinarily thrilling. But then, as his fingers pushed deeper, his tongue pressed more firmly on her clit. It was impossible to stop. Her hands held his head still, pushing him more firmly on to her as she began to scream uncontrollably. Her body convulsed. She felt completely overwhelmed and sank back. He was beside her instantly, wrapping her in his arms. He pulled her very close.

'My God, that was amazing. But, Christ, was I too loud?'

He laughed. 'Oh, we're well insulated and it's quiet

here at weekends. And I thought it was glorious.'

'But what about you?' She suddenly felt a twitch of nervousness.

'Oh, you really don't have to worry about that,' he said smiling.

'That sounds almost ominous.' But she was intrigued. 'I want to please you. I just am not sure how.'

'We'll make that very easy for you,' and he pulled her on top of him. 'Just sit on me. He'll find his way inside you easily enough.'

'Because you made me so wet, you monster?'

'Well it does help. He loved you being enthusiastic.' He closed his eyes. And he was right, she found it easy to let him inside her again and she sat down to take him as deeply as she could, feeling his cock head deep in her stomach, feeling her clit respond again already as she pushed down on to him. Again? Already? She thought. Then his hands moved from her shoulders to her breasts. He studied them, then looked in her eyes. 'You really do have the most beautiful breasts.'

She sat up straighter. 'What? These?'

'Yes, now I know why I've been trying to stare down your cleavage.'

'I don't show a cleavage.' She tried to sound indignant.

'Oh, it's modest and feminine, and even more alluring for that.' Then his eyes closed, his hands moved to her hips and she felt him pushing deeper.

'Come to me, closer, let me feel your breasts on my chest.' She pressed herself to him. 'Oh, wonderful,' he gasped, but kept his unbroken insistent rhythm going, holding her hips to allow himself to move more freely in and out of her. She moved with him, astonished to find how close she was getting to coming again. She felt his hands move to her arse cheeks, he moaned as he squeezed them. Then she felt his fingers move closer to the centre. She twitched. This was new. Was it what she wanted? But it tingled, it was pleasant, and as one finger slid gently inside her it became exciting. She found herself gasping and wanting more. She felt his rhythm increasing and he was pushing his cock and his finger deeper.

'Oh,' he gasped, 'I have to, I can't stop. Come with me, please come with me.'

She was gasping and moving with him. She knew it. She was coming too. She tried to wait until she felt him coming inside her. She just made it before releasing herself, shouting, almost screaming even louder than before, feeling the waves pulse through her, intense for long moments and then becoming slower and gentler but still insistent. She could feel herself dripping on to him. Feel him still giving her every drop – of his cum? Of his feelings?

Enjoy the moment she told herself, enjoy the

moment.

She slumped on to him and they slowly disentangled their limbs to leave themselves on their sides, facing each other, lips almost kissing.

'Oh, amazing,' he said, 'you move so beautifully. I thought I was in control. I hope I wasn't too quick.'

She laughed. 'Too quick? No way. I couldn't have held out a moment longer.'

She snuggled in to him, wrapping her arms around him, enjoying his warm and, she had to admit, slightly furry skin. It was gorgeous. She freed one hand to run her fingers through the thick chest hair.

'A little ape-like, I'm afraid.'

She kissed his chest. 'I love it, big ape, and the smell of your skin.'

He pulled her to him. She felt his not yet soft cock grope for her clit.

'Yes, and I love him too, apparently, but please tell me he's going to take a break now.'

He smiled and eased away slightly.

'We don't do multiples.'

'But I thought.'

'Yes, but it was a shock for me.'

'What, never?'

'Not never, no, but it's rare – and not so close together.'

'It's London,' he said, 'like buses coming together.'

She slapped him gently and they laughed.

'Cuddle in a while, or do you want lunch now?'

'Oh, cuddle me for a while. But I am keen to see you perform in the kitchen.'

'Ah,' – a glint came into his eye – 'a worktop moment. I hadn't planned…'

'Monster!' And she slapped him again and then nestled her body close into his.

She felt him stirring; she must have dozed. He returned from the bathroom with a white robe. 'It's mine. I thought you might feel more relaxed. And I shan't feel so stressed about my meagre lunch offering being adequate for your million-dollar outfit.'

'It's hardly that.'

'Well, you look it. And I don't want the cleavage getting me all agitated at the table.'

He had slipped on a tee shirt and some black gym pants. He looked very casual but still stylish.

'I fell asleep.'

'Me too, just not quite as long as you did.'

She grabbed her watch from the chair by the bed.

'It's only two,' he said, 'you're not going anywhere yet.'

She raised her eyebrows at him. 'Sir commands?'

'Yes, sir commands.' He smiled.

'Then what choice do I have?'

'None, you do as you're told here. This show of

consultative democracy that I put on for the office has no place here.'

'It's OK; I had guessed what the real you was like.'

'So, you haven't been surprised this morning?'

'Oh, I'm not saying that. But I'm more surprised by me than I am by you.'

'Ah, you're more wanton than you thought.'

'Something like that. But now I'm hungry. Can I shower first?'

'Of course, everything's in there. There's even a clean towel.'

'You were prepared.'

'I don't want to seem ungallant, but I think we both knew what would happen.'

She looked down coyly and nodded. 'True.'

The table was laid by the time she'd showered and freshened up her make-up. It was impressive, all cold but beautifully laid out and colourful: smoked salmon, huge prawns, Italian meats and a variety of small salads that he'd clearly prepared himself. A fresh glass of champagne stood winking by her plate. She had barely touched her first before she had been led away, so it was not yet time to worry about alcohol. He raised his glass to her.

'I'm afraid you still look beautiful,' he said.

'Afraid?'

He smiled. 'We should eat.'

'It looks wonderful. Did you have it delivered?'

'How dare you? Crack of dawn, Borough market. The carciofini sliced by my own fair hand. I'll admit I just picked out the others and let them put them in pots. It's not something I do often.'

'Ah, yes, we're in your monastic cell, just a diet of water and microwave meals.'

'I need the simple meals. You know the itinerary for the next two weeks and every night it's a restaurant dinner.'

'Poor you!' She smiled, but she knew there was little glamour to it. She'd booked it all for him: nine flights and five different hotels. 'Is it all bad?'

'Oh no, I know a lot of the guys so it's fun to touch base, but Malaysia and the Philippines are new, and I'll want to get out into the regions, I don't just want to stop in city centres, you know that plane, taxi, meeting room, hotel sort of trip is useless. I want to see the people and the countries. I think they know what I'm looking for.'

'I'm sure you'll make it very clear if they don't.'

He laughed gently.

'Well, you are very direct.'

'Was I too direct this morning?'

'I think you'd guessed what I wanted. Even the bits that surprised me.'

'Oh, was some of it new?'

'A little, but I didn't want you to stop. After all, I

had been warned about you being dirty and dangerous.'

'I'm not sure I understand what's meant by that, much less understand who makes comments like that. That's your coven, isn't it?'

She nodded.

'Well, who thinks they know? And what do they say?'

'I'm not telling you that. And I'm very happy finding out for myself.'

'What? What's dirty and dangerous, you mean?'

'Is there more?' She teased him.

He poured more champagne. 'We'll see how we can surprise you. But I'm sure you want to eat more first.'

'Oh, I do, and you can talk. Made up your mind about where to live?'

'I'm getting told Singapore, so I'll look around when I'm there. But it's not like I'll be there that much. I'll be in hotels all over the place.'

'Won't you get lonely?'

'Oh, there'll be plenty of people to meet – and anyway, that's where you come in. I really do want to keep ringing; I wasn't just saying that. You're OK about that, aren't you?'

'Of course, I am.'

But she wondered as she said it. She promised herself nothing after the morning – but she knew she would feel a wrench when he left. And she'd be wondering when she might see him again. And how she might feel about his new life with its distant liberties.

'I get a lot out of it, knowing you trust me and want to hear what I say. You don't always give the impression of being a good listener.'

'You don't think I listen?'

'Oh, I know you do but some people think of you as… well, quite a few words get used, not all of them uncomplimentary.'

'I expect arrogant comes up.'

'Yes, but I was thinking you'd see that as a compliment.' And they smiled.

'Well, I think I see things clearly and know what I want.'

'Yes, that was this morning, wasn't it?'

'That was the first part of it.' He smiled wickedly. Something twitched inside her. Perhaps the day wasn't over. Perhaps there might even be another day. But she drank and made herself remember that she'd told herself this was going to be the only day and it would be a lovely memory. So far, she'd been right, but she was feeling a growing apprehension about dealing with the aftermath.

'Are you saying there's more?'

He smiled and looked into her eyes, then let his gaze fall.

'I'd given you the robe to hide your cleavage.'

She knew it was fairly open and would not be concealing much. She liked him looking at her. He looked back at her eyes.

'Yes, I want more.'

'Today?'

'Yes, and you?'

'Are you asking?'

'Not really.' He stood up and held out his hands. She took them and stood up with him. The robe fell open and he pulled her body to him. His arms went inside the robe and around her body as they kissed.

'Come!' And he guided her not to the bedroom but towards the sofa in front of the big window. Then held her standing behind it, looking at the river. His hands moved to her shoulders and pulled the robe down. He cupped her breasts and fondled them gently. She reassured herself, they were high up and could not be seen and suddenly she was thrilled to be naked, feeling his hands on her breasts, his lips on her shoulders and his bulge pressing on her back.

'Let's let London admire your tits too.' His fingers squeezed her nipples gently. 'But right now, I want to admire your arse more.' He knelt behind her, she felt him nibble and kiss her arse cheeks. His hands slid to her hips.

'Bend over a little.'

This was new, to be standing naked in front of a window while a lover felt and kissed her body. And a lover giving quite clear instructions. She leaned forward, her thighs pressed on the sofa back, he held her hips tightly still, but she felt him sway backwards.

'What a fabulous arse you have.'

She felt thrilled and embarrassed in equal measure, but one hand slid slowly up between her thighs and she felt his fingers on her clit. She gasped, she knew she was quickly getting wet and soft. She felt his other hand moving up her back, pushing gently but firmly. She bent further forward. She felt fingers sliding into her again. He stood up behind her, somehow his pants had gone, and she felt him stiff against her cheeks. Her arms were now on the sofa back, her arse protruding towards him. She felt him slide easily into her. His hands moved to her hips and they began to move rhythmically with each other. She felt him very deep, his cock-head way up inside her. She heard him murmuring, 'Oh, beautiful, beautiful.'

He seemed then to force himself to slow down, easing his grip, not pushing so deep but she wanted more of him. She pushed back but suddenly he slid out and went to his knees behind her. His hands and arms were on her back, hips and thighs, clamping her. She felt his face push between her legs, his tongue reaching her clit. She shivered almost uncontrollably then she felt his grip relax and the pressure on her clit lessen. He began to lick her gently and rhythmically again, finding a way of keeping her on the edge of screaming wildly. It felt glorious. Then she felt his tongue inside her, his face pushing into her. Then his hands moved to her buttocks, stretching them apart. She felt a spasm of panic, wondering what would happen and he began to lick and kiss in that strange place, so new to her, but it tingled. It felt very intimate, intensely pleasant as she felt his tongue push inside her.

She felt him stand and hold her hips again, pushing himself once more, deep inside her. He murmured, 'Don't worry, just say stop if you want me to.'

And his stiff wet cock was rubbing between her arse cheeks, its head was tickling her hole. She felt nervous and anxious but also curious, and he was moving very gently. Slowly she felt its head push at her hole. It felt large; it began to feel uncomfortable. She gasped.

'You OK?'

'No, I mean yes, don't stop, don't stop.' It was intense and exquisite. 'Try a little more, please, I want to.' And she did. Her main thought had been to please him but now she was relaxing. She pushed back gently and knew she had his full width inside her.

He groaned and pushed a little deeper. She felt more; it felt huge but only uncomfortable, she felt full of him. And she felt him quicken, not pushing too hard but very obviously getting close to coming, then suddenly he was making the loud noises, his hands gripping her hips as he released himself into her.

He stayed stiff inside her long after his movements had stopped. His hands moved gently and tenderly over her skin.

'Now you have to stay like that for a while,' his voice was almost normal. 'I want to taste you. I want to feel you come.'

She looked up out of the window. It felt strange, the river and the city had been there all along, but they had been lost inside their feelings.

And suddenly her body was lost again. His hands and arms framing her arse and her sex. His face pushing into her, his tongue finding her throbbing clit. This time his mouth engulfed her, and she felt herself quickly move into the rhythm of her orgasm. She fell limply forward on to the back of the sofa. His face followed, still licking her gently, stroking her skin, letting her breathing return to normal.

Then he stood up and eased her up to face him, to be enveloped in his arms.

'I think the bed's waiting,' he said, 'come with me.'

And two naked people in one embrace shuffled to the bedroom.

They fell on to the bed and into each other's arms,

kissing with a gentle passion.

His arms pulled her tightly to him. Skin on skin felt glorious, especially where it slid over the juices on their bellies and legs.

'We probably shouldn't sleep,' she said as she felt him relax, 'I do have to go back this afternoon and I don't even have any shopping to show.'

'Shopping?'

'I said I would be shopping. I knew I wouldn't be driving straight back.'

'Ah, wanton and now deceitful. What have I done to you?'

'Much more than anybody else ever has.'

'You didn't mind?'

'Mind? It was amazing. But I shouldn't tell you that. You're conceited enough.'

'I'll take conceited. It would be perverted I wouldn't want.'

'Oh, you are that as well, but I seem to have enjoyed it.'

They laughed and embraced each other more tightly.

And now you're going away, she thought but stopped herself. Suddenly the hole that she knew would open when he left looked much, much bigger.

4

She kept busy, spending evenings reading the reports from the businesses in the Far East to try to understand what he would be dealing with. She also looked at organization charts and tried to memorise the names and faces of people he would be working with. She caught herself feeling relieved that there were few women and couldn't imagine him being attracted to the ones that there were.

But then, who can account for men, she thought. And he could find plenty of company away from work.

He was true to his word. He called most days, usually mid-afternoon for her, when he'd got back from dinner to his hotel. He was usually mellow and only sometimes tired. He was frustrated about not seeing more of the countries and the markets but knew that his first job was to get to know his people.

'It's tough, they're all so keen to impress and they want to tell me so much about everything but if I just sit and listen, I keel over with jetlag. I make them take me out and about after lunch just so I can fall asleep in the car between the meetings and businesses we're seeing. They're very nice about it. Well, so far as I can tell. It's not that they're inscrutable, like the cliché says, but most seem smiley and enthusiastic, and anything I ask for seems to get done straight away.'

'And it wasn't here?'

'You know you were an exception. That place did frustrate me, the culture of wanting to debate rather than do.'

'Did we debate?'

'Of course, these phone calls are debates – or they will be when you're up to speed. And I'm surprised already by how much you know. Have you been reading?'

'A bit.'

'Hmmm, that's probably a lot, you're always thorough.'

'But did we debate on the Saturday?'

'Ah, that's different. Did you find me dictatorial?'

'A bit, but I liked it.'

'At the risk of sounding ungentlemanly, you made that obvious.'

'Had you planned it all?'

'No, not beyond taking you to bed and making love to you.'

'So, you weren't planning your full repertoire?'

'Do you think that was the full repertoire?'

Suddenly she felt a little naïve and embarrassed. 'Gosh, there's more?'

There was a silence. Of course, how could he react? Was she pinning him with assumptions when he was barely escaping from other, older commitments? And this wasn't even a commitment.

'Do you want more?'

'Look, please don't take that too seriously. I'm honestly intrigued. You've pushed me way past some old boundaries and I loved it. But I know you're over there now. But you know that, even with the few chances I'll have, I'd love to do it again.'

'And explore more boundaries?'

'Yes, why not?' She had no idea of where that would lead but the man excited her and she felt very, very close to him. There was a silence. What was he thinking? She knew enough to wait and not to babble. But the silence lasted too long.

'Can I make it easier for you?'

'What do you mean?'

'I know you a bit, I think. And I'm pretty sure you had a wonderful time on Saturday.'

'It was fabulous.'

'Thank you, but don't interrupt, this isn't easy for me.'

'Go on then, I'm listening.'

'You're probably worrying about what my expectations are. You're feeling a bit responsible – and even a bit, well, caring.'

'Yes.'

'But I know it was a one-off. My eyes were open, and I knew I was doing something I hadn't ever done but I wanted it. OK, it was a little more than I expected, but even that was thrilling. If it doesn't happen again though, I will live with that. What I don't want is to lose this. I love the window on new worlds I get just listening to you.'

'I've told you how important that was to me.'

'That was before you fucked me.'

'It's probably more important now.'

'How so?'

'Well, there's more trust and intimacy now.'

'Ah, but now you'll start keeping secrets about your new life.'

'I admit I keep secrets. Do you want to know everything?'

'I'm feeling brave enough to say yes at the moment. I know I'll feel wobbly when you have a date but really, really, I want to know.'

'OK, I'll be as open as I can.'

'You know I'll know if you're not.'

'I do. But your friendship is very important, even more now. I love it here, but I can envisage getting a little lonely.'

'You won't lose my friendship. Really you won't. But I do have one request.'

'What's that?'

She gulped and steeled herself. 'Well, you can call it a demand.'

'Go on.'

'All right, all right, this isn't easy. I'm still a shy girl at heart.'

'It didn't feel that way on the back of the sofa.'

'That's it! You have to fuck me again when you're here next.'

There was a pause. Christ, she thought, what have I done? Then came his loud laugh. 'Don't mock me!'

'I'm not. I'd be absolutely thrilled to fuck you again and I'm delighted not to have to ask you. Can you get time to come to London? I'm there for two weeks before I move out.'

'I can get time.'

'Time for me to fuck you twice?'

'Fuck me lots! I know you're going. I can guess what you'll be doing but we'll deal with the tomorrows tomorrow.'

She knew how full his time would be when he was in England. Two weeks to hand over the business and get prepared to move to Singapore. Family time too, she guessed, time with his boys if not with his wife. Although even that might take some time. She remembered her break up and divorce and how much time and energy that had cost. But that had been years ago. Her mind was wandering. She was desperate for time with him, private time, but she was steeling herself for how hard that might be – and maybe how convenient it would be for him not to find the time.

There would be only ten work days and one weekend, and his evenings would be taken up with business dinners, saying goodbye to people, even a farewell party that she would have to organize and smile through.

Then came his email, to her private address:

I guess you know how busy the next two weeks at home will be, but I do want some 'us' time, and it may be best to plan it rather than wait for disappearing opportunities or have it squeezed by who knows what 'emergencies.' How can you manage your time? I'm hoping you'll say you can get some time free at the weekend, or at the very least an evening. I need to plan meetings and some family dates but if you can tell me what works best for you, I'll do everything I can to work around that.

So, it was important to him, she thought, a little excited and flattered, but aware also that it would make saying goodbye even harder next time. But if he was just enjoying the sex, well then, so could she. The scenes from the Saturday had revolved in her mind many times since. The memories excited her, his skin, his smell, his smile, his voice, his body's insistence in taking her so many ways – some of which she'd only read about before – and firmly rejected as ideas – but she had felt so close to him – and being so adventurous had made it feel even more intimate.

And in her quiet moments she found herself wondering how adventurous she was. She couldn't imagine being that adventurous with Dave, or Douglas. Both marriages had quickly fallen into simple, repetitive patterns with small and infrequent, and ultimately resented, outbursts of passion. She'd thought that normal, as it seemed for all her friends with children.

She'd been livelier in her teens and she began to kindle those memories to think of how she might surprise him. She remembered the late nights in clubs with Millie, the different boys who had taken them home, the fumbling in the cars, even the night when they'd shared two boys. She'd been shocked at first when Millie had unzipped one of them and begun kissing him. Her own partner unzipped himself and clearly expected something similar but, as she usually found, he came very quickly once she began to play with him.

They were nice boys, those two, not like the ones who put their hands up the skirt as soon as the car door closed. But they had both come quickly, paying little attention to the girls' pleasures and leaving them a little frustrated. They had Millie's house for the night while her parents were away and had thought there might be more to experience than two young men having to clean themselves up quickly. The boys, however, soon recovered and started touching and kissing again but were sent out to buy drink and a takeaway.

'Have you done that before?' she asked Millie as soon as the car pulled away.

'What?'

'You know. Had a boy in your mouth like that?'

'Of course. They love it.'

'I could see that, but what do you get out of it?'

'A mouthful of sperm if I don't pull away quickly.'

'And do you?'

'Not always, not if I like him and he's going carefully like Malcolm just now. I like to feel him getting excited. He's not usually that quick but I can always have more later. Haven't you ever tried it?'

'No. I know they want it, but I can usually make them come first anyway, or persuade them to do it properly.'

'What's properly?'

'You know. I like it in there. I want to come too.'

'And do you?'

'Well, not so often, I have to admit. They always seem so quick.'

'That's why I like controlling them a bit. I can make them wait until I'm ready. You should make them play

50

with you until you've had fun, then you can finish them off easily. Do you let them kiss you down there?'

'Well, no, I mean, no-one's really tried. Do you let them?'

'Let them? Wow, I want them to. Malcolm's lovely when he slows down. I've come three times in one night when he's been doing that. Why don't we swap when they come back? You should try it and I haven't had Kevin. He looks like I need to teach him.'

She remembered the conversation so vividly, although it was years ago, and it had made her curious. She was uneasy at first when the boys got back but after a few drinks and the food, it seemed more natural. And Millie had easily distracted Kevin and taken him upstairs.

Malcolm clearly fancied her and was obviously attracted by the idea of having two girls in one night. She didn't think of herself as having two boys since all she'd done so far was to mop her hand with Kleenex.

It was calmer now with Malcolm. They lay on the big sofa with their clothes in easy disarray. He'd eased her pants off her and was playing with her gently with his fingers. She was very wet already.

'Do you want to kiss me there?'

'Aye, you feel beautiful.' He slid fingers inside her.

'Then I want to do you, like Millie did.'

He smiled. 'Well, I'm not going to refuse that.'

She flushed a little. 'Look, just one thing,' the conversation was getting more difficult, his fingers were arousing her, 'I haven't actually done that before, so we need to go slowly.'

'Slowly? With your sweet lips on him.' He smiled again. 'I'll try my best. I would love to go slowly. And I'll be going slowly with you right now.'

She slid further down the sofa, he went on to his knees and she opened herself wide and felt his whole mouth on her. His tongue and fingers touched and teased. Her excitement rose quickly. She pushed his head on to her, his tongue squashed her clit and she found herself throbbing. She tried to stay quiet, Millie was upstairs, but she couldn't as his mouth and tongue moved all around her and made her scream. He kept licking even as her climax subsided. This was new. Normally it was a quick cuddle after she'd come, but now she felt a glow through her and knew already that she could get excited again. She lay back with her hips on the edge of the sofa. His tongue continued, Millie was right, it was gorgeous, and he was good. Then she felt him lift his head, their eyes met, and they smiled. 'That's lovely,' she said, wondering what she should say at a moment like that. Then he moved closer and he pushed slowly inside her.

'I like that, Malcs, I really do but didn't we have a plan.'

'Oh, aye, we have a plan all right, but I had to have him in your sweet pussy first.' He closed his eyes and pushed deeper. She could feel her mounting excitement again as his pelvis pressed on her clit. She could come again, she knew, but she wanted to touch him and taste him. She put her hands on his shoulders and pushed gently. He eased back.

'Come on, it's my turn. You sit back here.' He sat beside her and leaned back. She knelt between his knees and touched him with both hands.

She had fondled a good many boys – she'd recently counted to eleven when daydreaming idly – but this was her first chance to study a penis closely. He was quite large and very stiff; the purple head was gleaming with their juices. She moved one hand to his balls and stroked them gently. She heard him groaning, 'Oh, be careful.'

'Am I hurting? Sorry.'

'No, no, no, it's just gorgeous but don't we want to go slowly?'

'Yes, yes of course. Talk to me. Tell me what's nice. Tell me what's too much.'

'Well, you've a lovely touch. Just keep moving your hand like that.'

She was gripping him and moving up and down the shaft, trying to find the rhythm that best pleased him. His groaning and breathing moved with her. Now she had the time to study this fascinating object, the thick veins, the stretched skin, the shining bald head. She moved towards it and licked the underside and felt his breathing get heavier. Now she had to try it. Her mouth closed over it.

'Oh,' he gasped.

She pulled back.

'No, don't stop. It's wonderful. I just don't know about waiting.'

Neither did she. Best to do it, she thought. If I like it, we can always try again. And she took him in both hands and enveloped his head with her whole mouth and she could tell as he moved that he would come soon. And he did and she felt the blobs squirting into her mouth. He was pushing but not too hard and it was easy to control how much of him she took in her mouth. But she pulled back a moment, eager to watch the blobs.

'No, no, don't leave him.' She felt his hand on her head, insistent, and she took him again. His hand relaxed and she controlled his movements, surprised by how long he kept pulsing, having to swallow several times to clear her mouth, until finally, with a loud groan, she felt him soften and she moved up beside him on the sofa to cuddle him and feel their skin on each other through the disarray of their clothing.

They must have fallen asleep. 'Look at you two,' she heard Millie at the doorway with Kevin standing behind her. She was up quickly, covering herself as best she could. Malcolm had a drowsy smile on his face and was plainly not at all bothered by his semi-nakedness.

Mille and Kevin were dressed but looked reasonably contented.

'Come on, Malcs,' Millie said. We must tidy the mess up and you two will be useless.

Malcs wrapped his arm around her and nuzzled into her neck. 'What's the rush? We're having a lovely time.' She leaned back on to him, silently agreeing, but she knew Millie's parents might be back early and they couldn't leave evidence.

So, the boys left. It was three a.m. and although they both wanted to talk it was four before they'd convinced themselves that they had cleaned up thoroughly and then both fell instantly asleep on the beds in Millie's room.

She smiled at the memories. She'd seen Malcs a few times before he'd gone south. They'd had fun and she'd learnt more about controlling men and keeping them happy. But these were skills that diminished through the years of her marriages, much as the motivation had entirely subsided.

But now she would be seeing Jack again and, although it clearly wouldn't be new to him, she thought it might surprise and please him when she took control and pleasured him. He obviously liked to dominate – and she had delighted in being taken – but she was sure he would also love to be made to lie back and be pleasured. She found herself shaking her head. She was at work, at her desk, and completely lost in reverie, thinking of taking Jack's cock deep into her mouth.

5

She liked the hotel in Chelsea, she enjoyed the suites with their views over the marina and, with a conference to organize the next month, she had a good reason to be there. She'd asked Jack to keep the Tuesday evening free, telling him where she'd be. He replied quickly, he would come to her, there were some good food choices in walking distance. That was true, but that wasn't uppermost in her mind. She was thinking of his smile, of his voice, of the fuzz on his chest, of the feeling of being relaxed with him – but also of the anticipation of his body and hers together, wondering if he would stay the night.

He'd also surprised her in his reply, asking if she could still make time at the weekend. He'd love to see her on the Saturday as well, she was excited and knew she would find a way but wished he hadn't made the point quite so bluntly that his next trip to England would not be for some time. Of course, it wouldn't be, she didn't need telling, and she made herself more determined than ever to make the most of the time they had.

He was in the office on the Monday but there was only a smile and a few pleasantries for her until late in the afternoon when he asked her into the glass office.

'Can you help me with the flights for the next month?'

'Of course,' – she tried not to give her emotions away – 'but you'll have someone there wanting to do that for you, won't you?'

He smiled and shrugged. 'Yes, I'm dreading it, wrong connections, missed taxis, long stopovers.'

'You'll be all right, they'll have done it before.'

'Will you talk to them? Her name's Mai.'

'What, so I can tell her all about your funny little ways?'

They both smiled. She hadn't meant to be suggestive, but both their minds were clearly on what 'funny little ways' might mean.

'Noooo, but she asked who helped me here and if she could talk to you.'

'I'll call her, of course I will. But how long are we planning for now?'

'I'm clear about the next three weeks but I need to speak to more people out there to plan after that. Then there's the US in June.'

She'd realized that his focus would be Asia but also that he'd spend time at headquarters. It was still a jolt that she tried not to react to. His guarded look with that raised eyebrow told her that he was half expecting a reaction.

He'd written down his plan. 'I didn't want to email you with it because it's not fixed in stone. If some of the connections don't work, I can juggle the meetings and visits a bit. I'm trying to avoid becoming a travel zombie.'

She looked over the paper. The destinations were names from geography lessons and corporate reports. She felt a pang of envy but then tried to think of how missed flights in alien destinations might feel.

'And we're still good for tomorrow?' she wanted a little reassurance.

He looked a little serious, 'It's very important to me. Are you still OK with it?'

She smiled. 'I want to know more about your repertoire.' He smiled. 'I'll go up mid-afternoon, I have work there.'

That was true, she had work to do, but that wasn't relevant to her plan. She wanted to enjoy a long bath and pamper herself before he came. She had her plan to surprise him with her repertoire, limited though it was, but she was sure he'd be at least as appreciative as Malcs had been all those years ago.

But those were teenage fumbling, she told herself. What did people really do? She'd spent time at home at night on Dave's computer, looking at his porn sites, the ones he thought he'd hidden securely.

How did people give blowjobs? There were hundreds

of videos. She'd seen them only fleetingly, catching him furtively watching. But now she studied them, how the girls held the men, how they licked them and squeezed them, how deeply they would sometimes take them. My God, was that possible? She wouldn't try that, she knew, but most of it looked like what she and Malcs had done. And she was going to hold him and taste him and take everything. She wanted him. And, much as she had loved him controlling her and taking her, she wanted to control him a little.

The manager greeted her cheerily. She had run several conferences and events there and knew the staff well. They, in turn, seemed to appreciate a client, an attractive woman, taking the trouble to brief them all fully before any event and then to take time to say thank you afterwards. She did that all perfectly naturally but recognized nonetheless that she wouldn't have got the corner suite based on her business alone.

She looked at the rooms differently now. It was always pleasant to see the flowers and bowl of bright, glossy fruit and the bathroom's selection of Aqua di Parma toiletries, the big fluffy towels and the two bathrobes (always two, she'd never used the second one).

It wasn't yet four. She wouldn't expect him for two hours at least. She tried to think of timings, how she would greet him, whether he would want to go out and eat first – if he'd made a booking, he would hate to be late, if he'd had difficult meetings or heavy traffic, he might seem frazzled. She tried hard to put it all out of her head and ran the bath, dosing the foam generously. He liked her skin, he'd said so, she wanted it as soft and smooth as possible. She lay back in the hot water, the foam wetting her hair – ah, it needed doing anyway, plenty of time for that – half-reading her book, half thinking about the evening – topping up hot water now and again whenever the bath became merely warm – but mostly thinking about the man and, when she was honest with herself, about his penis. She had touched it and she had felt it deeply inside her, but she hadn't seen it to study it and she was curious, she wanted that intimacy with him. It wasn't right that the penis she knew best, how it looked, how it tasted, how it felt, belonged to a teenage boyfriend much more than a decade in the past. She thought again of Jack's, it's head deep in her belly, its size as he squeezed it in behind her – that had been completely new and unexpected, but she had wanted to please him, she wanted not to seem naïve, she was curious – what did lovers do with intimacy and passion? She was remembering him pushing in slowly and how he'd prepared her by licking her deeply – another shock – and, however gentle he'd tried to be, how uncomfortable it had been afterwards, how she'd had to find cream to ease the soreness. She smiled at herself. Tonight, she had lube in her case. If that was going to happen again, and she hoped it would, she was going to be prepared.

She dropped the book on the floor, she had hardly read a word in ages, and looked at her wrinkled fingers – time to get out. She wrapped towels around her head and torso, ran her hands down her arms to reassure herself that her skin felt good and looked at her face in the mirror – not bad, good structure, no lines, well, hardly any but well, it would need some work, like any girl's.

But she was quick. It came with the job. A pampering bath was delightful but a rare luxury. Normally she would be constrained by a ten-minute turnaround. Tonight, she had more time – my God, it was half-past five already – but she stuck to her habit, face in five minutes, on with the bathrobe and fix the hair.

She didn't hear the door because of the drier's noise so she was shocked when she turned to see him in the doorway, smiling.

'Gotcha!'

'I didn't expect you for…'

But he already had her in his arms and the kiss stopped her speaking. She gave herself to it and felt their bodies move together, his hands slipping open her robe, pulling her tightly to him.

She pulled away. She'd had a plan. It was falling

62

apart. 'Am I late? Do we have to be going? Have you booked anything?'

He smiled. 'No, no and yes.'

'Where are we going? How long have I got?'

'Calm down. We have plenty of time. I don't want to rush out to dinner, sit there looking into your beautiful eyes thinking wow, I wish I'd made love to her earlier, how soon can I ask for the bill?'

She breathed deeply; this was OK, she just needed to get control, she was sure he'd appreciate it. 'Ah, so you had an evil plan?'

'Oh, evil? You didn't seem to find it evil at the flat.'

'Oh, I did' – she smiled – 'very. But that doesn't mean I don't want to repeat it.'

Now he smiled.

'But anyway, Mr Stephens, I have an evil plan of my own. I think you can pour some drinks. No, second thoughts. I'll do that. You sit on the sofa and admire the view. It's not your flat but it is interesting, and I love seeing water and boats.'

'Me too,' he said, standing in the big window and looking out over the balcony.

She opened the half bottle of champagne. It was in an ice bucket, not in the minibar, and it never seemed to appear on her bill. She took the glasses to the window. He took his and they clinked. He put his arm around her shoulder and pulled her to him. She looked up and kissed him, her robe falling open easily. He leaned back, admiring her body and she felt, unusually, completely unselfconscious.

She sipped, then took his glass. 'You were told to sit down.'

'Don't I give the orders?'

'Usually, yes, but I think being controlled a little won't make you unhappy.'

'I'm intrigued.'

'I plan to make you more than that. Sit down,' she said mock-sternly.

He sat down. She kneeled in front of him, held his head and kissed him and then pushed him back. He looked surprised. He reached for her breasts. She slapped his hand. 'Look all you want but you're not touching yet. Lean back and relax.' She was already unbuckling his belt. She slipped it out of its loops and felt a strange frisson as the leather snaked free. She would take her time now. She was enjoying the drama and she knew he would like to grow before he was exposed. She could feel the bulge already. She rubbed it before moving to his buttons. She felt clumsy, he had been so adept with her bra.

'Shall I help?'

'No, this is part of the fun for me.'

'And for me.'

She knew he was smiling but she was concentrating

fiercely until the buttons were undone. Now she could pull the zip slowly down. Now his bulge was already fighting the waistband of his pants. She pulled that down to see the head, gleaming and purple again. She held him and looked up.

'He and I have some business. I suggest you lie back and enjoy it.'

He leaned back silently, and his arms stretched out along the back of the sofa. She pulled the waistband further down. She wanted to enjoy this uninhibitedly – and she wanted him to enjoy it too.

'We have to get through the inelegant part,' she said, as she held his cock in one hand and tried to pull off a shoe with the other.

'Am I forbidden from helping? I'm desperately keen to subject myself to your plan.'

'Go on then.' And in what seemed like a second, he had discarded everything below the waist and leaned back again, unbuttoning his shirt.

'You know, you amazed me at the flat by how quickly you got naked.'

'But are you keeping your bathrobe on?'

'A little,' she said but let it fall open and her breasts graze his thighs. She felt his cock twitch.

'They are gorgeous,' he said, reaching for them. She slapped his hands.

'Lie back,' she said sternly, taking his shaft in one

hand and cupping his balls with the other. He groaned and lay back. He murmured softly as she gently massaged him. She looked up at him, his eyes were closed, and his head swayed gently from side to side as she stroked. She could take her time. She could be as intimate with this man as she ever had been with anyone, she knew. And she wanted to experience all the tiny, human details to carry her through the months of long-distance phone calls. No, she thought, no tomorrows, I'm enjoying the now and she moved forward and licked the underside of his cock. He murmured louder. She leaned back. He was very stiff and shiny. She kept her grip gentle and her movements slow.

'Can you control him OK?'

'At the moment it's perfect. I'll warn you if it gets too close.'

She looked up at him. 'I think I'd like to control that moment.' And she leaned forward and took the head into her mouth, running her tongue around it, tasting his juice. She rocked slowly back and forth, letting him in and out, sliding her tongue under its head. She leaned back again to study him, the man she had always admired but who now meant so much more than merely that – his belly a little bigger than his vanity wanted, the hairy chest with the tail of fur running down to his pubis, his cock very erect; it would stand on its own, but she was loving touching him.

But how far could she go, she wondered again, she had thought of that embarrassingly often in the last few days. Now she tried, her lips felt the edge of the head, now she slid further down, her mouth was full, and she could feel him straining not to move, wanting to, but wanting her to have control of him. She tried to move as he seemed to want to, a little in and out but she could take no more. She pulled away, breathing heavily.

'Oh, this is incredible,' he gasped.

'Just stay there.' She was beginning to feel she had control, and with her hands rubbing him gently she could sustain it, keeping him on the edge until she decided to free him.

She studied it again, the skin, the head. A photo, she thought, not now, but before he goes away. Something I can keep and look at sometimes when he's six thousand miles away. She smiled to herself. She'd find a moment to tell him – and he was sure he'd be thrilled – and then he would want some of her. I would enjoy that, she thought, but I'd want him to tell me to pose for him and she imagined her new self in outrageous poses.

But here was this gorgeous manhood in her hands. She carried on looking, her hands keeping him thrilled, and thought that she'd never expected to admire a penis, let alone be so excited by the thing.

She went back to licking its head, taking it gently in and out of her mouth, while her fingers kept stimulating him. She let the flat of her hand rub under his scrotum gently and then let a finger slide up between his cheeks. She had enjoyed that surprise when he had played with her. How would he feel? She wanted to explore. He slid forward slightly, letting her access him more easily, she let her finger rub his anus, his breathing got louder. Her nails were a little long but, if she were careful... she remembered the lube she had in her robe pocket – it had been planned for him to use on her but now... she kept his cock in place with her mouth.

'Don't stop,' he breathed as she took her hands away, but she was quickly back with a large dollop of lube on her middle finger, she eased it slowly into his arse and then pushed it in and out in time with her hand and mouth on his cock.

His voice croaked, 'You're in control, Miss Claudia, but I don't think I can hang on much longer.'

She looked up at him and smiled. 'Oh, I was going to put you out of your misery soon.'

'It's anything but misery, I assure you. It's wonderful.'

She smiled again, this time to herself, and moved her head forward to take him as deeply as she could.

She heard him groan again, louder this time.

She looked up. 'It's time now; I want all of you.'

She didn't want him to hesitate about coming in her mouth, she wanted to taste everything, to swallow everything.

He began to move more forcefully, still cautiously. Her hand held him firmer, her mouth kept its head. She knew he was coming. She pushed her finger in as deep as she dared. His noises grew louder, his movements stronger, she felt the twitches and the warm blobs coming into her mouth. She felt it pulsing and pulsing. She wanted his cum, all of it and she kept the whole head in her mouth until the pulses began to slow, then she pulled back a little to let it fall on her lips, and to let her tongue lick the slower drops that were easing out now after the early flood. Her hand held on to him, he kept moving rhythmically, he was still full and slightly firm but not the rock of before. She licked the wet head again to savour his taste.

He bent forward, his hand moved under her arms, he pulled her to him. Now she could relax, and she moved to lie lengthwise on him as he stretched horizontal on the sofa. She felt his softening mound on her belly. She pushed her clitoris down on his thigh, not so much to excite herself, that could come later, but she wanted him to feel how excited she had also been, how utterly wet she was.

His arms were round her, he pushed her robe down and ran his hands over her skin. It tingled and she cuddled in to him.

He moved one hand between her legs. She held his wrist. 'I do want you,' she said, 'I want you very much, as you can tell, but I think I can wait until later, if you're not dashing off home.'

'I'm not dashing anywhere.'

'Good. You have to make love to me later – and do everything you want.'

'Hmmm,' he said and kissed her, 'I'm beginning to adore you.'

That was a jolt for her, but she knew enough about men to know what got said at moments like this. She got up and pulled her robe around her.

'Aren't you going to feed me?'

He smirked at her.

'No, that doesn't count! What are we eating?'

'Indian OK?'

'I love Indian.'

'I know.'

'You know?'

'I do listen sometimes.'

That was actually true. He always seemed so decisive at work but, she had to admit, he had usually listened before he gave directions.

'You want to shower?'

'I think I will. And shave, I'm taking my girl to dinner.'

He disappeared into the bathroom, leaving her to sit and look out at the city. She stood and went to the window. She loved looking at the boats. She felt strangely thrilled. She ran her tongue around her mouth and tasted him again, thinking of how she'd made him come – she had never been in control like that. It was an exciting memory, how many more like that might she have? But it had been the 'my girl' remark and the fact that he would shave that had also thrilled her. He was making things special. Which would not make his leaving any easier. Then suddenly he was behind her again, naked, she could see the reflection in the window, with his arms around her. 'Bathroom's free,' he murmured.

'You're going like that?'

He smiled. 'I have a change in my bag – and some smellies, didn't think you'd appreciate me stealing yours.'

She left him to fix her face again. Not too much damage, she thought as she confronted the bathroom mirror.

He was dressed when she got out, and on the phone. It must be the US at this time of day. He had his patient voice on. He no doubt thought it was patient, but it seemed patronizing to some. She smiled to herself and went to the wardrobe in the bedroom: loose top, Versace skirt, holdups, killer heels (she knew it was a taxi ride, not a walk) and the new knickers. Well, one of the many new knickers. It was only after she'd been shopping that she realized she might get the chance to show off only one or two. She'd felt a little silly but shrugged it off.

She went to the main room and stood in front of him.

'OK, Mary, I have to go. I think we're done, or do you want me to call again later?' He was looking up at her and shaking his head. Mary ran finance in the US unit and was famously long-winded. 'OK, I'll call tomorrow morning then, bye.'

'Wow, you look fabulous, a twirl please?'

She twirled.

'Love the heels, guess we're taxiing.'

'Yes,' she said decisively.

'Wait, I haven't seen everything.'

'My jacket's hanging… what are you doing?'

He was raising her skirt. 'That must surely be obvious. This is the knicker check. Nice,' he said admiringly, leaning back, 'but sadly superfluous.' And his thumbs quickly pulled them down to her knees.

She reached down to pull them up. He held her wrists.

'No, no, madam, you've enjoyed your control. Now I say what goes. You're going commando, like me. Now step out of them.'

She hesitated.

'Are you waiting for a please?'

'I suppose that would be pointless?'

'Completely. Just go with it.' He looked up at her, smiling. 'Done this before?'

'Of course not, never.'

'OK, just another little step on our journey.'

He stood up and held her hand for balance while she extricated herself.

It felt strange walking through the lobby. She felt a little exposed and vulnerable – ridiculous she told herself – but also more than a little excited.

6

She'd read about Rasoi and knew he'd been there more than once. She was almost prepared for the feeling of walking into someone's house as he walked up the steps and rang the bell by the front door. It was answered quickly, and they were ushered in to the narrow hallway.

'Ah, Mr Stephens, so good to see you again, sir.'

The thought buzzed her like an irritating mosquito, how well known was he here? She knew enough about restaurants to know they practiced these easy deceptions – only one table for two at eight o'clock made it an easy guess. But who had he brought here? She knew she would have to manage these feelings much better in the coming months.

It was fairly full and there was not much space between the tables, but they were cosy in a corner by the front window. He ordered champagne when the maître d' came, then looked at her. 'That OK?'

'Of course.'

'You look wonderful, by the way.'

'Thank you, sir,' she said, 'although I do feel slightly underdressed,' and she smiled at him. It was weirdly intoxicating.

'How did you find this?' It was in a small side street off the Kings Road.

'The usual. Look up the guide for the best Indian anywhere. I love it, I admit, I'd have wanted to come anyway but it's handy for your hotel.'

It had been less than ten minutes in the cab.

The menus came, the a la carte folder and the wooden block with the tasting menu listed.

'I don't like appearing stingy but, even though they're small portions, I do run out of steam on the tasting menu.'

'That's a relief. It looks wonderful but a mite overwhelming.'

'I promise you I can eat anything on the a la carte so you can order two starters and two mains, and we'll share, or I'll take the one you less like the look of when they come.'

They studied the menus in silence briefly, but she didn't want to dither. 'It all looks amazing. Why don't you order then we can do what you suggest?'

He put down the menus.

'Have you decided already?'

'Yes, 'fraid I'm like that. Now would you like wine or beer?'

'What do you normally do?'

'Beer. It's the only place I do it, but you don't have to worry so much about matching tastes up.'

'I'm good with that.'

The waiter brought tiny, delicate poppadoms, mint yoghurt and an exquisitely chopped but threatening looking onion and chilli bowl.

'Are you ready to order sir? Madam?' He looked at her and she nodded towards Jack.

'We'll start with the cod and the scallops and then go with lobster and duck breast.'

He wrote slowly. 'And to drink, sir?'

'We'll just have Cobra with the food please, but you could bring two more glasses of champagne before we start.'

'It's amazing. I've never seen dishes like that. Have you been here a lot?'

'It's my younger son's favourite and he has an appetite for the tasting menu.'

'Oh, an expensive night out.'

'That's not the half of it. He wants wine and not beer and still has his student drinking capacity. And I once had one of those silly party buttons that said *Life is too short to drink cheap wine* and he's never let me forget it. But we have fun.'

She had asked the question artlessly but was now glad that she had.

'And I like to bring the foreigners here, very few of them have ever had anything like it and almost all of them end up raving about it.'

That was true. They had many international visitors and, if they were staying in town, he would take them to dinner.

'What's your favourite food?' And they fell into an easy conversation. She knew he had dined all around the world, but he made her talk about what she liked eating, what she liked cooking. She did like cooking but in truth her more adventurous attempts went unappreciated at home. That took the conversation into domestic issues but they both stuck to discussing children.

The main course came.

'Oh, they look wonderful,' she said, trying not to sound too out-of-town enthusiastic.

'The lobster for madame, please,' he answered the waiter's questioning look.

'Are you sure? I like duck breast too.'

'Well you can have some if you want but I am trying to spoil you.'

'Thank you, sir,' she said again, trying to perfect the gracious nod.

'Oh, I think I've been very spoiled already, thank you. This is the least I could do.'

'I rather thought you had more on your mind.'

He raised his eyebrows.

'For later, I mean.'

A big smile lit his face. 'Ah, when I regain control, you mean?'

'Yes, when you regain control.' They looked into each other's eyes.

She was glad it was a short taxi ride. He had got the bill with the coffee and asked them to call the cab, so it was waiting by the door. Having restricted themselves to chaste finger touching across the table, they now fell on each other passionately. Their arms were around each other but between kisses he looked in her eyes and moved her hand to his crotch. She felt his bulge, and he had clearly been right about going commando. 'You've recovered quickly,' she said smiling at him. He lifted her knee across his, exposing her as her skirt slid up. He slid his hand gently up, letting his finger first graze her clitoris, then rub her and push gently at her entrance. She wanted to push towards him but started looking at the driver and their surroundings. They were in shadow but still exposed as the taxi passed buses and pedestrians. His hand slid away again, he wrapped his arms around her and kissed her, more tenderly than passionately this time, letting his tongue merely brush the tip of hers.

Then he smiled at her again. 'I think she wants to play now, doesn't she?'

'She's wanted to all evening, but I had a plan.'

'Ah yes, your plan. I don't really have one for tonight beyond showing you, as you put it, more of my repertoire.'

'I may regret that. That was way more adventure

than I'd bargained for last time.'

'That's a relief. I think I may have used all my ideas up.'

She kissed him again. 'Somehow, Mr Stephens, I doubt that.' And she was both nervous and thrilled at his wicked grin.

She hoped they didn't look too dishevelled as they moved quickly through the lobby. They were in the lift before she could pause before a mirror to reassure herself. Not too bad, she thought, and then realized that late night hotels would see much, much worse. He was behind her with his arms around her while she checked herself. She could feel his cock hard against her. She wiggled at him. He smiled and squeezed her breasts.

'Cameras,' she said. He slid his hands up the front of her top and merely laughed.

The turndown team had been in and the room was shining and neat, and a new bottle of champagne was in the ice bucket. She went to it and lifted it from the ice.

'They're good to me. I do so much business here. So, they normally give me a small bottle for free. But a bottle of Taittinger?'

'I ordered that,' he said, 'don't worry, it's paid for, it won't appear on your bill.'

'You're very sweet, thank you.' She looked at him quizzically. 'Did you know it's my favourite?'

'You'd made a comment once at some event you'd

organized.'

'And you remembered?'

'Well, it's my favourite too.'

'Ah, so you'd actually ordered your favourite,' she teased him. 'It's a coincidence, or you're just lucky I said that. What if my favourite was Krug?'

'I'd have ordered Taittinger.' He smiled, lifted the bottle and popped the cork carefully, pouring them two glasses, handing one to her.

'And now, Claudia Jane,' he said as they sat together on the sofa, 'we're going to find out if you really do like being controlled.'

'What do you mean?'

He leaned back on the sofa, looking steadily into her eyes. Sometimes his look gave him away, she knew she could read his body language as well as anyone, but mostly, when he was neither smiling nor frowning, he seemed, not cold, but just inscrutable. Now this man who she'd long felt so close to had become her lover, her intense and passionate and adventurous lover, like nothing she'd ever experienced before – and, she thought, after one or two more weeks, like something she might never experience again. Or maybe she would. But right now, she could explore herself and find out more about the woman who was surprising her, the woman who had daydreams of this man taking her, the woman who demanded to have him, who had loved taking him all in her mouth, this man who made her feel so relaxed and yet so excited. She tried to look calm and returned his gaze.

'I think you know. I think you've been discovering more about yourself these past few weeks – and there's more you still want to know.'

'That's true,' she said, sipping her champagne, and tempted to say more but restraining herself. She felt so close to him. She wanted to know where he would take her.

'Well, you did a wonderful job of controlling me and I do believe I followed your instructions exactly. True?' She nodded.

'Well, now you're going to do exactly as I tell you. Just nod.' She nodded again.

'You have a wonderful body.' She had only just begun to believe that. 'And now it's mine for an hour. Later we will cuddle and sleep, but now you are my sex slave. I don't need you to agree any more. You can stop any time you choose. But while we're making love – and it may not always feel like that, but I promise you that's what we're doing – you will do everything I tell you to do.' He raised his glass to her; they clinked and sipped. This was making her nervous but also desperately thrilled. What would he do? What hadn't they already done?

'First I want to admire your wonderful body a little

more closely.'

He stood up, picked a cushion from the sofa and stepped over to place it on the desk by the window. He sat again on the sofa beside her.

'Now you walk over there, bend forward onto the desk and lift your skirt up to your waist. You have the most beautiful arse and you're going to show it to me.'

She hesitated but he was looking firmly at her. She began to slip her shoes off.

'No, no,' he said. 'Keeping them on will make it look even sexier and you'll be at the right height for my subsequent plans.'

He's right, she thought, and now I know he's going to fuck me and not just stare. She regained a measure of composure; she could make this very sexy for him although she'd never shown herself off so brazenly before. She walked a few tiny steps to the desk then turned her head to look over her shoulder at him. He was focused on her arse. She shouldn't rush this. She eased herself down on to the cushion. It wasn't comfortable but it was certainly better than the plain wood. And he was right about the shoes. They kept her hips above desk height. Now she wanted to show off to him and this would let him see everything.

She reached for the hem of her skirt. She tried to think of the strippers she'd seen. She should do this slowly. She moved her knees rhythmically as she inched the skirt up. It rode up at the back anyway, she would be showing everything soon. She looked over her shoulder again. He looked calm but enthralled. Now she lifted the hem up to her waist and pushed her arse back towards him.

'Wow, I was right, you have the most beautiful bum.'

She smiled to herself and looked out of the window. Maybe they were overlooked from distant rooms, but that thought made her feel naughty rather than nervous.

'But I also think your pussy is very beautiful. I want you to move your feet apart so I can see everything better.'

She moved her feet apart and felt much more naked. He must be able to see everything very clearly. He sat for a while, clearly studying her. She began to move her hips and thighs to some imaginary music.

'Delightful,' he said. She heard him standing and could see him, reflected in the window, moving towards her.

He pulled the leather belt from his trousers.

'That makes me nervous,' she murmured to herself but loud enough for him to hear.

'Oh, I wasn't planning to use the belt today.'

She looked up at him quickly and saw him smiling.

'I'm very pleased to hear it,' she said but wondered, deep down, whether she really was.

'I want to admire and enjoy your unblemished magnificence,' he said, kneeling behind her, placing his hands on her hips. 'But I also want to taste you and, hopefully, excite you. Reach back and hold your cheeks and then pull them as far apart as you can.'

This was still very new, and she hesitated. His hands moved to stretch her. 'Like this,' he said.

She moved slowly but did as she was told. It felt very odd, but his face moved in between her cheeks and she felt his hand move up to her pussy. His fingers fanned her mound and his thumb pressed on her, by now very wet, clitoris.

'Stretch yourself wider,' he said, 'my tongue wants to explore you.'

She pulled her cheeks wide and felt his tongue rimming her, entering her. It was strange and thrilling. She relaxed and let his tongue and fingers move. It was extraordinary. She tried to move to her inner music to stop the excitement mounting too quickly. Occasionally he would lean back a little and exhale, 'Beautiful,' before pushing his face in again to lick her everywhere and just as she reached the point of wanting him inside her, he felt him stand. She heard the zip and could sense the trousers drop. She felt the stiff bulge against her hip.

'I think we both want this now,' he said as he stood directly behind her.

'Mmm, oh yes, oh yes please,' she gasped as she

felt him slide easily and deeply into her.

His hands held her hips firmly and he seemed to move with her music. Then he began stroking the skin on her back, keeping a firm grip to keep their movements together.

After a while his movements slowed, and he pushed less deeply. 'I'm going to leave you here for a moment. Stay exactly where you are. Now, if I'm not mistaken, you've kindly provided some lube. I hope you won't regret that.'

She smiled to herself and thought, no I won't, not now, this is the new me.

He left her and went to the bedroom, she could hear, she straightened and was about to call when she heard him go to the bathroom, where she'd left the robe. She was looking at him when he came back in. She was almost standing, and her skirt had fallen halfway down her buttocks.

He looked serious. 'Claudia Jane, you were clearly told to stay exactly where you were, weren't you?'

'Yes,' she said quickly, 'yes I was.' And she leant forward and lifted her skirt all the way up to her waist.

'That's very nice, but I was completely obedient earlier when you were in control.' And she felt a sudden fierce stinging slap on her right buttock.

'Jack,' she called out and tried to stand but found his free hand in the middle of her back holding her firmly down on the desk. She tried to gather her senses. That had been a complete shock and had really stung. The sting stayed with her but slowly suffused into a warmth. His hand did not move from her back. His other hand gently massaged her burning cheek.

'It's a first offence, Claudia Jane, the punishment is only two.'

'Two,' she gasped as his hand slapped again, this time on the other cheek and, if anything, harder than the first. 'Ow, that really stung.'

'Yes, it was meant to, this is my control time,' and she felt him position himself behind her and slide his very stiff cock deep inside her. The shock of the slaps was quickly forgotten, and she moved in unison with him, his hands were on her hips, locking them together, then one hand moved and picked up the lube he had dropped on the desk beside her.

'I had a thrilling time at the flat,' he said, 'I'm afraid it's become almost an obsession these past few weeks to have you like that again. Reach round and pull your cheeks open.'

He pulled back slightly but kept his cock-head moving slowly in and out of her. She reached round and spread herself. She felt dollops of cold lube drop between her cheeks, his thumb massaged them around and inside her. She had found it so strange and unexpected; now she found that she too had been waiting for this again, that tingling around the rim as he entered her, the feeling of complete fullness as he slowly, carefully slid half way in.

She gasped, he waited.

'A little more,' she murmured even though her whole insides seemed to be filling up.

He pushed a little more. She gasped again.

'Those are lovely noises,' he said, 'but they make me want to push even further.'

'Go on,' she whispered, although she felt she couldn't take any more, but as she felt his belly on her cheeks and his thighs on hers, she knew he was completely in her and she felt completely full of him.

'This feels utterly wonderful,' he whispered, beginning to ease himself in and out of her. She felt always full, but the tingling of his movement increased and excited her.

'I've been dreaming of this,' he said, 'but in my dreams I can control myself. This feels so wonderful that I know I can't keep it going for long.'

'I don't want to wait, I want to feel you coming.'

'I want you to come with me.' His movements were becoming intense.

Her excitement was mounting. 'I'm not sure I can, I'm not sure I can. I've never done this before.'

His movements slowed, he pushed less deep.

'Reach between your legs. Touch yourself.'

She hesitated.

'Claudia Jane. I'm finding it very hard to control myself like this, but you will do as I say.' And he slapped her arse, gently this time, to remind her of what might happen.

She reached under her belly and touched herself. She hadn't touched herself in years, but it was instantly electrifying.

'Good girl,' he breathed, he held her hips firmly again and resumed his deeper thrusts, this time his movements more pronounced. She was aware of his thrusts and his noises but more aware of the intense feelings in her clitoris and her arse. She knew she was coming. She found a rhythm with him and slowly felt the rising waves of feeling as her orgasm began to overwhelm her exactly as his was overwhelming him. She was almost screaming; he was moaning loudly, thrusting on and on even as her orgasm began to subside, until his groans lessened to a heavy breathing and his thrusts began to slow and become gentler.

He slipped from her, moved his hands to her shoulders, pulled her up to him, turned her, embraced her.

'Amazing,' he whispered, 'come with me, let's lie down, I have to hold you and your beautiful naked body.'

They walked slowly to the bedroom, his arm

around her waist, and fell on the bed together. He slowly unbuttoned her shirt and easily removed her bra, pausing for kisses between the languid movements. She unhitched her skirt while he leaned back to admire her. She snuggled into him.

'The holdups look wonderful, but I'd like your naked leg skin wrapped around me.'

'I want your skin too,' she said, sitting up and rolling the stockings off before cuddling in tightly to him again.

'Are you OK? Not sore, not offended?'

'Not offended, heavens no. A little bit shocked, I suppose, and yes, I am a bit sore.'

'From the spanking, or from me pushing him where he doesn't belong?'

'Oh, the spanking doesn't smart now, but you've made my arse sore.' She cuddled him tightly. 'But I think it's exactly one of the places where he does belong now. Christ, I'm surprised to hear myself say that.'

'It wasn't the first time?' She looked up; he looked a little shocked.

'No, no, of course not,' she said, smiling, 'that time at the flat was the first time.'

'Oh, sorry, I should have been more cautious.'

'I would have said no but I was curious – and I like being close to you. I'm not going to ask about your first time. That obviously wasn't it.'

He looked guarded.

'It's OK, please don't start getting all tactful with me. I am loving this, but I know it ends after next weekend. You are going to fuck me next weekend, aren't you?'

'I thought we had all day Saturday planned.'

'We do. Are you still OK with that?'

'Definitely. I need to know what else is in your repertoire.'

He laughed. 'Well, not much more really. I may get some toys in to make sure you get fully stimulated. Do you use a vibrator?'

'I have one. It was a present at a girls' night out, but I've never used it.'

'OK but leave it all with me. You gave me such a wonderful time before dinner I want to see how I can excite you and keep you on edge.'

'Oh, you were doing that very well just now, thank you.'

'Ah, but I was having a thrilling time too, probably even more than you were. I'm afraid I liked bossing you around and you really do have the most fabulous arse.'

'You have a strange way of showing your appreciation.'

'It looked even lovelier with two big red handprints on it.'

'Is that standard repertoire?'

'It doesn't have to be.'

'I don't know about that yet. I liked you just taking control of me. I liked having to do what you said. It's funny, that's not really like me.'

'I know that from work – telling me to fuck off if I get too arrogant.'

She smiled remembering the incident, thinking for a moment that she was bound to be fired, watching him turn away, saying nothing and then coming to her desk half an hour later with a cup of coffee and an apology.

'But that wasn't really my question. Look, I know you're going away, and I know already, unfortunately, that I'll find it hard with you having a new life but, if you can do it, and if we really are going to stay phone friends…'

'We are, of course we are. Christ, you're the only person I can really talk to.'

'I'd like to believe you, I honestly would, but I can only do that if you're open with me. Not just honest – you can find your diplomatic ways of avoiding untruths – but open. Let me know what you're really up to.'

'Hmm, that doesn't sound like me.'

'I know, but I think we have a fairly unusual friendship, don't we?'

'That's very true.'

'So, how about trying this openness thing?'

'OK, we'll try.'

She looked at him cautiously. She was uncertain.

She didn't know how brave she really was and how she would react when he talked to her about new people he would undoubtedly meet. But she knew enough to know that too many secrets would be the death of friendship. There would be a relationship of sorts, a friendly one, but something at the centre of what they now had had become very special to her, unique even.

'We'll try, hmm, that doesn't sound very committed, Mr Stephens.'

'Well, it will be pretty new for me. A bit like you having a cock pushed up your bum.'

'That's not the same thing at all,' she said, laughing.

'How can I reassure you?'

'You can start by telling me more about your repertoire. How many women have you spanked?'

He smiled. 'All who deserved it.'

'And how many deserved it?'

'Well, it's more accurate to say all who wanted it.'

'Gosh, is that many?'

'It's probably more than you think.'

'Oh.' And she fell silent, unsure about whether pursuing openness was such a good idea. 'Did you think I wanted it?'

'I didn't know. It was easier to ask for forgiveness than permission. If I'd asked, you'd have said no.'

'Probably. Do you normally ask?'

'Please can we get away from the notion that I do

this all the time? I've had a few relationships, that's all, and it's come up in some of them. And to answer your question in our new spirit of openness, no, I don't always ask. Once or twice I've been asked.'

'What? They ask you to spank them?'

'It's happened. That's how it first started for me. I was intrigued, I suppose I've always been an arse man and I'd thought about it, but I was suddenly confronted by a request.'

'She actually asked you to spank her?'

'Look, we weren't standing by the baked beans in Tesco, we were in the middle of a fairly intense affair, and at one particular moment she cried out spank me! So, I did – and then she said harder! So, I did again – and yes, I did enjoy it.'

'And that became part of your routine?'

'Yes, it did. Look, are you really up for this openness?'

Claudia moved her hand to his cock. 'Yes, I want to know more. How did you spank her?'

'Well, the first time, when she called out spank me, I'd been inside her, but later, when I realized how much she enjoyed it, I would put her over my knee. I guessed that was what she wanted, correctly as it happened. She would play pretend naughty and expect me to respond that way.'

'And did you hit her as hard as you hit me?'

'I don't like to think I hit you. I spanked you. I

wouldn't ever hit anyone.'

'OK, you spanked me, you didn't hit me. How hard did you spank her?'

'Harder.'

'Harder?' she spluttered, squeezing his cock.

'Careful,' he said.

'Sorry, but I can't work out anyway if he's growing again because I'm holding him or because you're getting excited by your own memories. I'd better leave him.'

'No, please don't do that, you have a lovely touch.'

'OK, but harder, tell me. Much harder?'

'No, I think I slapped you pretty hard.'

'Yes, you definitely did. I was struggling to think what harder could have been like.'

'Well, the paddle was harder.'

'The paddle?'

'Yes, she bought a paddle and wanted me to use that.'

'And you did?'

'Of course. Look, I love looking at your bum. I always did, by the way, I'd often look at you in the office and admire it, but I'm afraid I love it even more now when it's naked and bright red.'

'And did you admire hers too?'

He hesitated. 'This is an easy one to answer. It's in the past, it's non-threatening and, as it happens, her bum was a bit big and she had saddlebags, but if we're going to do the openness thing, I'm going to tell you things exactly as they were.'

'And as they are. I want this for the future. I know it'll be hard, but I'm sure I can handle it better if you tell me that some little Chinese woman with a perfectly pert bum has draped herself over your knee and begged you to spank her.'

She wasn't actually sure it would be better, but she felt certain that imagining things herself would be worse. And while her mind turned over some strange images, her hand was massaging him into life again.

'Come and sit on me,' he said.

Without letting go of his cock she straddled him and then eased him into her. He had grown stiff again, but she took him in easily. Had his story aroused her? She could think about that later. Right now, this man was smiling up at her and she was utterly enjoying riding his cock. They moved slower this time; his fingers ran gently across her nipples, which grew harder, then his hands cupped her breasts.

'You really do have lovely tits,' he whispered. He stayed relatively still, she was moving harder, pushing herself down on to him, feeling greedy for him again. She leaned forward, pressing her breasts to his chest. His hands moved to her hips.

'Slap my bum, please, I want it again.'

His left arm gripped her waist and pulled her up his torso slightly. His right hand moved to her arse. He patted her gently twice and then freed his arm to deliver a stunning slap.

'Ow,' she cried, and twitched, almost losing his cock before pushing down again. 'Go on, I want more, just like this.'

He spanked her again, just as hard but she twitched less this time and waited for the next. He waited too but held her waist firmly and then delivered another slap. She held him tightly. It stung fiercely but she wanted more. He spanked her eight or nine times, feeling her excitement grow, then moved his hands to her hips again to move with her as she orgasmed again, pushing herself passionately down on to him, holding him tightly until her movements stopped and she could roll off him and feel his arms around her as they lay side by side.

She nuzzled her face into his neck. 'Er, I don't know what came over me.'

'You found the story exciting?'

'I suppose I did a bit. But I'd never thought about being spanked before.'

This wasn't quite true, she remembered. Mandy had been spanked at home, she knew, and when she found out she'd had some very strange feelings about what that might be like. Mandy had resented it, and she herself found it unimaginable in her own home. Her parents were gentle people and even a harsh word was rare. But at the time she'd had one or two nights, playing gently with herself, when she imagined being told by a master at school to bend over for him and lift her skirt, then she'd tried to think of how that might feel, how it would sting but, when she found herself being too stirred by the thoughts, she switched her focus to boys and what they were trying to do when their hands moved between her legs. And in her dreams, she let them, and it felt warm and very pleasant as she played more intensely with herself.

'You got very excited about it.'

'I did, didn't I? But was it a story? Were you just making it up?'

'No, that really happened.'

'I don't know about the over the knee stuff and the paddle, though.'

'You wanted to know more about what you call my repertoire. I've told you that bit but don't get carried away. I don't have that much history.'

'But does everyone get put over your knee?'

He laughed. 'No, if it happens it's mostly a bit like tonight, caught up in the passion of the thing. It just adds spice. I've only known two or three who wanted that role play sort of thing.'

'But you enjoyed it.'

He breathed deeply. 'Yes, I admit I did, but it's not an essential part of a relationship for me.'

'What's essential then?'

'Well, we've had a relationship for one or two years now I know, fortunately, people wouldn't call it that but since I've been spending more and more time away, I've found you were the only person I could talk completely openly to. That's what I want. So, you are asking for openness is odd, because in many ways you've had it. I admit though it hasn't covered ground like this, and it's been, to my shame, very one way.'

'What do you mean?'

'I haven't asked you much about yourself.'

'Well, you hadn't told me much about yourself. Most of the talk was about business.'

'That's true, but a lot of my heart and soul is in that. And my ego, I suppose,' he added ruefully, 'so you're getting, like it or not, a pretty clear view of what I'm about and what I think of things and people. But you don't give much in return,' he laughed gently, 'you're always very tactful when I get nosey about people. I can't complain, it's one of your many great virtues, but it does frustrate me when I think there's some dirt and I can't get information.'

'You know enough, I think.' She had always been impressed by how he would walk round the business, talking to anyone and everyone, and it gave him, for a boss, an unusually good picture of what was going on and how people were feeling.

They cuddled in to each other. He fondled her arse

cheeks. 'Sting?'

'No, it just feels warm now.'

He moved. 'Let's look. Have I left a mark?'

She turned to let him.

'Wow, you recover quickly.'

'Really? Do you normally leave marks?'

He laughed again. 'I am going to stress, I don't have wide experience, but I have known people where it takes days to disappear.'

'I suppose it's handy if it doesn't show but it's not like anyone's going to be studying my bum any time soon.'

'Not at home?'

'It's a while since we slept together, or even in the same room.'

'Should I know more about that?'

'Maybe. Do you want to know more about it?'

'Well, I don't just want one-way openness. I want to know what you're thinking and feeling, and what you're going through.'

'OK.' She felt pleased, she wanted it two-way too. 'But I don't have any stories like yours to entertain you.'

'Oh, I'm sure there are a few things. You can think about it. You can tell me on Saturday about the naughtiest things you've done.'

'It'll be brief and, as I said, not very spicy for you.'

'Well, I still want to know much more, even the ordinary stuff. I'd love it now, but I sense we're both getting sleepy.'

'Are you staying?' She'd been reluctant to ask, and now it slipped out. She wanted to nestle in to his body and feel him sleep, to smell him, to listen to his breathing.

'Is that OK?'

'Of course, it's OK. I like you here.'

'I will get up very early to go to the flat to change and shower. I can't turn up in the office in yesterday's shirt.'

'Do you need an alarm?'

'No, I always wake very early.'

And he did.

When the sun angled through the blinds and woke her, she turned to an empty space and felt hugely disappointed, but the card at her bedside propped against a glass with a flower he'd plucked from the vase in the other room said: *Thank you for a wonderful and unforgettable night.*

She hugged herself, delighted to still feel sore in unnatural places.

7

She had meetings all morning at the hotel and was glad to be busy, but there would be occasional physical reminders of the night and she hoped, when the memories caught her, that she wasn't smiling.

The meetings went well, using the place a few times made organizing events and conferences easier. She understood what the hotel could do, and they understood what she was striving for so she drove home that afternoon looking forward to a long bath in the evening when she could shut herself off and think of the night again. Dave would watch TV and probably drink too much and the kids, once she'd fed them, would be happy to play computer games and wouldn't comment that the usual restrictions were not being applied.

She lowered herself gingerly into the bath; there was enough residual soreness to remind her to be careful and, although the hot water burnt when it touched her skin, it made her smile rather than wince. She had checked her arse in the mirror and, he was right, there were no marks left from the spanking but, where he'd pushed that big cock in deep behind her, that still smarted a lot, however much lube he'd used. She closed her eyes and lay back. It was still three days to Saturday, she would be ready for more then.

And the irritating mosquito thought about what happened after, when he would fly off to a new home, briefly buzzed her brain again. She would deal with that, she told herself, but wasn't convinced – but she did manage to focus her thoughts only on their next meeting.

If they only repeated what they'd already done, it would still be more than she'd experienced before, yet he'd hinted there could be more. Toys? Really? A paddle? She thought not. But his story had left an image in her head. It left her a little excited and a little jealous. That was a dangerous combination, she knew, it made you do silly things, and she remembered her times back home. Maybe that was the naughtiest thing she should tell him about. She'd been out with Malcs and Millie and Kevin in one of their favourite pubs. They hung around as couples for a while. There was sex but not exclusive relationships. She might have got closer to Malcs, but she didn't take him too seriously. She knew he saw other girls and he would be going off after the summer, so she had been caught off guard by her reaction when another couple joined them, and the girl sat next to Malcs. The girl let her hand stay on Malcs' leg, stroking him, and Malcs had not moved away.

'Who was that?' She asked, as coolly as she could when Malcs was driving her home.

'Who?'

'The tart with her hand on your leg in the pub.'

He laughed, 'Ah, Alice. She's no' a tart but she's good fun.'

She bristled but was determined to show nothing. She put her hand on his cock and rubbed slowly. 'Am I good fun, Malcs?'

'Oh, aye, and if you keep doing that, you are splendid fun.'

She could feel him growing quickly. She moved her hand to his zip. 'I think you should stop the car, Malcs, there's a layby up by the wood.' A plan was forming slowly; it was dusk on a warm summer evening; many things might be possible. They turned the bend and she was relieved to see the layby was empty. During the day it would have been full of cars, people stopped and took picnics up through the wood to the top of the hill. But now, once he stopped the car, she could relax and unbuckle him and ease his cock out of his pants. It was stiff by now and the head was already wet and shiny. She felt him ease his seat back as she took him gently in her mouth, more teasing than tasting. She heard the odd car pass them as she licked and stroked him.

She looked up suddenly. 'Come on, Malcs, we're going into the woods.'

She was glad she'd worn a skirt and the wedges weren't too impractical on a dry path. They got out. Malcs buttoned his jeans but didn't zip them. She took his hand and led him through the gate. They didn't go far before he stopped her by a tree and pulled her towards him. An arm went around her shoulders, and he kissed her but put his free hand up her skirt straight away to touch her pussy. She was wet already, she knew, and she soon felt his fingers on her clit as he pushed the flimsy fabric aside. She unbuttoned him, pushed his pants down while they were still kissing and freed his cock. Sex outdoors had crossed her mind sometimes, and once or twice she had masturbated to the thought, but she hadn't imagined actually doing it. Now she had his sweet cock in her hands, and her pussy was wet and waiting. She leaned back against the tree, they were more or less behind it and partly sheltered from the road, but she didn't care, she could show Malcs what fun was. She pushed his jeans and pants further down. 'Put it in me, Malcs,' she whispered to him. He lifted the front of her skirt and, keeping her pants to one side, he pushed himself into her. She pulled him to her, trying to get comfortable. He was bending at the knees; she could feel the bark scratching her back through the thin shirt. She wanted him deeper, she wanted to make him come, but standing up, the first time she'd ever tried it, was awkward.

'Malcs, Malcs, shhh,' she whispered, moving less herself, getting him to slow down. 'Malcs, I want you deeper in me, let me turn around.'

He leaned back to look at her and smiled, still

leaving his cock inside her.

'Nice,' he said, his smile widening. He pulled back. She turned and bent over, bracing herself against the tree. Malcs quickly lifted her skirt. 'You have a lovely arse,' he said and quickly slipped her pants to her ankles, helping her take one foot out to leave her free to move. She felt his cock quickly penetrate her, free to go deeply now and she knew she was easy to enter. His hands pushed her skirt up higher. He was no doubt admiring her lovely arse as he kept pushing firmly into her. And Malcs was very good; he could keep going for ages, she knew. She wanted to make him come. She reached between her legs and stroked his balls. He pushed harder and began moaning loudly.

'Oh, honey, that's gorgeous.' But still he kept thrusting, so slowly she bent deeper, gripping him tighter. 'Oh, Christ, that's wonderful, wonderful.'

She felt even fuller, but she knew she was gripping him, he fitted tighter into her, getting noisier all the time. She bent right down now, almost toe touching, she could feel his fingers digging sharply into her hips. 'Oh, I can't stop now,' he yelled suddenly and began thrusting very violently as deeply as he could. She felt uncomfortable, but a little triumphant. She eased herself up a little while Malcs continued inside her. He was always very copious, it always made her smile, but these pants tonight would have to be washed very carefully, they were under her shoe now and would soon be soaking up lots of his cum.

Finally, he eased himself out and she stood up and turned around. 'That was amazing,' he breathed, 'absolutely amazing.'

She leaned back against the tree again, breathing heavily. Malcs put his arm around her and slid his hand to her pussy, gentler this time. He was sweet like that, he always thought of her pleasure as well, and she was feeling very excited, the smell of the wood, the feel of the cooling evening air on her skin, the excitement of an outdoor fantasy, the feel of his fingers on her wet clitoris. 'You're beautiful,' he was muttering, 'just amazing.' But she was focusing on feeling his fingers on her; she was regaining that rhythm they had found a few moments ago.

She knew she was coming, she clasped him to her, rubbing herself on him as much as he was touching her until her orgasm broke over her and she was screaming, 'Oh, oh, oh, oh,' into the gathering sweet dusk.

She sat up in the bath and added more hot water. Her naughtiest memory? Possibly, but anyway it would do if Jack wanted a story on Saturday. And maybe, just maybe, she'd be in the big window at the flat, looking over London and squeezing Jack's cock with her pussy just as she had squeezed Malcs' into submission all those years ago.

8

She looked out of the big window. It was a bright, breezy day and white clouds were scudding quickly across a brilliant blue sky. The city, with so much glass on the newer, taller buildings, dazzled as a backdrop behind the river and the parliament buildings.

He was making coffee. They had embraced passionately enough when she had arrived, the same concierge with the beaming smile had again shown her into the lift, and Jack had been waiting at the open door. Her thoughts about him had become even more intensely physical since the night at the hotel; she wanted a day of passion, maybe her last?

After the long kiss in the doorway, he had led her to the sofa and asked how long she had. She had a good story about having to work in town all day, preparing for the meeting in a few weeks. Dave never questioned deeply, merely grumbled about the time she spent at work.

She leaned back and looked at the river, muddy looking but somehow sparkling in the sunlight. She felt almost uneasy that she wasn't being ravished, she'd come with such expectations of pushing her own boundaries.

And he was making coffee.

He came with the cafetière on a tray – and some biscuits on a plate, for God's sake – and even a jug of milk, although they both drank coffee black.

He sat down at the other end of the sofa, looking slightly uneasy, or was she just imagining that?

'I've got stuff in for lunch, but it'll show you what a boring caterer I am, it's the same as last time. Would you rather go out? There are some quirky places nearby; you can imagine the people from MI6 on neighbouring tables secretly swapping their briefcases.'

'I enjoyed the lunch last time and I'm very happy to do the same. I hadn't imagined going out. I mean it's a lovely idea. I'd like to try and spot the spies. Do you really think they meet there?'

'There are a couple of places under the railway arches and I'm sure the MI6 people go there. When the trains are noisiest overhead, I look for the men leaning closer together, and I speculate on what secrets they're sharing.'

'I like trying to spot the clandestine, but I'm a bit greedy for time on our own, to be honest. What's up? You seem a little distracted.'

'I'm not distracted. I'm completely focused on you.'

'But?'

'No, it's an and. I want to make sure you have a perfect day.'

'Ah, and coffee and biscuits and lunch over the road would be a perfect day, would it?'

'I don't know when we'll get the chance to have another normal day.'

'Mr Stephens, what do you think of as normal for us?'

He hesitated. 'I thought you might like to have a day doing normal couple things.'

'Ah, like biscuits and lunch,' she smiled, 'and you hadn't noticed that my new normal is having my brains fucked out by you?'

'Well, that thrills me, of course, but I didn't want you to think this was all about sex.'

'It isn't – if I believe you. I can find out about that in long phone calls in the next few months, if I still get the smiley voice and the outrageous observations. What I can't get then is your cock and your dirty imagination, you'll be pointing that somewhere else. I want them for myself today, thank you.'

He still looked a little guarded.

'Are you worried I'm going to get needy and clingy on you? Is that it?'

He relaxed a little. 'Something like that. Look, this is something a little special, well, it is for me. It's grown in a special way, I don't like letting my guard down, but I'm open with you in a way I never am with anyone else. I know I'll be a bit needy and clingy, as you call it. I'd already got that way with you when I was travelling and needed to talk to you, and that was before all this. So, I don't know how I'll feel on lonely nights in Singapore.'

'You'll feel like you should go out and get some company and have your fun and then you can go back to your plush apartment and feel guilty about little me, pining away at home, watching telly with only the snores of a drunken husband for company.'

'I wasn't thinking about it quite like that, but I have started to worry about you.'

'Jack, I'm a big girl. I love it that you're concerned, but I knew this day would come, the day when I have no idea what happens next. But I'm not going to spoil today by worrying about tomorrow; I've done too much of that. I want some memories to feed on for my lonely nights, for heaven's sake. Now, are you going to take me in the other room and fuck me?'

He leaned back and laughed, then reached for her hand, 'You are adorable – and unique, I've never been propositioned like that before.'

'And I've never propositioned anyone like that. So, don't disappoint me.' She stood up.

They were naked quickly, her almost as quickly as him, and they were kissing and embracing affectionately, rather than passionately but his cock found its way into her very soon. She was on her back, looking up at him, lifting her knees to get as much of him as she could. If he'd seemed reluctant when they were on the sofa, there was no reticence about his cock, which pushed slow and deep inside her. He held his weight on his hands and was looking into her eyes, smiling.

'This is what I came for today, you oaf. I want to feel him inside me all day. I want some dirty tricks, some of your naughty ideas. But mostly I want to just feel you inside me.'

'Everywhere?'

'Of course, everywhere, now you've made me realize what a greedy slut I am.'

'Well, we'll see if we can make you feel even sluttier.' He was smiling even as he was pushing his cock deep into her. Without breaking his rhythm, he reached to the bedside cabinet, and she heard a drawer open. She raised an eyebrow at him.

'There's lube in there for later.'

'Just lube?'

'No, not just lube,' he smiled, 'you wanted a dirty repertoire, you will get a dirty repertoire.'

'Finally, you get it. You're a dirty monster, Jack Stephens, and I want to know how dirty.'

'Let's try this first.' He'd taken something from the drawer, now he withdrew from her and sat back on his heels.

'What's that?'

'It's a cock ring. It's got a mini-vibrator on it. It'll

buzz on your clit.'

'And what does it do for you?' she asked as he fitted the thing down on the base of his very erect penis.

'Oh, it should make me feel bigger and let me keep going longer.'

'I suppose I asked for that.'

'Never mind what you asked for. You'll get what you're given now. Lift your bum up. I'm going to put pillows under you.'

He slid two pillows under her and adjusted her hips. She heard a buzzing noise just before his cock entered her again. His hands went behind her knees and pushed them up towards her shoulders. Suddenly he felt incredibly, almost uncomfortably deep. She felt the vibrations from the ring as his pelvis pushed it on to her clit.

'Oh,' she gasped, twitching, moving to get comfortable but he kept her pinned and pushed, if anything, deeper. 'Oh, easy, Jack. It's wonderful but a little easier please.'

He eased back and released her knees and took his weight on his hands. He looked at her, smiling, but kept the pressure on her clit. She closed her eyes and let herself focus on the vibrations, still feeling his cock very deep inside her.

'God, I want to come already. Is that right?'

He laughed. 'Everything's right today,' he said, 'that was your idea, I thought.' He pulled back a little and the vibrations became a gentle tingle. 'I planned to make you come a lot but maybe we'll make you wait a bit for the first one. Come on' – he pulled out of her – 'sit on me. You can control yourself a little better that way.'

'That's true but I thought you were going to control me.'

He gave a mock evil laugh. 'Oh, I shall do, my dear, and part of that is making you wait for your first orgasm.' He kissed her and rolled on to his back, pulling her on to him. 'Now sit down on him and show me your tits!'

Now passion had become fun and she felt she'd pulled back from the edge, but as she eased herself on to him again and felt the vibrations on her clit, she realized she was still close to coming.

He did too apparently. 'Let me turn the buzzer off.' He groped down between their bellies and the noise stopped. 'Push down; you'll still feel the bump on your clit.'

She pushed down. He was very deep, and he was right she could move and feel the ring's bump pushing on her exactly where she wanted. But as high as she was on the thrill of it, she wanted to wait, to keep going like this.

They found a rhythm, her pushing down on him, occasionally bending to kiss him, sometimes leaning back to let him touch her breasts.

'You do have fabulous tits,' he breathed, 'but now I'm going to play with your bum while I fuck you. Can you reach the lube in the drawer?'

She leaned across to the cabinet, keeping his cock deep inside her.

She saw the lube and reached for it. 'Gosh,' she gasped, 'that's a pretty full drawer.'

'Just a few things for your entertainment.'

She pulled out the leather paddle. 'This is for my entertainment?'

'No, that's if you're naughty.'

She sat down firmly on him again. 'But I think I'm being naughty anyway. Are you punishing me for this?'

'No, I'll punish you for disobedience.'

She dropped the paddle back into the drawer.

'No, no, Claudia. Hand me the paddle!'

She looked at him quizzically.

'The paddle,' he repeated, looking serious, mock-serious she thought, but she wasn't completely sure.

'The paddle,' he said again when she hesitated. She took it from the drawer but held it away from him.

'I didn't hear a please.'

He grabbed her wrist and pulled the paddle from her grasp. His left arm shot round her waist pulling her down on to him, and suddenly there was a loud noise and a searing pain in her buttocks.

'Ow,' she screamed, 'Ow. That really hurt. Hurts. It stings.'

He put the paddle down on the bed beside them.

'Of course. Now hand me the small dildo from the drawer. Please.'

She leaned over to the drawer and pulled out a blue vibrator.

'Wow, what's the black one for? It's huge.'

'That's for later, when I get tired.'

'But—' and she hesitated.

'Oh yes, it's much bigger than I am, but you'll be very relaxed by then.'

She handed him the blue one, he placed it by the paddle, and they settled back into the rhythm they'd had earlier, and she pressed on him and on the ring's bulge, moving closer to her edge again. She felt his hand rubbing her bum gently.

'Sore?'

'It still stings but it's more of a glow now.' She thought for a moment. 'It's quite pleasant now, actually, but that was really painful, you know.'

'I know,' he nodded and carried on stroking her skin.

She leaned down on to him, squeezing her breasts on to his chest.

She felt him fumbling with the lube and then his fingers were massaging a large cold dollop around her anus. She sighed, she'd come to love the feel of him touching her, of him playing with her. She wiggled her hips to encourage him. His hands were on her bum, pulling her cheeks apart. She felt him slide a finger into her, it tingled delightfully. 'Yes, yes,' she gasped, 'a little more please,' and suddenly she was stretched a little wider.

Now his arm moved to her waist to pull her higher up him, and he eased his fingers deeper. She felt very stretched but more and more excited.

His fingers left her, and she heard a buzzing noise again, a different one this time and there was something hard pushing at her arse. That dildo, she thought, and she held him more tightly. Moving further up him to let him do what he wanted – what she wanted – the thing was inside her now, almost as big as he was, and he was pushing it deeper. She felt very stretched and very full and very, very excited.

'I have to!' she screamed, 'I have to come now.' And the waves crashed over her as she ground down on his cock. The dildo slipped away. His hands gripped her hips. She was over the peak of her climax sliding gently down, able to feel and enjoy him rising to his. Now he was loud; now he was thrusting and grinding. Now he was pulsing into her. She clung to him, moving slower now but trying to squeeze every drop from him as his heavy breathing slowed, and his arms moved around her waist, and he began to kiss her lips, and she still felt his lingering fullness in her.

They lay motionless for a long while, his cock not subsiding, tenderly rubbing his hands down her back and her bum, kissing her shoulders, her face, her lips.

'Is he ever going to go down?' she asked, 'I'm loving it, but doesn't it get painful for you at some point?' She pushed herself up to look into his eyes.

'Well not yet, I'm very happy to say, but you are right.' And he threw the various artefacts off the bed and slid her off him, pulling her tightly to his side.

'Wow,' she said, 'that was wonderful, wonderful.'

'All of it?'

'Don't make me say it.' She looked up at him.

'Well, I thought all of it was wonderful,' he said, smiling at her.

She nuzzled her face into his neck. 'Yes, I thought all of it was wonderful.'

He may have slept a while, she certainly did, but they hadn't moved when she was awake again. She smelled him, kissed his chest, rubbed her fingers through the fur, slid her hand down his belly to touch his cock. It felt full but not stiff.

'It might take him a little while yet.'

'Oh,' she said in mock disappointment.

'His big friend in the drawer is waiting,' he said mock threateningly, 'but I want to hear some stories from your dissolute youth. You said you would.'

'You said I would,' she contradicted him, 'my youth wasn't dissolute.'

'That was a pretty wonderful blowjob at the hotel for a young innocent, madam; you're not going to tell me that was a first.'

'No. I had a good friend when I was young. He was good for me, I think. Oh, he liked his fun as he used to say, but he used to think about me as well. And the other girls apparently.' She laughed lightly. 'But everyone knew that, so no-one got too hurt.'

'And I've him to thank for your blowjob skills?'

'Mostly, I suppose. It's not something I've practiced lately.'

'Ah, vanilla sex. I've had years of that.'

'You?'

'Yes. I've been married and contrary to all the stories I've been faithful most of that time.'

'It doesn't sound like it.'

'No, it's true, but that's a story we can spend hours on when I'm away and we're phoning. I want to know more about your youth and this boyfriend. What was his name?'

'Malcs. Malcolm.'

'You must have stories.'

'Funnily enough, yes.'

And she told him the story of the trip to the woods, without giving him the detail of how she'd bent over

118

completely to make Malcs come. She would save that for later when she had Jack in the big window. But she liked telling him about her skirt being lifted in the woods and the cool, fresh air on her bum. He was enjoying the story; she could feel his cock rising and pressing on her hip as she spoke. She straddled his thigh and pushed her clit down on to him, aware that she, too, was getting excited again. She felt his hand between her legs, his fingers sliding into her pussy. It was very wet, she knew.

'Pass me that big one.'

'What?'

'You know. It's in the drawer. I can't reach, I'm busy.'

That was true. One arm was round her waist, pulling her to him. His free hand was playing with her, making her more excited.

She reached for the large black dildo. She took it from the drawer and examined it, the shaft very black and modelled with veins, the head an unnatural brown colour. As her hand surrounded it, it was clearly much bigger than anything she'd touched, as big even as some of the men in the porn films she'd researched. They'd made her wonder what that would feel like.

Jack lay back, massaging her gently, intrigued to watch her studying the object.

'It's huge!'

'You're a big girl,' he said with a wicked smile, sliding another finger inside her, 'hand it to me!'

'Or?'

'You know or,' he said, 'the paddle's not far away. But actually, I think you'd like a really big cock.'

'You don't know that.' But he was manoeuvring her a little higher, allowing his hand to play with her more freely. She smiled at him and handed him the black cock. She positioned herself more at an angle on him with her legs a little wider. She could be a big girl. She felt his cock stiff now against her belly. There was a buzz; this thing too had batteries. She felt its head push into her wet, wet hole. She felt a little full, but it had gone in easily.

'Stick your bum up higher.'

She pushed her clit down on his thigh.

'I like this.'

'You'll like it more when I'm playing with you. Get your bum up.'

She arched her arse higher, feeling quite slutty and wanton but thrilled too to be told exactly what to do.

She felt him push the thing slowly and deeply into her. It wasn't difficult at all. She felt delightfully full and then his fingers began to massage her clit while his hand moved the dildo in and out. She pushed her arse a little higher to let him play more easily and to let herself feel excited more easily. She swayed back and forth.

Moaning softly, fucking herself gently on the huge thing, feeling his fingers touch her very gently, not letting her come, just keeping her on the edge of that delightful precipice. She was more across his lap now, focusing more and more on the sensations in her lower body, feeling them radiating out through all of her, up to her head, up to her heart but, as his fingers now began to press her more firmly, and his hand pushed the thing deeper, she focused again solely on her cunt. She knew this was going to make her come. This orgasm was coming from a long way away; she could feel it rushing in from a distant horizon with a power and an inevitability that she could wait for and thrill to. She was screaming as it hit her, she knew, but she let it all out, pushing her hips back and forth to feel the thing, to feel him touching her, massaging her excitement, which was going on and on; but she was breathing more deeply, moving more slowly, still feeling thrilled by that huge cock inside her, by his fingers still playing, even as she lowered herself slowly down to rest her belly on his thighs. She felt herself still twitching from it all as he slowly pulled it from her. He stroked her, her arse, her thighs. She loved his hands, his skin. She moved to feel more of him, to be able to kiss him, to wrap her arms around him, to feel his cock stiff under her belly.

'Wow,' she said, 'wow.' And she moved, rubbing his cock with her belly. 'And I want to give him some wow time too, but you'll be better off waiting till later.'

'I know I'll be better off waiting. He doesn't have the stamina or recovery powers of his black friend.'

'Oh,' she said, mock disappointed, smiling as a heavy hand slapped her bum again.

'I liked your story,' he said when they sat down to eat. He'd been right, the food looked very like what he'd served before, even the champagne was the same, but at least it was Taittinger. And she loved the food, the salmon, the meats, the cheeses (ah, they were a little different) and the colourful array of salads. It was a very relaxing way to eat and, now they were closer, she'd been in the little kitchen with him, laying it out, taking glasses and plates to the table, dressed casually in a tee shirt of his and a new pair of knickers – she was managing to wear the selection. She was glad she'd brought several with her, glad to have showered before lunch.

'It was a true story,' she said, slightly defensively.

'Oh, I assumed that,' he said, 'it made me want to take you out in the country this afternoon.'

'I have a plan to simulate the experience,' she said teasingly, 'I think you'll be a little bit thrilled later. But I don't think the countryside's on for our last day.'

He fell silent for a moment. 'I don't like to think of it as a last day.'

'That's nice of you to say, Jack, but I have to face the fact that I've booked your ticket for next week and we've no idea when you'll be in the UK again. I'm having a lovely time but I'm not going to let myself think about next Saturday.'

He took her hand. 'Well, can we just agree it's not a last day?'

She fought with herself, squeezed his hand, took a sip of champagne. 'I'll agree with that Jack but...'

'Go on.'

'Look, you probably won't be here again for ages. You'll have a new life to organize. I'm sure it'll be mostly work, work, work, it's what you do. But you'll also meet new people, and some of them will be ladies. You're obviously separated from your wife now. You'll enjoy life – and I'll want you to. But if we're going to continue in any form, then I want to know what you're up to. I want the openness I've had for the last year or so. I'll find it hard, of course I will, but I don't want all this shit about wondering and speculating. If you fuck somebody, I want to know.'

He raised his eyebrows. She smiled.

'Then you can come and fuck me whenever you're here.'

He laughed, one of his loud laughs, the ones that woke up the office. The office had its best days when he was around. Or maybe she had her best days when he was around.

'OK, if it happens, I'll tell you.'

'No, Jack, not if, when.'

That got a gentle laugh from him. 'I promise. But you'll tell me what you're doing.'

She snorted, 'I'll tell you, Jack, but it won't be very interesting.'

'We'll see,' he said.

We'll see, she thought, maybe we'll see.

They spent some time in silence, eating, drinking, occasionally looking at each other and smiling.

'I'm enjoying what I'm learning,' she said suddenly.

He smiled. 'And what are you learning?'

'What do you think I'm learning?'

He paused and looked a little serious. 'I'm guessing a bit.'

'You with your remarkable powers of insight?'

His face softened. 'Two things.'

'Two things?'

'Well, two areas.'

'Ah, two areas.'

'The first one is easy. I think you've found out that you can get much more pleasure from your body in many more ways than you thought.'

She nodded. 'Well that wasn't difficult, was it? That's been blindingly obvious. I've been thrilled with everything you've tried.'

'Everything?'

'Yes, everything. Don't make me spell it out. I'm

not sure I want to talk about it, not all of it, but I have found all of it thrilling.'

'Well, that kind of leads me into the second area. But I'm more out on a limb here.'

'Go on. I won't bite.'

'I see you as very capable and competent. You could do much more at a much higher level.'

'Tell me about it.'

'You deal with everyone very well and stand your ground when you need to.'

'Like telling you to fuck off?'

'Like telling anyone to fuck off, I guess. You stand your ground, you get things done, you're ever so capable.'

'I don't disagree; I don't want to be stupidly modest. I think I run the place when you're not there.'

'I know you do. So do the VPs, they're terrified of you.'

'Seriously?'

He smiled. 'Well, not terrified exactly but they treat you with immense respect and always go along with whatever you organize for us all.'

She felt gratified and a little bucked. 'OK, but what's this got to do with area two?'

He paused. 'I think, despite all that, despite taking the lead in the office – and I'm sure you do at home.'

She laughed. 'Definitely at home.'

'But sometimes you just want to be told.' He waited, to let it sink in, or to wait for her to argue, she wasn't sure. But she nodded slowly.

'You remember the last sales conference?'

'Of course, I do. You had a sexy little black dress and a snazzy hat. It really stood out.'

'Ah, with all the sales ladies in their slinky ball dresses, I don't think so. You were looking at some of them.'

'Not denying it. But I thought you looked hottest.'

'Well, I thought you looked hot. And if you'd told me that night to go to your room so you could fuck me, I'd have gone. I wanted you to. I tried to show you, but I'm not good at that. I'd dreamt of you telling me. I'd dreamt of coming to your room as you'd ordered and being told to strip for you. I'd dreamt of you staring at my body and then doing whatever you wanted to with me. So yes, maybe you're right. I do want to be told. I think I knew that. But you're the first man I've actually dreamed of telling me. It's the first time I've wanted someone to do all those evil things to me. You can just make me do whatever you want. I want to please you. I want, even when you take my clothes off, to obey you.'

She looked down at their hands.

'But I still want to be able to tell you to fuck off when we're working.'

And they laughed, leaned together and embraced

each other.

They worked their way through lunch, funny and serious by turns, talking about their pasts, their marriages, people at work – he surprised her by knowing far more about them than she'd thought. He surprised her by how long he'd kept his marriage going. She was much more than ten years younger but was already failing at her second. But then, as he was talking and laughing and being charming, as he sometimes could be, she realized that he'd had his distractions during his married time – a very itinerant life gave him far more opportunities than she could have had. But she wouldn't have taken them, she thought, wouldn't have looked for them. She'd not been unfaithful to Dave. She'd only been unfaithful to Douglas when they were already apart. In her life, in her marriages, when the love went you didn't look elsewhere, you just didn't look.

Then why was she here, drinking and laughing with this man, already wanting to touch him again?

'What am I doing here?' she asked suddenly – a question out of the blue, it was out of her mouth before she could stop it, he'd been talking rather cruelly about an American VP with a weight problem.

'Because you…' and he stopped. He'd been about to respond in the glib and sometimes funny way he responded when caught off guard or when not wanting to reveal anything. He took her hand and looked into her eyes.

'Do you have an answer to that?'

'No, I don't. Don't worry. Silly question. It just slipped out.'

He waited, looking serious for a while. 'Well, I don't think you're just on a voyage of self-discovery' – he smiled – 'much as I'm enjoying that. Are you worrying about next week?'

'Of course, I am. I've been telling myself that today is today, and tomorrow is tomorrow, and I'm not going to spoil our time by letting it get to me, but I can't hide it all the time.'

'It's bothering me too.'

'Oh, I believe you, but you fly off first class to an exotic life, new job, new people and I'll try to coax my little old car to get me back to a snoring and indifferent husband and some wonderful memories that have suddenly become just memories.'

He touched her hand again. 'And you're just making it worse. I'm sorry. I'm being completely stupid. What I'm actually doing is having the time of my life, I suppose I'm just wondering how it happened.'

'I've thought about that.'

'You've thought about it?' She was genuinely surprised.

'Yeah, I think we've been falling for each other for ages. We've kind of grown together without noticing it.'

She laughed. 'Well, I'd noticed it. I told you, I wanted you to order me to your room at the conference. I might have made a bigger play if I hadn't assumed you had somebody already back there.' He pretended to look shocked. 'No, I wouldn't have. I'm too shy really.'

'I didn't see too much of shy at the hotel.' He smirked.

'That's what you do to me.'

'My fault again.'

'No, it's not your fault. You were saying, about falling for each other. I liked that.'

'I meant it. But we have plenty of time to get serious in our phone calls. I want to know what you've got planned for me this afternoon.'

'That'll come later. I've lots of time. Oh, are you free? Do you have to be anywhere?'

'No, todays for us. I'm doing a family day tomorrow.'

'With all of them?'

'Yep, wags as well.' One son was married, she knew, she assumed the other had a girlfriend. 'We're being quite civil about it. Everyone seems happier to have a clean break. There's not all the unsaid stuff now to poison things and make people awkward.'

'Will they visit you?'

'The boys? Yes, I think so. Dad'll buy all the tickets, of course, so the girls will push them to come.'

'And if I visit you?'

He didn't look as shocked as she feared.

'Would you? Could you get away?'

'This corporate project I'm working on. I want to do more anyway. That might let me travel, maybe Singapore, maybe DC. Would you see me if I did?'

'I'd do more than see you.'

'I know, you'd fuck me senseless.'

'Well, I was going to say I'd take you to dinner and show you around, but yes, of course I'd fuck you senseless. And I'd find out more about the woman who wants to tell me to fuck off sometimes – and who sometimes wants to be told exactly what to do.'

'I do, I meant that.'

'I know you did. I'm going to enjoy that.'

Suddenly she was hesitant. 'Why? How? What are you going to do?'

'I'm not going to tell you exactly, but we've come far enough now. This is going to go on somehow and we're going to find out more about ourselves. I know I'm a little kinky, potentially, and we don't seem to have found your boundaries yet. I know when I looked at you in your little black dress, I wanted to tell you to go to my room. I had a fantasy that night about having you. But I didn't have a fantasy about ordering you to strip.'

'What was your fantasy?'

'You knelt down and unzipped me.'

'Without you ordering me to?'

'Oh no, I told you exactly what to do.'

'And did I make you come?'

'Well no, that was the funny part. I couldn't just see you as a sexual object. Even in my fantasy, I wanted your active participation. If I'd known you like being told what to do.'

'Only by you,' she said hastily, 'I've only had these thoughts since we started.'

'Well, I could have conjured some really exotic ideas.'

'And now you do know?'

He looked serious. 'Well, we're going to find out. Not today, I'm already looking forward to your plans for the afternoon, but somehow, before I go, we're going to find out a little more about where we want to take this, emotionally and physically.'

'But you're busy all the time until you fly.'

'It looks that way, so you'll have to be ready.'

'Ready for what?'

'Ready at a moment's notice to do exactly as you're told.'

His voice was cold, but his eyes were smiling, and he was holding her hand gently.

'I don't know... I don't know if—' her stomach was knotted. It was a strange mix of thrill and anxiety.

'I know you don't know. We're going to find things out about you. But that's for next week probably. This afternoon we're going to relax and then think about simulating woodland. I'm afraid I find it a very sexy thought that a young man has you bent over against a tree in the woods and he's got your beautiful arse all bare and wiggling. I assume you wiggled.'

'You're about to find out. But doesn't it make you jealous to think about that?'

'A bit, of course, even if it was a long time ago. But I do get a bit of a thrill about thinking of you being fucked.'

'You are kinky,' she said smiling.

'I haven't denied it. We're just finding out how much.'

'I don't have anything too kinky planned for this afternoon. You just have to do what I tell you.'

'I had a wonderful time the last time you did that.'

'Well, it starts the same way. Get over to the sofa and get your pants off.' It gave her a thrill to see him walk across the room, just as she'd told him.

He turned to face her. 'Are you coming?'

'Eventually, but you were told to get your pants off.'

He slipped his pants down. He was already half erect. She'd wanted to touch him and kiss him from the start but obviously the discussion, and maybe her instructing him had already begun to turn him on.

She walked slowly towards him. She liked the idea of being in control and of exciting him. He turned as she approached him round the sofa. They were in profile in the big window. It excited her to think they could be seen but it was a safe excitement, the other buildings were too far away, the traffic too far below. But if some pervert with a telescope had the luck to be looking, she was about to give him a rewarding display.

'I shan't need these,' she said and pulled off her tee shirt and threw it on to the sofa. She looked at his eyes; his eyes were on her breasts. She looked at his cock; it was rising. Now she slipped down her pants and stepped out of them. His cock twitched. She knelt on the soft rug in front of him, taking his shaft in one hand and cupping his balls in the other. She looked up at him. 'Try to go slowly, I want to enjoy this,' she said, smiling up at him, wickedly, she hoped.

'I'll try, but I got very excited last time.'

'I remember, but I'm supposed to be getting him ready for your woodland experience.'

'He's pretty much ready now.'

'I can feel that,' she said, rubbing his shaft which was already firm enough, 'but I want to suck your cock first.'

His cock seemed to grow stiffer. 'I love you talking dirty.'

She'd thought he would. It had been worth the effort of overcoming her inhibitions to feel the pleasure she was giving. But she needed him to go slow. She wanted to look at his cock, to lick it lingeringly, to taste it, to feel it thick in her mouth, to run her tongue around its head, to remember every tiny detail for her fantasies in the months ahead.

She took him in deeply, her hand holding his thrusts. She listened to him moaning gently, but evenly, he seemed to be controlling himself. She massaged his balls very gently. His moaning got louder. She stopped. 'Yes, you have to stop that, it gets me too close.'

She pulled back a little. 'Yes, I can feel that,' and she took his cock in her mouth again. He was very ready, and she could feel how wet she was growing. She leaned back for one last long look. 'OK, now you have to fuck me.'

She stood up, turned and bent over, supporting herself on the armchair.

'I want you in my pussy.'

'Can I lick you first?'

'No, now stick that cock in me.' She couldn't believe her own words but felt thrilled to be saying them. Even more thrilled when his hands were on her hips and she could feel him pushing deeply into her.

She wiggled, trying to get him even deeper.

She felt his hands move to her buttocks stretching them. She heard him sighing deeply. 'Oh gorgeous, gorgeous.'

She leaned down a little more. He felt huge, but she felt she had him gripped tightly inside her.

'Oh, wow, careful,' he whispered, breathing more heavily. His hands moved back to her hips. He could clearly see everything he wanted now.

She let him find a new rhythm. His movements were shorter, he couldn't move as far; and quicker, his excitement was rising. Now was the time. She moved her hands to the chair seat, bending as deeply as she could.

'Ah, ah, ah,' he breathed in staccato bursts, 'ah, I can't stop, I'm coming, I'm coming.'

'Come on,' she heard herself say, her own excitement mounting. 'Come on, fuck me, fuck me.' She felt him start to pulse inside her. 'Fuck me, fuck me, give me everything.'

His hands gripped her hips more tightly. His thrusts, still short, she had him gripped so tight, went on and on. She eased herself up slightly, enjoying the feel of his skin on hers. The easier movements as his still stiff cock could move more freely in and out of her. His soft moaning becoming gentler and slower as he continued to pulse into her.

She felt his hand move up her back to her shoulder. He pulled her up and slid out of her. 'Come here, wild child, let me put my arms around you.' And he pulled her to him tightly, caressing her back and her bum voluptuously, then pulled her down on to the sofa on top of him where they could enjoy each other's skin and kisses.

'That was amazing. I couldn't have held back. You had all of him wildly excited, you were squeezing all his nerve ends. And I love looking at your bum while he's completely inside you.'

'Yes, I'm a bit jealous of that. I'd like to see it.'

'You want to video us?'

'I want something to look at while you're away.'

'I'm afraid that chance has gone. Or do you have any other wild teenage memories to wake him up with?'

'I'm afraid that's it.'

'Hmm, just as well, I don't think even you could coax life back into him.'

'So that's the last one,' she said and instantly regretted it.

'No, it's not the last one, unless you want it to be. I told you, I have an idea for next week. You'll have to do as you're told.'

9

But when next week came, he was busier than ever, in the office very early talking to his new people in Asia, staying until very late talking to the Americans, in particular his successor, who would stay living in America. That would mean the UK headquarters would become a backwater, making her current job, already frustrating for her when Jack wasn't there, even smaller.

He smiled at her often but had no time for more than small talk and slowly she gave up hope of any directive from him, any orders she had to obey. She'd spent time early in the week wondering what he might conjure up but gradually gave up hope of getting anything. And maybe that was good, she told herself, Saturday had been a perfect day and maybe that should be the day she should remember until the next time. The next time?

On Friday, in early as she was, she picked up the letter from the middle of her desk. The handwritten 'Claudia' was obviously from him. He was sitting in his glass office already on the phone. He saw her and waved. She felt reassured, her first thought had been that this was a goodbye letter, a real goodbye, not a see you in Singapore or Washington goodbye. She found a quiet corner, it was only seven, and there were few people around, and opened the letter.

Darling Claudia,

First an apology. I had meant to get some time together. I had even developed some evil plans. But I didn't want to squeeze us into just a few minutes. Also, although I will want to be inventively naughty at times in the future, and I do have some interesting ideas to test your desire to do as you're told, I didn't think it quite the right way to say goodbye now.

It's been a wonderful few weeks, waking up to what we'd become to each other and waking up too to some interesting tastes in how to make love.

I am excited about going, I can't deny that, the region excites me, as you know, and the people already excite me: all that enthusiasm, all that optimism. I am looking forward to all of that.

But I hadn't expected to be leaving with regrets – and now I will, one very large one.

I have meant everything I said. I do want this relationship to go on, even if it's mostly phone calls in the next couple of years. We'd become very good, I think, about sharing thoughts and feelings in those conversations. But if I'd known what I was missing... well, that would not have helped one iota given the work relationship we would inevitably have wrecked!

I will respect your wish for openness even though

it's not, as you know, my natural style. As a quid pro quo I want to hear more about your teenage years and anything exotic that happens in your life, however you deny that it might (remember I'm kinky, I like to think of you in the woods).

But the central point is: you've become very important to me, and I don't see a mere six thousand miles diminishing that in any way.

Jack

She folded it back into the envelope, went back to her desk and put it discreetly in her bag. She looked at him – fortunately he didn't see her – and then turned away to mop the small tear that had formed in her eye.

Are you packed? She wanted him to be awake. It was only six, but she knew he woke early.

It was a while before his text came back: *No. The plane's not till this evening.* She knew that, she'd booked it.

Are you up?

I've been up. I'm drinking tea in bed.

Good. How much time do you have?

I'm in no rush. Why?

Lovely letter, thank you, nice thoughts but you need to fuck me.

Where are you?

Around the corner.

Come up. I'll tell concierge.

It wasn't her usual smiley man. The older man was surly and stayed behind his desk, merely nodding as she walked to the lift. On another day it might have disturbed her, but today she was all steely resolve. Dave had questioned why she would be away so early on a Saturday morning, she'd responded dismissively – the hotel conference story still had mileage, and this would be the last time she'd need it.

Jack was waiting in the doorway but, surprise, wearing only a tee shirt. That flustered her slightly – two neighbours shared the landing – and she was caught between looking at his smile and looking at his cock, which was already slightly awake. Did it start the day like that or had her text provoked him? She fixed on his smile. He embraced her and closed the door.

'I'm not going to ask what I owe this pleasure to. Your text made that clear. You want the services of my penis.'

'Not just that,' she said, leaning back to look at him. His eyes narrowed. 'Don't worry, not much more than that. Make some tea, I'll explain.'

They moved to the kitchen. He put the kettle on. When he turned back to her, she touched his cock gently. 'Does he wake up before you?'

'Sometimes. But he was intrigued by the text. That certainly gave him a start.'

She let go of him. He made tea for her.

'I just want to explain what I want. Can we go and sit down?'

'Of course,' he said, but she was already walking to the sofa in the living room.

When they sat down, she suddenly felt hesitant. She was fully dressed; he was half naked. What had been so clear when she had the idea the previous evening, even clearer on the drive along empty roads on a brilliant spring morning, was now not so obvious. But she was here. She could ask for what she wanted. He might say no. He could say no.

'I did appreciate the letter, really I did. I was a bit disappointed that we couldn't manage something, but I felt the same way, really, it wouldn't have been a good way to part.'

'But here you are.' His eyes narrowed. She felt challenged, but now her resolve returned.

'Yes, here I am, and I'm not here for a needy teary goodbye, I'm here because you're going to fuck me.'

'But not just that.'

'No, not just that.' Now she relaxed a little and she could smile at him. She took her phone from her bag and tossed it to him. 'You'll need this.'

He looked quizzical, but it was clear that the idea was dawning on him.

'I love how you appreciate my body, how you take time to admire my breasts, how you very obviously

141

admire my arse when you're behind me.'

'Oh, I do, especially when you bend right over like the other day.'

'Well, I want to see that too. I want to watch you sticking him in me. I want some little memories to study when you're away.'

'So?'

'So? Don't be thick. You're going to do everything to me, put him everywhere, and I'm going to have the pictures.'

Now she was hesitant again. She could keep her resolve only to blurt things out. But he was smiling and nodding slowly.

'Is that OK?'

'Of course, it's OK. I think he and I will rather enjoy the idea. But I have one question.'

'Question?'

'Yes, are you the director, or am I?'

He was smiling broadly now, and his cock was rising at the thought. She felt confident now and in control. 'I'm the director. It's my film.'

'Good. Act 1, Scene 1 then.'

'Well, I'm the director. You're the cameraman. I'm going to play with your cock now' – she knelt down between his knees – 'and I want shots from different angles.'

'Ah, now I see why you've tied your hair back this

morning. What's my best side?' He smiled as she looked up at him.

'Just try all the angles.' Then she focused on his cock, one hand on the shaft, one cupping his balls. She was getting to know it very well, the shiny purple head, the thick veiny shaft. She massaged him gently and listened to his gentle moans and the click of him taking photos.

'You have to concentrate now. I'm going to suck you. I'm going to lick his head and then I'm going to take you as deep as I can, but I don't want you coming yet. I have a plan for that.'

'I'll try.'

'I'll pull away if I think you're coming. I want all these photos. I don't know when the next time will be.'

He leaned further back, his buttocks almost over the sofa's edge, his cock erect in her hand. She moved slowly, licking its underside gently. His breathing was slower, his moans softer, but the clicks had stopped.

She looked up. 'Yes, I do expect you to enjoy it, but I want my photos.'

'Sorry.' And the clicks began again as she licked its head. Then she pushed her lips on and off it. It was beginning to fascinate her. Before it had been an instrument, now it was an object of desire. Before it had been her way of pleasing him, now its feel and its taste gave her a thrill. She could feel him moving gently, clicking from different angles. Now the harder part, how deep could she take him? She slid her head down, enjoying its fullness, then easing back only to take it again. The clicking was getting faster, just like his breathing. She pulled back and looked up at him. He breathed a heavy sigh.

'Yes, you needed to stop there.'

She smiled up at him.

'Show me.'

'Show you?'

'Yes, the director wants to see the rushes.'

He offered the phone to her.

'Oh no, you show me. If the shots aren't good, you may have to take more, and I'm sure you don't want me having pictures of him all floppy. I've got to keep him in shape.'

He got the photos on the screen. They looked strangely biological, the veins, the hairs, her nails, her lips but, as she went through them, she could feel her excitement rising, she was growing very wet.

'Happy?' he asked.

'Very happy,' she said, 'I think I'd like to move on.'

'You still directing?'

'Yes, why?'

'I have a few ideas and I think you should do as I say.'

It was his magisterial voice, oddly not at all out of

place even though he was leaning back half naked with her hands on his cock. And she realized, once again, that it thrilled her to be told.

He eased himself up slowly while she kept hold of him.

'You should have more faith in the expectation you generate. He'll stay that way until we get to the bedroom, I promise.'

He took her hands to help her stand and guided her to the bedroom. He pushed the curtains wide but left the lights on. 'I think we need maximum illumination.' He turned to her. 'Now take all of your clothes off.' He was holding himself, keeping himself firm. 'You can do it slowly.'

She felt self-conscious. She'd imagined being ordered and enjoying stripping for him, but she'd never practiced trying to do it seductively. But she simply went slowly, watching him as she did. He was looking intently at her body, still holding himself. She turned her back to him as she slid her pants down and kicked them away. 'Beautiful,' she heard him say gently, 'but now you kneel on the end of the bed and stick your arse out for me.'

She knelt with her knees near the edge. He was taking photos again.

'Bend right down, knees further apart.' She settled in the new position. He was taking too many shots of just her; she wanted his cock in the frame. She soon felt him move behind her. The clicks stopped as she felt his hand on her hip and his cock sliding in.

'You're not clicking!'

'You're on video, darling, and the sound is probably on.' They both laughed even as his cock pushed deeply into her.

'High as you can.'

She tried to bend lower.

'Lovely.' And she could feel his exaggerated movements as his cock almost left her and then pushed very deep again.

'Have a look,' and she felt the phone land beside her elbow. Both his hands were on her hips now, and he moved with a gentle, steady rhythm. She eased herself up to inspect the film and enjoy his cock inside her.

A little out of focus some of the time and even in the bright morning light some details were lost but mostly she was happy, that lovely cock moving in and out and yes, her arse didn't look half bad.

'You're right,' she said, 'I have a nice arse.'

'Yes, but it will look a little different in the next scene.'

'What do you…' but she felt him move to the side and realized, just before the slap landed, what he was doing. He had her waist gripped with one arm. There was a searing sting on her right buttock, then came another on her left. He waited a while, clearly inspecting them, holding his grip firm.

'It's looking good,' he said, 'but you'll have to take at least a dozen to get the effect I'm looking for.' And he began to spank her rhythmically, heavily, and painfully she thought. They were heavy slaps; they stung seriously, his grip was very tight, she couldn't move but, as the warmth suffused into the pain in her behind, she realized she didn't want to. He stopped after a while, his grip relaxed but not enough to let her move.

'Enough?' she asked.

'Mmm, maybe, let's just wait a moment.'

'Why don't you make sure?' And she bent deeply again.

'OK, we'll make sure.' He tightened his grip again and resumed spanking, even harder this time. It was painful but she was thrilled, she was loving it and could feel her excitement rising higher.

'I have to fuck you. That looks so fabulous.' He grabbed her hips and pushed himself deep into her.

'Give me the phone.'

His thrusting eased as he set himself to film them, then she felt one hand move to her hip, and the deeper thrusting began again.

'That looks so, so fabulous, I promise you. And now you must stay very still for the next part. I'm going to come soon. Stay still.'

He was pushing deeper and groaning louder. She would love the soundtrack. He was about to come, she could feel it.

'Stay still.' His hand left her hip. He pulled out of her.

'Stay still, I'm coming.' She could hear him groaning, feel his wet cock-head on her bum and then she felt the blobs squirting on to her still very tender skin.

'Oh, that's wonderful, stay still, I'm coming, I'm coming.'

And she stayed still until she felt his cock begin to soften and he slid its head across her skin.

'Oh, it's wonderful. Lie down flat and let me get all that.'

She lay down flat on her belly. He sat on the back of her legs.

'I always thought your arse looked wonderful, but I have to say, bright red and with all that cum on it, it looks truly fantastic. And you're welcome to have those comments on the soundtrack.'

He lay beside her, put the phone down and put his arms around her.

'Turn over.'

'But I'll wipe all that lovely cum off.'

'It's on film, turn over.'

She turned over. He looked in her eyes then handed her the phone.

'Open your legs very wide. You can film this if you want but my main intention now is to make you come.' He slid down the bed, and she felt his mouth envelop her pussy and his tongue slide into her and then begin to play with her clit. Sod the phone, she thought, I'll just remember this. And her orgasm, never far away, quickly overwhelmed her.

She fell asleep for a while. When she woke, she could hear him in the kitchen. She found a tee shirt, huge enough to cover everything, and went to join him.

'I can't offer you much breakfast, I'm afraid. I've been running stocks down. I assume you haven't eaten.'

'Right, but I'm happy with toast' – she'd seen the half loaf he'd got out – 'and you do like to serve coffee.'

He looked at her quizzically.

'With biscuits, do you remember? When I just wanted you to fuck me.'

He smiled. 'I remember. I was just trying to be sensitive to the situation. But now I know that's not what you want.'

'Oh, it is. You just should have known that I wanted you to fuck me.'

'I get that now. I'll just go right ahead next time and do exactly what I want.'

'I hope you will' – she paused – 'next time. I'm not going to ask when that's going to be. Are you keeping this flat?'

'Oh yes. I'll want somewhere to come back to, for visits and long term.'

'So, will you fuck me when you visit?' But she worried as she said it that it sounded like pinning him down.

'Of course, I'll fuck you when I visit.' He was making the coffee; he sounded light-hearted. Good, she thought, he wasn't going to take her seriously this morning. But then he turned and leant back against the window sill. 'I will fuck you when I visit. And if you visit me anywhere, I'll fuck you there as well but…' he paused.

'I know,' she said quickly, 'life goes on. I know it does.'

'For both of us.'

She stifled a hollow laugh. 'Yes, for both of us. Look, I know you've got lots to do…'

Now he laughed. 'And you've got what you came for.'

'It's not that,' she said quickly, before she saw from his smile that he was teasing her.

He put his arms around her. 'It's not an easy day for us. Let's have a leisurely breakfast.' He looked around. 'OK a leisurely meagre breakfast, and just pretend we're seeing each other next week. We'll be talking anyway.'

She hugged him tightly, burying her face in his neck, willing for it to be true but not really believing.

10

The week was going slowly. The office was quieter now. The business would be run more from America and the place would become less important. Jack had built up the US and Asian businesses, and that had seemed exciting at the time, but it would have the effect of making what had once been its headquarters a mere backwater – and of making her role smaller. There were many reasons to throw herself more into the work she had on the team running biannual corporate events. She had fun with it anyway; their business had pioneered it, encouraging and rewarding people who did that bit more, who made things change. But the other regions had struggled, and her counterparts complained of sluggishness by the managers and incomprehension about how the programme would work.

She was getting increasing numbers of calls for advice and pleas for support, and in the last meeting she'd attended in DC, the programme head had asked her to take a lead in some key sessions. He had subsequently come under pressure to get her to travel to help the other regions and had already arranged with Jack to get some of her time, while he made a travel budget available to her. All she had to do now was make sure the new business head was just as keen on her wider role, but when he rang her to make contact and arrange his first UK visit, she discovered he'd already been spoken to and was very positive about her helping. The rest of the week felt much brighter. But there was no Asian phone call.

That came the following Monday. It started with an apology of sorts.

'I waited till the weekend to make sure I had plenty of time but then I got worried about where you'd be and how you'd explain a call.'

'You can let me handle that, Jack, don't worry about it. How are you?'

'Oh, snowed under. I'm trying to choose a flat and trying to catch up with reading and I'd like to get around the place more. But getting on top of the job is the main thing, and that's going to take a while.'

And he talked about where he thought his problems would be and how his travel plans were looking. They sounded horrendous to her, but she knew he'd always loved travelling and the excitement of new places. First class seats and chauffeured cars would ease any discomfort, she thought, but it would still be demanding, and it would strain any marriage that hadn't already failed to function. But those were background thoughts; she was caught up in his stories about the new people and of the places he was planning to travel to. He was bright and enthusiastic although, she looked at her watch, it was eleven thirty in Singapore.

'Jack, it's late. Aren't you tired?'

'Nah, I'm running on adrenalin. It's much less tiring than alcohol.'

'No saké tonight?'

He laughed. 'Not much, I've been careful, it's too draining, and I have a lot to get done.'

'You should sleep.'

'No, tell me what you've been doing.'

'Oh, things have been very quiet, but I do have one piece of good news.'

'Go on.'

'Well, your successor knows I'll have more time, and he's happy for me to work more on the corporate project.'

'That's brilliant.'

'I'll be travelling more,' she said cautiously. There was a silence. She felt a pang of worry.

'That's even more brilliant. If you're coming here, and I seriously hope you are, you'll have to make sure I'm here when you come.'

'You don't think that had crossed my mind?'

She loved his laugh and she felt warm and relaxed.

'I love to listen to you, but I'll feel guilty if you don't sleep.'

'OK, you win, I admit I need it.'

'But, Jack,'

'Yes.'

'Call any time, don't worry.'

'I will. Goodnight.'

'Goodnight, Jack.'

More phone calls came but less frequently than she wanted. They did, however, fall into the old pattern. It would be late at night for him. He'd generally been out to dinner and was mostly happy and garrulous and fun to listen to. Occasionally he'd talk about more difficult problems and once he spoke about his wife divorcing him. Relief had seemed to be his overwhelming reaction, but she didn't ask questions. If he wanted to talk more about that, he would.

'So, you'll be a free man then?'

'Ha, well you and your coven thought I'd been behaving like that anyway.'

'And you hadn't?'

'Not for a long time before us.'

It was the sixth week, and he'd rung only about six times, and it was his first reference to 'us'. He'd been talking about the job, his people, the countries but it almost seemed like 'they' had never happened. She was hesitant about opening that part of the conversation, she worried about frightening him away, and most calls came in the afternoon while she was still in the office.

It was much easier to let him talk, although the girls would nod and smile when she put the phone down. They knew who she was talking to, one even looked theatrically at her watch after one conversation, and she realized it was too obvious. Still, at least he wasn't ringing that often.

'Jack, I've something to ask you.'

'Yes?'

'I might be making a trip to Singapore in September. Will you be there?'

'I can be. The sooner I know when you're coming the easier it is for me to adjust. Have you got dates?'

'I'm trying to pin people down. Johan needs to be there and the people from your big markets.'

'Johan?'

'He runs the whole programme, he's corporate staff.'

'Oh, Johan, of course. Sorry, I was being thick.'

'But you think you can be there?'

'I know I'm in the region then. I don't go to DC until October, but there will be some meetings in the diary already that I won't easily be able to change. Are you going to try to stay over a weekend?'

'Well, I can get cheaper flights like that.'

'Ah, saving money, of course.'

She assumed, and hoped, he was teasing. 'Well, I want to of course.'

'Well, dummy, I want you to too. I told you that.'

He had, it was true, but a weekly phone call wasn't offering much reassurance that the offer still stood.

'You did. I'll work on the dates.'

'Please. And email me as soon as you know.'

That sounded like a close of the conversation and she wanted to get straight on to fixing dates. 'I will. Goodnight, Jack.'

'Goodnight, sweetheart.'

He'd never called her sweetheart. She wasn't sure she liked it, but she felt better when the text arrived soon after:

You rang off too quickly. Wanted to say how much I want to fuck your brains out when you're here.

That made her smile.

Three days later she had her dates. Not all of Jack's people had confirmed, but she knew they would try harder once they knew that Johan would be there – and if they knew Jack would be in the office.

She emailed him, telling him the dates and asking if he could start the meeting up. It would be a big help to the programme if the head man was seen to support it, so she couldn't be accused of asking for any selfish reason.

Works for me and delighted to help was the unexpectedly terse reply – but corporate emails weren't necessarily private.

She felt better when the text came:

I'll have some toys too in case you tire me out.

But it was still four months away!

It would be a long four months. Home was getting harder. She found herself more irritable than ever with Dave. In her calmer moments, she knew he was no worse, but now she compared everything he did with what Jack would do. And the family trip to the local Indian brought strange and difficult echoes of sitting down in Rasoi with no knickers and Jack's taste in her mouth.

'What the fuck's up with you lately?' was Dave's aggressive question as soon as the kids were upstairs on their return.

'Nothing's up with me lately, Dave,' was her equally aggressive response. She didn't recognize herself at moments like this, but she couldn't stop herself. 'Nothing's up with me lately that hasn't been up with me for a long time.'

When they'd still been talking, she had tried hard, but any setback sent him scurrying to his den and his whisky bottle. The last few times they'd had sex, so long ago now, she knew she'd been unenthusiastic and that had certainly added to his problems but feeling warm towards him, wanting him to touch her, encouraging him to try before he was already half drunk, that was all beyond her now. Now she was merely relieved to see him turn to his room. She went up to the kids to lose herself in mindless telly.

Later, with them in bed and Dave presumably sleeping

on the camp bed in his room or still drinking and watching porn – did he really assume she didn't know? – she had time to herself to check messages and catch up on Facebook. The new message stunned her: Malcs wanted to be friends! Malcs! How many years? But he still looked good, still had hair, still looked lean. She smiled to herself, they were good memories, and no one had got hurt. Then she thought about what she'd learnt and how that had helped her with Jack.

Her finger hovered over Accept, held back by her own mistrust of herself. If it were so straightforward why should she feel a nervous tremor in her stomach? She'd liked Malcs. He was very open, as well as good looking and a little charming. But the memories she had were not just the fun with their friends; she was also remembering her sexual education and her sexual daring – she had led him into the woods. Somehow being with Jack had made her think intensely not just about Jack but also about sex, something that had not been in her mind for years. Now here she was, thinking not just about making love to Jack but smiling at different memories from years ago. She left the page. She could think about that some other time. Now was the time to lie back in bed and think about Jack touching her, and about touching him. She missed his skin, the fur on his chest, his voice, his laugh and yes, the feel of his cock stiffening as she held him.

11

The thoughts came back to her the next time he made contact and made her feel silly; she should stay on her guard. It was a week later, and he had sent a text.

You still at work?

Yes, just packing up. What are you doing? It's late.

Just got in.

Call but I've got to get home for the kids soon.

Understood. Let's talk tomorrow.

She walked to the car telling herself it was hard to get feeling into a text message. But not even an xxxxx at the end though, that was unusual. And she hadn't put xxxxx either, deliberately avoided it when the thought had come to her. She was somehow on her guard.

When he did call it was Friday, three days later, also quite late, one o'clock for him, but on Fridays the place emptied early, so it was easy for her to take the call undisturbed in the old glass office.

'I'm sorry it's late. Do you have to go now?'

'No, Jack, I can stay a while and please stop saying sorry. I know you're busy.' But she'd detected the drink in his voice. Even in the old days she could tell from his first words how sociable the evening's business had been. But today was Friday, an unusual evening for business meetings. 'What have you been up to tonight? Business or pleasure?'

'Both really. It's a group of businessmen who meet for dinner every month. They're expats mostly just chatting about doing business in the region and how they cope with the expat life.'

'And do they cope?'

'Oh, most seem excited to be here. Some have been here years and don't want to go back. But a lot of the wives are homesick.'

'They bring wives along?'

'Yes, more than half I'd say, most in fact. We bachelors are a minority.'

Typical Jack, he'd found a way of telling her he'd been there on his own.

'And are they all unhappy?'

'I've not really spoken to many, but it feels like a majority. Well, not the local wives, obviously.'

'Local?'

'I'm guessing second marriages. The Asian ladies get together and twitter like birds and smile all the time. The expat wives tend to look a bit dourer until they've drunk too much. Expat husbands too, there are a few women in big jobs here who bring their husbands along. It was a woman who brought me in the first place in fact. She's head of the bank we use.'

'And is her husband there?'

'Ah, no, interesting. I can't work out if she's a dyke or just anti-men, but she's civil enough in business and I'm glad she brought me. It's got me fixed up for my first game of golf this weekend. It's months since I played. I hope it's not too embarrassing.'

And he talked about the people he'd be playing with, he told her their stories and how they were living there, and her thoughts were with him, trying to imagine that strange life, so far from home, meeting so many new people. But at a different level, her mind was already thinking of the women he would meet, had already met maybe, and whether they would attract him. It was a given for her that he would attract them, especially so freshly single.

When he rang again, more than a week later, she asked him about his golf date.

'Oh, I enjoyed playing, I'm not doing enough in the fresh air, but I was terrible. The guys were nice though and they don't play enough either. Everyone's terribly busy. But I did get asked back for dinner by the American.'

'And does he have an unhappy wife, or has he already found a replacement?'

'You don't miss much, do you?'

'Well, I had a very vivid picture of the party you went to.'

'It wasn't a party.'

'Get-together then. But I could almost see the miserable western women and the happy little birds, I think you called them. So, what about your American couple, are they happy?'

'It's funny you ask that. They seemed to be. They've been here a couple of years and have a clear route back next year so there's not the tension you find in those who feel trapped here.'

'Seemed to be, you said.'

'Yes. It was strange. She called me a few days later about something we'd talked about. It was a restaurant, and she was asking if I'd like to go there. I said yes, of course, I can't have them here for dinner and it would give me a chance to pay them back, I thought. But when I said that she said it was difficult to pin Rick down, that's her husband. I felt a bit uncomfortable, but I'd sort of committed.'

'So, when's dinner?'

'Next week sometime.'

He sounded vague – but Jack was almost never vague – and she let him change the subject.

But the thought stayed with her and grew. She would have to ask him, she knew, but she would do it very carefully. Maybe if he was going to get up to something, then best if it's with someone whose time was limited. The American wife would be going home next year.

It was a weekend when he next rang. He'd texted and she'd told him that the kids were out with their dad.

'It's nice to have you sober,' she said.

He laughed. 'I do have my first G&T in my hand. I was on the balcony but it's too warm so I'm on my sofa enjoying my cityscape view.'

'Is it like London?'

'Not really. I can see a little water, but it's not the Thames, and I'm higher up.'

'And are you overlooked?'

He laughed again. 'Oh, there might be a few more spectators for your gorgeous arse when you're here. How are those plans coming along?'

'I've got everyone committed now. They all agreed quickly once they knew you'd be there.'

'Well, it's a few months yet.'

'What do you mean?'

'I mean their diaries won't be fixed that far ahead, they'll have flexibility.'

'And you'll still be there?'

'Of course, I'll be there. It's an important meeting.'

'You're teasing me.'

'Only a bit. I do think it's important, but that's not the only reason I'll be here. I want to show you the view from my apartment. Funny, isn't it? In London it's a flat, here it's an apartment.'

'And has anyone else seen the view?' She couldn't

stop herself; then she was seized by panic when his response was slow.

'I've had a few guys up here on odd occasions. It's pretty central and it's nice to meet up before dinner.'

'And the American woman?' Now she was driven by indignation. He'd promised openness, she had a right to ask questions.

'Yes,' he was guarded, 'she came up. She wanted to see the place.'

'Ah, Jack, she sounds dangerous.'

'Yes, she is, a bit.'

'So, she came on to you?'

'Yes.' There was a pause. 'But I resisted nobly, of course.'

'Of course. When are you seeing her again?'

'No plans,' he said abruptly.

'Why do I get a weekend?' She wanted to change the subject.

'I've been travelling all week and I didn't have quality time, as they say. God, I hate that expression. But I wanted to relax and chat and it's nice to sit here and think about how I'd like to fuck you here.'

'Tell me.'

'Tell you what?'

'How you'd like to fuck me.' She wanted him to paint that picture with words. She wanted him to talk dirty.

'I have a low, wide sofa and a thick, soft rug. I would lean back and let you kneel and unzip me. But first I'd make you stand in front of me and strip completely naked. If there is anyone with a telescope watching, I want them to enjoy your body, especially when you bend over to lick me, and you stick your arse out for them. I'm not really very overlooked but I like the thought of you showing your arse off, so I'm imagining a Dr Perv opposite who has a high-resolution telescope trained on your arse and pussy while your head's bobbing up and down on my cock.'

'Is there a man with a telescope?'

'No,' he said quickly, 'I told you. It's just my kinky mind.'

'But you liked that, on the sofa at the hotel?'

'It was wonderful. I shouldn't have asked where you learned that.'

'No, you shouldn't have, but it's mostly intuitive anyway. I was learning by doing.'

'Well, I have you on your knees, furthering your education and I'm trying very hard not to come.'

She heard the car on the drive. 'Shit, Jack, I'm sorry, I have to go, the kids are back.'

He laughed. 'Ha, coitus interruptus. Don't worry, sweetheart. I'll call again soon. But you have disappointed our little man, he was getting quite excited by the story.'

'So was she, Jack, so was she. Talk soon?'

'Yes, I'll call next week.'

'Promise? No, don't promise, just do what you can.'

'I promise,' he said. And she was glad but wished he hadn't.

12

She tried to put the thoughts out of her head, but the American woman was obviously making herself available. So, then she thought about how they had avoided commitments and how she'd said she wanted openness. Did she really? It was hard. She threw herself into work; she was getting more involved in the international project. She had more trips planned, mostly within Europe but they were exciting, much more so than the job in her unit. She was managing to avoid Dave at home even though he seemed more morose and withdrawn than ever. The kids, however, teen and almost teen, were getting easier and more independent – cheekier, true, but less needy – more precarious, she thought, it wasn't a time to get complacent, but they were good mostly, and she was for the moment avoiding the problems other parents seemed to be having. And she had time most days to listen to their school gossip, watch telly with them, adjudicate between the claims for different programmes but, more and more, they'd be playing games by themselves on their tablets.

It meant that every evening had its few hours when

she was on her own. That was the time she would think about Jack in the first days and weeks after he'd left. She'd looked at the pictures on her phone and smiled, but now, with them downloaded and hidden on her computer, she was avoiding them. Trying to think about other things than Jack. And when she was thinking too much about the American woman one evening, she went on to Facebook and left a message for Malcs.

But Jack did call the next week. Not until Friday, it was true, but he'd texted the day before to say he would and to check that she'd be in. She'd replied that it was a good day, the office was always quiet Friday afternoons.

He would remember that, but nowadays it was much worse, the life was going out of the place.

He rang at three.

'Gosh, you're early. It's only ten o'clock.'

'Not just early, sober.'

'No dates tonight?' Why had she said that? She told herself she wouldn't.

'No, no dates. Just late in the office and a microwave meal. I'm starting to cherish quiet evenings.'

'And the weekend? Playing golf?'

'Yes, matter of fact I am.'

'With whatshisname? Rick?'

'Yes, and the others. Looks like it might be a regular thing. They used to have a fourball, but one guy's just gone back.'

'Isn't that a bit awkward?'

He hesitated. 'Yes, it is a bit awkward. You mean about me having a meal with Joanna?'

'Joanna, so that's her name. Well, it sounded like it was a bit more than a meal. Does Rick know?'

'I don't know.'

'So, if he brings it up tomorrow.'

'I don't think he will.'

'Well, it might come up.'

'It won't come up.'

'It might come up, then you could look silly.' She sensed his evasiveness. 'Has she asked you not to mention it?'

'Yes, she has. How did you know that?'

'Jack,' she said slowly, 'she's a woman and she obviously fancies you. She came on to you she said.'

'She did a bit.'

'Have you snogged her?'

He hesitated. 'Yes.' There was a pause. 'Things did get a little out of hand.'

'After dinner?'

'No, not after dinner.' Another silence.

'It sounds like trouble, Jack, and what about the commitment to openness?' She'd gone over an edge, she realized, but her imagination would be worse than the truth, she thought, even supposing that he would tell it.

'I did say I wasn't terribly good with that.'

'You did, but you said you would try. Have you fucked her?'

'No,' he said sharply, 'no. But things did get out of hand.'

'Now I'm imagining all sorts of things. What happened after dinner?'

'Not much, I've told you. She came on a bit and we snogged.'

'That sounds dangerous, but not bad.'

'It wasn't. But she came around for a drink one evening this week.'

'Where was Rick?'

'Away, he travels most weeks.'

'So, she called in?'

'She rang first, to see if I was free. I wasn't as it happened, I had a dinner meeting, but she rang again as soon as I got home. I'd had a few drinks. It was easier to say yes.'

'But you haven't fucked her.'

'No,' he paused, 'but she is American.'

'What does that mean?' She was trying not to sound aggressive, part of her wanted an open conversation, but she was feeling threatened.

'I'm not sure about this, Claudie. She's not a happy woman, I know, but she's fun to spend time with.'

'Fun?' She knew she sounded prickly.

'Look, it's the first female company I've had for a long while. It's totally non-threatening. I have one romantic relationship, and I'm excited about seeing you in September.'

'But you can have fun with other women in the meantime?'

'You're making too much of this. It's getting like the conversations I used to have with my wife before I learned to avoid them.'

'You're right. I'm sorry. I've no right to pry.' She'd gone too far, she hadn't meant to. She'd meant to do everything to stop herself. She'd wanted him to be open, she wanted to try and deal with that but if she pressurized him the truth wouldn't emerge anyway.

'Well, you have a right to know what's going on. We said we'd talk about things openly, but when it feels like an inquisition it's hard to respond like you say you want me to.'

'I know. I'm sorry. I know you can't live like a monk.' There was a long silence. 'Are you not talking to me any more?'

'I'm talking. Maybe I should have had more to drink before I rang you.'

'Well, I must admit you don't seem to hold back when you've had a glass or two. I love you being funny and outrageous.'

'And now I'm just dour and prickly.'

'No. Well, yes actually but it's my fault.'

'Let's try again tomorrow, shall we? I get picked up very early for golf and it's been a heavy week. I'm tired and obviously a bit irritable.'

With late night visitors you obviously would have been, she thought, but managed to say nothing but, 'Yes, you sound tired. Ring when you can. It might be tricky, but you'll understand if I put you off.'

'Of course, I'll understand. Sorry I've been so touchy. I'll call you tomorrow.'

But he didn't, of course.

13

It was two weeks before his email came. It had been a tough two weeks, and there had been many times when she'd been tempted to write. She knew it wasn't pride that stopped her; it was knowing just how useless it would be. If she meant anything to him, he would call her. Next time she wouldn't talk about his social life. It meant she would just imagine things but her pleas for openness had brought her only this, not just the nervous misery of waiting for the next call but the duller ache of assuming it wouldn't come.

But at least she had Malcs. They had talked twice now and had laughed about memories and passed on their sketchy knowledge of the people they had known. He was still in touch with Kevin but hadn't seen him for years, just as she hadn't seen Millie, still in Scotland, settled with two kids. It was a pleasant distraction, and maybe they would meet up some time, he was only forty miles away. He'd hinted he'd like to, but she knew it was a dangerous temptation. She decided she wouldn't but looked forward to him ringing again.

Then the email came:

Claudie,

I prefer the old-fashioned phone. Well, I prefer face to face, but at least on the phone, I have your voice and that window on your feelings. But we didn't do very well last time and I didn't know how to approach the next conversation. I want to keep talking. It means a very great deal to me to have someone I can talk to about anything.

And yet I couldn't. I let you down, and I'm sorry. We'd said we'd be open, and I wasn't. As you know, I was only reluctantly committed but committed I was.

What we had (have, I hope) is special but it can only stay that way, I suspect, if we make that openness work for us. So, I'll take the cowardly path of writing a few things now and you can tell me how you want to move forward, or if you do.

I do see other people here. I am mostly in crowds socially, or with men at golf or in bars, but I've had a few dinner or drink dates – with a few people, not just one. It's friendly, and it's fun and I'll talk about that if you want me to, but nothing comes close to what I've had for a couple of years now, someone I can to talk to about anything and everything. Well, almost everything – and it can be everything if you want it to be.

I'll sign off before I repeat myself again and wait to hear what you want. I want to keep talking. Let me know that you do, please.

Jack

PS I've talked a lot about us talking. I can't sign off without also saying that the sex has been mind-blowing, and I miss it terribly))))))).

She smiled as she finished reading.

Jack,

I want to talk, you idiot. I spoiled it last time, I'm sorry. I want to be a big girl about this. Just call me, tell me who you've fucked, and we can get on with it.

Claudia

PS Yeah, I thought the sex was OK)))))))))

She wasn't sure she was a big girl, but she knew it was the only way forward.

'So, who have you been out with?' It was a daring opening for her when he did finally ring, but she thought being brazen was the only way to get through it.

'A few, nearly all married, nearly all western. Hell, it's not half a dozen, why am I being coy? I've had dates with five people, all enjoyable, none of them serious.'

He seemed to be rising to the challenge. She found a quiet room and settled down. Somehow being direct did make it easier. It was a disembodied conversation, as if they were talking about other people.

'How many have you fucked?'

'One.'

'Joanna?'

'No, not Joanna.'

'But you've snogged her and she wanted more.'

'Yes,' he said slowly. She hoped he wasn't going to clam up. She was being a big girl, he had to respect that. 'But I told you she was American.'

'That's obviously some sort of shorthand for you, Jack, but I don't understand it.'

'Haven't you read in magazines? American girls keep their virginity before marriage by having only oral sex. And married women don't think they're being unfaithful, apparently.'

'Jack!' and she laughed. It seemed ridiculous. 'So, she sucked your cock?'

'Well, Claudie, ten out of ten for bluntness, but yes, she sucked my cock.'

'And is she any good?' She amazed herself at how direct she was being. Brave, she thought.

He laughed, it didn't seem appropriate, but she was glad to hear it.

'I'd say she's had plenty of practice so yes, she is good.'

'And what does she expect from you? Oral too?'

'I'm not finding this easy, Claudie, but yes, that's the deal.'

'And she thinks you're good at that?'

'I suppose so. She's been back since.'

'I don't know why I asked. I know you're very good at that. Is she coming back often?'

'I think she'd come by more if she could, but I

won't see her more than once a week.'

'And her husband, are you still playing golf?'

'Well, that hasn't worked out, fortunately.'

'So, who have you actually fucked then?'

'Martha. She's the bank head that introduced me to those businessmen's evenings.'

'Oh, I thought you said she was a dyke or a man hater.'

'Well, that's what I thought – and there is a bit of the latter about her.'

'But you've fucked her.'

'I am admiring your bluntness, but I have to admit to finding it a little disconcerting. Are you all right with this?'

'I'm doing very well, I think. I'm going to find it entertaining as long as you tell me how lovely I am at the end.'

'I'll tell you that now. You're very special.'

'Yes, yes, yes, I know, but tell me that at the end. Tell me now how you fucked Martha. No, first tell me what she's like.'

'She's American too, dark-haired, slightly heavily built, a little older than you.'

'Married?'

'Not any more and dead against it.'

'She says.'

'Oh, I think it's genuine. She's done it twice and it

was bad both times.'

'Ha, that sounds familiar. But anyway, does she suck cock?'

'Of course, but that's not her big thing.'

'Just a minute, how many times have you fucked her?'

'A couple.'

'Is that two?'

'Yes, it's two.'

'And what's her big thing?'

'Well, that was a surprise. I have to say, setting the scene, that this is a powerful woman. It's a big job, she runs all the bank's operations throughout Asia, and she comes across as direct and quite dominant. Either impressive or scary, I guess it depends on how timid you are.'

'And you don't do timid.'

He laughed. 'No, I suppose I don't.'

'So, this domineering woman, what's her big thing?'

'She likes to be dominated. It's funny, I've seen her with her people at the bank and in gatherings with some quite powerful men, and she's very comfortable centre stage. But when I took her to dinner – no, let's get this right, when she took me to dinner, it became obvious that she wanted someone to take charge. I got the impression her husbands were weak men who got rolled over by her, and she ended up despising them.'

'So, she didn't just get the bill and tell you to take her home and fuck her?'

'No, it wasn't like that at all.'

'Ah, Jack, so now you have to admit that you made the first move.'

'I did.'

'So, what did you do?'

'You sure about this?'

'No, but we've started now and I'm not letting you stop. What did you do?'

'We got a cab back to her place and I told her I was coming up for a drink.'

'Smooth talker.'

'No, I wasn't. I liked her, we'd had a fun evening and I'd made a guess that she wanted something more. She didn't seem surprised; she just led the way up to her apartment.'

'And you fucked her.'

'It was a bit like that, yes. I just pushed her on the sofa, kissed her and stuck him in. We were still fully clothed. Really strange. No words, barely a kiss and there I was on top of her. We stayed like that for a while.'

She tried to deal with the picture in her head, an elegant apartment, no doubt, a couple, older but still attractive – well, Jack was, of course, and he wouldn't go to dinner with anyone who wasn't – lying on a sofa with dishevelled clothing, just fucking. She was still managing to keep it detached. It was a funny scene if she could put out of her mind that the man was Jack.

'And then?'

'You know there's an and then?'

'Come on Jack. I love fucking you, especially because it's never short and it's never simple. I bet you took her to bed.'

'Yes, I did, of course.'

Of course, she thought, but this was what she'd asked for, and however hard the next few weeks might be, she wouldn't have to wonder about him. Or think he was hiding things or lying to her.

'I told her to go to the bedroom and get undressed. When I got there, she was still wearing underwear.'

'Not disobeying you, Jack, surely?'

'Well, I guess it's part of the game we play. You do the same to tease me sometimes.'

'It's true. I do. That's 'cos I like to be on the end of the dominant you.'

'Yes, well I kind of guessed that's what she wanted. So, I ordered her to take off her knickers and kneel on the bed.'

'And she did?'

'Of course.'

'Of course, she did.'

'And you got to work.'

He laughed loudly. 'Well, that's a way of putting it. Yes, I got to work. But that's when it got a little stranger.'

'Stranger?'

'Yes, give me a second.' He paused. 'Sorry, just getting my drink. Are you comfortable, by the way? I seem to be going on a bit.'

'Oh, I'm surprisingly comfortable. My coffee's finished but I'm not letting you stop now.'

'Well, her arse was a little big, I think I'd told you that.'

'You'd said she was a little heavily built.' This was Jack of old, scurrilous and gossipy but his old stories and speculations had never directly concerned himself.

'OK, it's a big bum, but quite attractive and I couldn't resist slapping it a little.'

'Oh, imagine my surprise.'

'Yeah, OK you know me. I left a couple of big hand prints on there and she wiggled and asked for more. So, I slapped her again and she said harder again. I ended up standing to one side to swing as hard as I could.'

'Harder than with me?'

'Yes, it was stinging my hand but she was getting loud and excited so I couldn't stop. Anyway, she came like that in the end.'

'She came?'

'Yes, just from being spanked, well, she was touching herself as well, but it was the spanking that took her to the edge. She was loud and very wet, and her arse was bright crimson, but she came and then collapsed.'

'Leaving him standing with nowhere to go.'

'Yes, but she took care of him soon after. I'll admit he was excited by the exercise, so it was pretty easy for her to send him over the top.'

'So that's her big thing, being spanked?'

'It seems to be, yes.'

'You said you've fucked her twice. Did she want that the next time?'

'Yes, but you're getting ahead of the story. Do you want more gory details?'

'Oh, definitely gory details.'

'Well, we calmed down and chatted and she thanked me, said it was so rare to find someone who understood her.'

'Ah, a dangerous woman.'

'Claudie, you think they're all dangerous. I'm on my guard anyway. I told her about you.'

'About me? What did you say for heaven's sake?'

'I said I had a girlfriend, a serious relationship.'

But you'd just fucked another woman, Jack, she thought but managed to stop herself saying anything.

'And she was happy about that?'

'Honestly? She seemed delighted. She said she wasn't looking for a relationship. The ones she's had took too much effort and didn't make her happy. She wanted to meet someone to see occasionally, especially if they understood her needs.'

'And you obviously do.'

'Apparently. I have been back. You want me to be open?'

'I want you to be open, Jack.' And she was surprised to find that she still meant it. 'So, what happened the next time? Was it like the first?'

'I was a bit better prepared. I went to her place and she cooked. It was very nice, not too elaborate. I need to admit to a pang of guilt here. The champagne before dinner was Taittinger, and that gave me a problem.'

'Which you surmounted heroically?'

'Yes, which I surmounted heroically. So, we sat on the sofa after eating with coffee and cognac.'

'And she started getting close?'

'No, not really, she doesn't like making moves. I just told her I was going to fuck her again.'

'And she liked that?' I would have liked that, she thought.

'She looked surprised and then smiled. But I told her she had to do something for me first. I'd seen a long-handled wooden clothes brush in the hall cupboard where I'd hung my jacket. I told her to fetch it for me.'

'And she did?'

'Of course, she did. She went slowly, but she'd nodded straight away. The thing was long and smooth and shiny. I'm afraid I'd thought of its alternative use straightaway, and I'm only guessing but, knowing what I know about her now, I think she may have had something like that in mind when she bought it.'

'So, she brought you the brush?'

'Yes, and she stood in front of me and held it out to me. I told her I was going to put her across my knee and spank her and she lay down across my lap. I told her she would have to take twelve and that it would hurt. She just buried her face into the sofa cushions and pushed her bum a little higher. I went quite slowly for a while here. I admit I was enjoying it and I was making it a little more dramatic. I pushed her skirt up slowly and then slid her thong down. That was unnecessary, really, her cheeks were fully exposed but pulling the elastic down over the hips and cheeks is always very sensual I think.'

'So do I.'

'I know, it makes you wet.'

'Come on, Jack, get back to Martha.'

'Well, there we were, her arse completely bare over my knee. I waited a while, her arse may be a little big, but I still like looking, but she wiggled more and more. She wanted me to start. So, I slapped the brush down pretty hard. She gasped and a nice big red mark formed across her bum. I slapped again, a little harder next time. She gasped a bit more but settled for the next one.

'After twelve, her whole arse was bright red and she was moaning very loudly, and she just cried out – you can't stop there, you can't stop there – so I didn't, I just kept spanking slowly but pretty hard until she came like crazy. It was extraordinary.'

'That's never happened to you before?'

'No, nowhere near. You know I've been with girls who wanted it, but nobody's ever come from it.'

'Wow. And then she had to deal with our little friend?'

'Yes, but you don't call him little when I'm squeezing him up your bum.'

'No, he certainly doesn't feel it. I was just using a term of affection.'

'I want to make love to you.'

'You've just been talking about another woman.'

'I know. I want to make love to you, though.'

'I want to make love to you too, Jack. It seems ages away.'

'I know Claudie, but I really do want you here.'

And she let that idea stay with her amongst all the turbulent, difficult thoughts of the following days.

14

The email, when it came two days later, helped a little:

My Claudie,

I'm having regrets about being open.

At the time it seemed the right way forward. We'd made a poor job of not being open, and that seemed to threaten 'us'. Also, I had drunk almost a bottle of wine, and you know that makes me more talkative – you have other words for it: outrageous; scurrilous. But I did want to talk. These things sit on my conscience – not the activities themselves, although maybe they should – but saying nothing about them when we'd agreed we'd be open. I was reluctant but that doesn't matter, I had agreed. So here we are, living a difficult life that I can't see changing much for a while.

But what we have is very important to me and I'd like it to grow and not wither. I admit to enjoying other company, but I am not looking for another relationship. I do love and value what we have. It had become very important, but after our last few weeks it became, I thought, extraordinary.

I suppose I'm looking for guidance – unusual for me. Is it still what you want? We can talk, and we will talk – but a few considered words from you in an email might help us both.

You are wonderful.

Your Jack

That she was nervous and excited when it came told her about her true feelings. Excited because it was from him, nervous in case he was thinking better about the situation. Now it was clear he wasn't. But her plea for openness, apparently so successful, was now giving her sleepless nights and unwelcome thoughts.

Her reply, written almost instantly, waited three days in her draft folder.

She didn't change much when she finally sent it:

Jack,

I saw being open as being the only way to nurture this. 'This' is something I'd unknowingly wanted. It's very special to me and I'd hate to abandon it.

I'm not going to pretend the conversations were easy, but I will say that the second, where you were so open, was vastly preferable to the first.

Yes, it has left me with some difficult images in my mind, but I knew when you went that I'd have to be a big girl if this was going to continue and, as you say, to grow and not wither.

I want to keep trying, and I want to keep listening and, above all, I don't want you to keep anything hidden. That would surely make it wither.

So, keep talking – be scurrilous, be kinky, be pervy because here is where I must be open. I have utterly loved all the naughty things you've done to me and I've discovered many new things about myself in the last couple of months, and I'd like you to help me discover more.

Your Claudie

PS Do you have a long-handled clothes brush?)))))

She wasn't sure about the PS, but it would make him smile – and it was a thought that kept recurring.

It wasn't something she talked to Malcs about when they finally did meet. He was often in London and she had to be there occasionally, she hadn't had to be too inventive about coming up with a date, and she felt on her own territory in the Chelsea hotel.

He looked good and instantly recognizable even after twenty years. She had seen Facebook photos but the man, in the flesh, was more like the boy she'd remembered.

'You're looking good, Malcs.'

'You're looking fabulous.'

'Thank you, kind sir.' He's lost some of his accent, but it was still distinctive. And the dangerous smile was still there.

'They fuss around you here. What's that about?'

'I use the place a lot for conferences and events, so they know me quite well. I've got one in two weeks, actually.'

'You're big business for them?'

'Not really. I just make a fuss of them. They're very good. It doesn't hurt if I tell them.'

They ordered lunch. It felt slightly bizarre, like they were still two teenagers playing at being grownups. But when they covered the twenty years, they'd both left a lot of wrecked or disturbed adulthood behind them. He had a daughter from his first marriage but none from his second which had also failed. 'My fault, both times,' he'd said with a shrug.

'Not fifty-fifty?'

'Not even sixty-forty.'

'Always the naughty boy.'

'Aye, I suppose so.'

'And now?'

'Now I have a partner.'

'You live together?'

'Mostly weekends. But we don't get too hung up on that. We spend time when we can and when it suits us, but we keep our own places.'

'She's happy with that?'

'At least as much as I am. She's been married twice too, and I think they were worse than mine. So, it works well for us, we don't tie each other down, we can do what we want but we're there when we need each other.'

'So, you see other people.'

'Of course. We've proved the other way doesn't work. But what about you?'

'Well, I'm still in my second marriage.'

'Happy with it?'

She laughed, then thought she should be careful. 'Oh, like most other people, I suppose. It sort of works and the kids mean a lot to us.'

He looked rueful. 'Yeah, I don't see enough of mine.'

'Your fault, or your exes?'

'Sixty-forty?' he said, but the smile was still a little sad. 'She doesn't make it easy, but I could do more. Do yours both have the same dad?'

'Yes, my first husband was an arsehole and, fortunately, I realised that before the question came up.'

'Is that why it failed? Because he was an arsehole?'

'Seventy-thirty.' He smiled. 'I'm saying that to try and sound fair. I don't really believe it. I think at least eighty-twenty. You might remember him, anyway. Douglas?'

'Oh, aye, yes. I remember hearing about that. I was still in touch with Millie. I was a bit surprised. You could have done better.'

She laughed. 'Well, you'd buggered off.'

'You wouldn't have had me anyway. You always were too sensible for that.'

'That's true,' and she laughed again, 'but we had a lot of fun.'

'Oh, we did that. You surprised me. You were sensible, but not too sensible.'

'No, I learnt a lot, and I knew you'd go off anyway.'

'I still think about the trip to the woods sometimes.'

'Oh, you've probably had many more trips to the woods.'

He nodded slowly, smiling. 'Yes, a few. It gave me a real taste for the outdoors. But can I tell you something?'

'You're going to anyway.'

'Yep,' he smiled, 'nothing's been like the first trip.'

She knew she was blushing slightly. 'Of course, me and my perfect arse,' she said as coolly as she could. 'Are you having coffee, Malcs?'

'I will, if you've got time.'

'Yes, I'm working here anyway but someone's coming at two.'

'Just got time then, yes please.'

He was gone by two, but she had no appointment. She'd felt slightly disturbed by the memories. Malcs, despite all he got up to then, and clearly since, was one of the few men she'd taken the lead with and it had thrilled her. Just not as much, she reminded herself, as being ordered by Jack – to do anything. She sat looking out at the marina, thinking about how she would do anything for him but then the ugly thought came back to her: obviously other people had similar thoughts. She was thinking of Martha and trying to picture her: well groomed, no doubt, like all successful American women; loud, forceful, brash; but that wouldn't have appealed to Jack, so she probably wasn't. And he'd taken the lead, sod him! He'd told her he was coming up for a drink. He'd told her to fetch the brush.

Would she have done that? Jack had loved the paddle but, once he'd started, so had she. So much was surprising her, how many new things she enjoyed, how she wanted him to try more. Yes, she would have fetched the brush, she would have lain over his lap, she wanted to feel his fingers pulling her pants down over her bum – and she wanted to feel that sharp bitter sting of her arse being spanked by him.

15

On the Friday after, he rang again.

'Good time for you?'

'Friday's always good, nearly everyone's gone by three, I have the place to myself. I just take the phone into your old office. But it's early for you.'

'I've just flown back in, dropped my bags and picked the phone up.'

'Where've you been?'

'China this week. It's a good team with a good guy running it but they could do more and I'm just trying to push them a bit. They're working on next year's plan, and they're sandbagging. I'll get some stick if I take that to DC in October. Are you going to be there by the way?'

'Don't you want to get September out of the way first?'

'No. You're being deliberately thick, aren't you? You want me to say something nice.'

'Heaven forbid, Jack, you? Say something nice? Never happen.'

He laughed. 'I'll just say that I will want to see you again. And although I'll be in the UK for a few days on my way back here, I think we could make time for ourselves better in the US. We'd have to be careful, though, these relationships are still a bit frowned on.'

'What's the UK for?'

'I have to catch up with lawyers. Can we leave that point?'

'Of course. Tell me about China.'

And he did. It was like old times. He was sober, it was true, but plainly excited by the place and fascinated by it. He seemed to be getting on with the people and she had no doubt he'd cajole them into more ambitious plans, it was what he did, always push, but always help people win. Something big had gone out of their business when he left.

'And now a quiet weekend?'

'I'll try. There's lots to catch up on and a couple of invitations I haven't responded to. One's for lunch on Sunday. Well, I call it lunch, but it spreads through the whole afternoon. We'll have to do it when you're here. Make sure you can stay for a Sunday. All the hotels have these fantastic buffets. They get fully booked. You must be careful, there's every imaginable style of cuisine, all done brilliantly. It's very easy to feel completely stuffed and yet feel like you've missed out big time. The trick, I think, is to go every week and eat nothing else on a Sunday.'

'And who do you go with? I'm not prying,' she

added hastily, 'I'm just trying to picture it.'

'One of the wives organizes it. One of the Asian ladies. She books a table for twelve every week and sees who's interested. It's great for me, I meet different people every time. I'll take you along.'

'Aren't you worried about us being out together?'

'What, work you mean?'

'Yes. We couldn't do that here, or in DC.'

He paused, 'Well, I probably will introduce you as a visiting dignitary, but I'll enjoy going out together.'

'So will I.'

'But how about you now, what have you been up to?'

'I had a lunch date.' She said it quickly, she'd been tempted to say nothing and knew how she'd feel later if she didn't. And then she paused.

'Ah, with a man.'

'How did you know?'

'Because you didn't say. Who was it? Am I going to be jealous?'

'It was Malcs.'

'Malcs the old boyfriend?'

'He was never really a boyfriend.'

'I wish I'd had girls who weren't girlfriends take me into the woods.'

'Stop it. You've had adventures I don't want to talk about.'

'But you did want to talk about them. Are you regretting it?'

'No,' she said slowly, 'I'm not regretting it. Like I said, it was easier to deal with the second conversation than the first.'

'Well, I want openness in both directions.'

'I've nothing I need to be open about. I've told you everything. I met an old friend. We talked about old times. That was it?'

'Seeing him again?'

'No plans.' There were no plans, but she was feeling awkward. Yet why should she? 'And nothing happened.'

'But you met.'

'Yes, we met. That's all. And it's not wrong, is it?'

'Of course, it's not wrong. It wouldn't be wrong if you'd done more than just meet.'

'But we didn't. And I wouldn't.'

'That's OK too.'

'Why do I think it's not OK? Why do I think you're almost goading me? It's like you want me to go further. Are you trying to make it easier for your conscience?'

'I wouldn't say that.'

'Is it something else? You did say once that you liked to think of me fucking someone else.'

'I did, that's true. I'm not saying it's normal, but I do find the thought of the girl in the trees very exciting, even when it's someone else fucking her.'

'You're kinky!' And she tried to laugh but she was disturbed by a few diverging thoughts: she wanted Jack, with all his kinky, dominant ways; she wasn't happy about his Singapore life but she was glad she knew about it; her own life was dull mostly and sometimes tense and difficult; she'd enjoyed having lunch with a man; she'd liked to be reminded of her naughty youth.

Not really very naughty, she told herself, nothing compared to what Jack was doing now.

'I've said what happened. There's nothing to it.'

'And if there were, you'd tell me?'

'Yes, I'd tell you. I'm the one who wants openness. And if I ever even thought of anything, it wouldn't be on your scale.'

'OK, just asking. We're good?'

'We're good, Jack. As long as you don't mind me saying I miss you.'

'I miss you too, lots.'

She didn't say it sounds like it and, although sarcasm had been her first thought, she was glad she avoided it.

'I have to go, Jack. The kids.'

'I understand, of course. And I've had a heavy week. Talk soon?'

'Ha, talk soon, of course, if you can. Goodnight.'

'Goodnight.'

16

It was a week, Friday again, when he rang. Not exactly soon, she thought, but it was the best time.

'I'm honoured. It's ten o'clock for you and you're not out and about.'

'It seems like it's a good time for you.'

'So, you stayed in for me?'

'I stayed in for you, of course,' he said with a touch of indignation.

'Sweet. But now you're going to tell me about your other evenings this week. You've been out, I expect. Oh, and how was that buffet thing?'

'It was excellent, as usual.'

'Anybody I know there?'

'Anybody you know?'

'Anybody I know, yes. I am being ever so good, Jack, but I think I want to know if Joanna or Martha were there. I've got the names right, haven't I?'

'Yes, you've got the names right. And Joanna was there.'

'And Rick?'

'No, he'd had to travel that morning.'

'So, she sat with you.'

'No, she didn't. She's married. She doesn't want people talking. Neither do I. I do tell people I'm in a relationship when they ask. So, I don't want to be seen with other people. That would look silly.'

'But you still see Joanna.'

'Yes. Like I said, less than once a week.'

'Counting these social engagements?'

'Not counting them. OK, give me a moment. I'm coming clean. She came to my place after the buffet.'

'All right, thank you for saying. You can leave me to make my assumptions about what happened next.'

'Good. I'm getting used to the openness thing, but I don't want to repeat every detail.'

'But you'll tell me if anything changes? If anything threatens to get serious?'

'It won't but I would tell you. Same as you'll tell me?'

'Of course, I'll tell you.'

'Good. I'm looking forward to hearing about you fucking Malcs again.'

'Jack, no! You're just kinky.'

'Not just kinky, no, Claudie. This is a lot more than that. But I am a bit kinky, yes, and I do think about you with other men.'

'I don't think it's going to happen and right now we're talking about your week. So far you've had your cock sucked on a Sunday.'

There was a silence.

'Thank you for the confirmation. I'm dealing with this quite well.' And that was surprisingly true, she thought. 'Now I want to know what else happened.'

'I did see Martha again.'

'Dining out, or her place?'

'No, she came here actually. She wanted to see the apartment.'

'And did she approve?'

'Yes. It's quite plush, more spacious than London but not as big as hers.'

'So, you entertained her.'

'After a fashion. You know the range of what I provide. Just cold.'

'That wasn't the entertainment I was thinking of.'

'I know but you've just said you want me to tell you if anything changes and it hasn't.'

'So, you spanked her again?'

'Yes. I know that's also a bit kinky but we both enjoy it, and we both know we're not drifting towards any other sort of relationship.'

'I'd like you to tell me more about it, Jack. Do you have a brush?'

'No, I don't.'

'Was it just a bare hand?'

'OK, Claudie, full details but then you have to tell me how you feel. If it's going to impact us, I'll have to rethink.'

'There's a few things going through my head, but I want to know what you did.'

'I bought a cane and I played the dominant.'

'You bought a cane? Have you ever caned someone before?'

'Yes, sort of playfully, but I'd guessed Martha wanted it a bit seriously.'

'Were you sure?'

'No, but that didn't matter. I was intrigued, and she could always have just stopped me.'

'But she didn't?'

'No. I let her clear up the things after we'd eaten and told her that she would be severely punished later. I could tell she was nervous and excited, she doesn't normally do meek, but she was quiet in the kitchen, and she dropped a glass. That helped the atmosphere; it stretched the time out to let her think more about what I was going to do to her after she'd cleared up and it gave a little pretext for the game.'

'Had you told her about the cane?'

'No. I'd just said severely punished. I had it across my lap when she came back into the living area. I told her she had to bend over the back of the armchair, and I would put a dozen stripes on her arse.'

'She took it?'

'She wanted more. You know she likes to make

herself come while she's like that. I was a bit surprised by how much she wanted. I was careful at first but, by the end, I was caning really hard. She was making whimpering noises but still asking for more. Her arse was all colours at the end, but she came really loudly.'

'And you?'

'I came too. I admit I got very excited by it, so I just pinned her there and stuck him in. That bit was over pretty quickly.'

There was a silence.

'What's going through your head now?'

'A few things, Jack, but first thank you for telling me' – she paused– 'would you cane me?'

'Are you serious?'

'I liked you spanking me, I like you dominating me. Yes, I'm serious, I want to try. I just want you to think about whether you can do it in our relationship. Or is it something you can only do when you feel detached – as you say you do with Martha?'

'I do feel very close to you, that's true, but I already felt that way when I spanked you. I honestly think it's the best way of exploring our sexuality, but I've never had a relationship where anybody was so willing to explore and experiment.'

'Martha seems willing.'

'Yes, but neither of us wants a relationship with the other.'

'You sure?'

'Yes, I'm sure. The peck on the cheek partings after these sessions kind of amuses me. There's no move on anybody's part to show any passion or even affection.'

'I do want you to try it with me. Will you promise? I want to find out more about me as well as more about you.'

'I promise. But we won't go any further than you want to. You do amaze me, it's an unexpected delight. One other thing though. I don't want you to force yourself into anything you don't really want but I would like you to fuck someone else and tell me.'

'But I don't actually want to fuck anyone else. Look, I don't feel the need to get even or anything. I'd rather you were spanking me and not Martha, but I'm managing to live with that. I just don't fancy another man. Does that put too much pressure on you?'

'No, it's not that. This is just about exploring sexuality. Yours and mine.'

'OK, Jack, if it makes you happier, the next time some slim dark-haired gigolo crosses my path I'll fuck him senseless and tell you all about it. OK?'

'Yep, I'm getting excited already.'

'But now I'm thinking more about the kids' tea than any gigolo.'

'Oh, you have to go?'

'Soon I do.'

'I wanted to hear more about your week.'

'Well, it doesn't compare with yours, obviously.' She told him about work and home and plans for the holidays and he asked enough to make her feel he cared and then suddenly she looked at her watch. 'Jack, Christ, I really do have to go.'

He laughed. 'I know, don't worry. Get away. But I do love talking – even about the difficult stuff. And I miss you.'

'I miss you too, Jack, and thank you for being honest.'

'Thank you for being honest. I was looking forward to September enough anyway. This could be a very interesting trip.'

'I think so too. Just one last thing, Jack.'

'What's that?'

'I want my own cane. You can't use hers.'

He laughed loudly. 'OK, Claudie, I promise, your own cane. Goodnight.'

'Goodnight, Jack.'

17

Her head was spinning through the weekend and into the next week: difficult images of Jack in Singapore; strange thoughts about what she really wanted – she'd been honest with Jack about that, she thought; and meeting Malcs and wondering whether she would sleep with him again; and work was suddenly busy – the next weekend would be conference weekend and the preparation was intensifying.

But at night when the house was quiet and her door was shut – there was a lock and key, Dave had never tested it, but it was good to know he couldn't surprise her – she thought hard about Jack and what she'd asked him to do. She pushed her pillows under her belly and stuck her arse up, she slowly slid her pants down and imagined him admiring her arse again, then she tried to think of him pinning her down with one hand while his other brought a cane down sharply across her cheeks. It was so strange, but she was desperate for him to have her, to cane her, to hurt her and then to ravish her, to push his cock in everywhere and come copiously over her tits where she could see the blobs drop on her. Her hips were moving vigorously; she had to touch herself and, for the first time in many years, she made herself come.

By Thursday she was calm and very focused, preparations were coming together well in the hotel. The delegates wouldn't arrive until the morning, but she had the day before to check everything through.

She'd stopped for a break in the café in the afternoon when the manager came to her, accompanied by a younger man, tall, sandy-haired and well-dressed.

'Mrs Brodie, this is Mr Jeavons. I believe I mentioned that he is organizing a conference here soon.'

'Ah, yes, you did.' She stood up and offered her hand.

'You did say you'd spend a little time with him, if you remember – I'm afraid I did go on so much about your events here that he was very keen to meet you.'

'You're in the middle of things, Mrs Brodie. I wouldn't want to disrupt you now.'

'I've got a couple of minutes, we can at least find out what you're interested in and maybe fix a time for later. It's Claudia, by the way.'

'Thank you, Claudia. I'm Alan. And thank you for introducing us, Mr Evans.'

The manager smiled politely. 'Would you like tea or coffee? I'll send a girl over.' And he left them.

She sat down. She had a table in the window – that view of the marina again – the irresistibility of water and boats.

'Have you used this place often? He talks as though you do.'

'Maybe half a dozen times. They're geared up for it and do a very good job.'

'He talks very enthusiastically about how you go about it, though.'

'Oh, we have a mutual admiration society. But I've used many other places and they're, well, crap, frankly.'

He smiled.

'What's your conference about?'

'It's technical. We get our scientists together once a year and they talk about what's going on in their different areas. It's a very mixed gathering, and it can get to be a tower of babel with all the languages. I went to the one last year, it was my first, and it was' – he smiled again – 'well, it was crap, honestly and they fired the guy who organized it and told me to do better next time.'

She laughed. 'Ah, no pressure then.'

He laughed with her. 'Right! No pressure. I'm looking forward to it, honestly, because it could be so much better, but I'd love to talk more to someone who understands these things. I've got a team at work and many opinions from the scientists, but I want to come up with an overall scheme and then sell it to them; otherwise it'll be a group designed camel. Could you help?'

'Well, I'm intrigued, but it sounds like a big project.'

'I know, it is, but maybe I could buy you dinner tonight and we could spend some time on it? You're staying here I think, the manager said.'

She was taken aback, but it was work, and anything was preferable to trying to dine alone in the hotel. She usually took room service to avoid being hit on by sleazy men on their own.

'Yes, I can do that,' she said. 'Can we make it a bit later so I can make sure everything's ready for me for tomorrow?'

'Oh, we can do any time you want. I'm very grateful, really. Is eight thirty OK? Please say yes, then I can get out of your way.'

'Er, yes, I'm sure that'll be fine but, tell you what, why don't you come down to the conference suite around eight, then I can show you a bit about what we're doing and how I approach these things.'

'Oh, brilliant, thank you.' He stood up and offered his hand. 'I'm really looking forward to this. I'll see you later.'

'Yes, see you later.' She watched him leave; tall, broad-shouldered, quite handsome really, just not her taste.

In the shower later she caught herself thinking:

would I normally do this? Conference preparation was a jeans and tee shirt thing, she and the crew were very informal. But I couldn't go into the restaurant like that, she thought. When she caught herself in the mirror taking particular care with her hair, she smiled to herself – well, he's a handsome young man.

When he came down to the suite, he'd changed out of his suit, but he still looked fetching in chinos and a fresh shirt. Fetching? What was she thinking? But she knew that Jack had managed to plant a thought in her head. Could she enjoy time with someone else?

But then her work enthusiasm took over. She showed Alan the main room and the breakout rooms, how all the exhibits linked to the main theme, how she would keep everyone active and focused, how no-one would be allowed to coast or merely listen, how she had picked the tasks and the team heads to keep everyone thinking and talking.

They were clinking wine glasses at the dinner table before she felt she'd even paused for breath.

'My God, you have let me rabbit on. I haven't stopped talking.'

'Oh, I absolutely didn't want you to stop.' He had been asking lots of questions as they'd walked around. 'I think I've learnt more in the last hour than I have in months. You've given me so many ideas.'

'I think I'd be happier if I'd only given you one or

two.'

'No, I get your point on that. There's a big point about making sure everyone knows why they're there and what the overall purpose is. They're not just here to be scientifically disputatious and then get drunk in the evenings.'

'That was your last conference, was it?'

'Yes. That makes you smile?'

'Oh, two reasons for that. I've been at conferences like that, but also you reminded me of someone.'

He looked at her quizzically.

'An old boss of mine. He loved words like disputatious. He didn't make many concessions to the multilingual gatherings – even though he told everyone to keep communication simple. Anyway, tell me more about your business, let's see if we can find the right theme.'

He talked, and she sensed his excitement. She'd not worked in pharma, but she had always seen it as an exciting area to make real differences to people's lives, but she recognized the scientists who he was describing, where jealousies and competing priorities could make for friction and destructiveness, just as they could in any area.

They were getting animated and a little loud, she thought, and noticed that a second bottle of wine had been opened.

'Alan, you're a naughty boy.'

He smiled like a naughty boy.

'I've been telling you about keeping all your delegates sober and here you are plying me with drink.'

'I just wanted to keep you talking.' He was still smiling but more earnest now, no longer naughty – or had she just imagined that? 'I've learnt so much. And I think I can see a way forward now. I was honestly getting a bit desperate before Mr Evans started singing your praises. Would we be able to meet again when I've got my thoughts a bit clearer?'

'Of course, we can,' she said and realized that she was taking an interest in his project, but also in him.

He turned and made the signature sign to the waiter to get the bill. Just as Jack would, she thought.

'I think we'll leave the last half bottle,' he said smiling at her. 'You've given me something of a guilty conscience.'

'Heaven forbid I give you a guilty conscience.' She looked over her glass at him as she took a last sip of wine. He smiled slowly and, standing up, he offered her his hand. A chivalrous gesture? She took it, rose, and was still holding his hand as they stood to go. He squeezed. 'I really can't thank you enough.'

'Go on. I've had a great time thinking about a different business.'

'Well, I enjoyed hearing about yours very much and, forgive me, but you are wonderful company.'

She looked down quickly, knowing she was blushing.

When they got to the elevator, she was glad there was another couple waiting.

But they got out the floor before hers.

'Which floor are you on?'

He looked deep into her eyes. 'I'm on your floor.' She felt her insides twitch.

'I didn't—' But his kiss stopped her speaking, his arms were around her, their tongues were touching. The elevator stopped. She pulled back. 'Well, we're here now.'

His arm was around her shoulders still as they got out.

'Which way?'

'It's at the corner there. Where's yours?'

'It's on the fifth floor.'

'But you said—' And he was kissing her again. She gave herself to it. When their lips parted, he said, 'I said I was on your floor because that's where I want to be right now. Can we go to your room? I want to kiss you again but not so much in public.'

She fumbled for her key card in her bag as they moved slowly to her door, his arm still gently around her.

'Alan, I…' But he had pushed the door open after she had swiped the card, pulled her in with him and kissed her again more passionately than before.

He was gone when she woke, a strange echo of her last time here, and she smiled to herself as the two sets of memories mingled. But where the evening with Jack had been almost choreographed, there had been a real spontaneity to sex with Alan and the soreness and the aches she felt reminded her that it had been long and varied.

They had made it to the bed quickly and he was fucking her before they'd undressed – had she really said 'Fuck me! Fuck me!' as he lay on top of her and pushed between her legs? – she smiled, she certainly had, and he'd come almost straight away. They lay back on the bed in each other's arms; he'd apologised for coming so quickly. She'd told him that was fine, he just had to promise to come again later and make sure she was happy. She felt a strange thrill in being so forward; he was a sweet and tender young man who had nevertheless rather masterfully got her into bed. But she felt quite safe and that she could trust him. This would be a one-night stand with no complications. She had fallen in love with Jack, but she was enjoying this other man's body.

She had told him to undress and enjoyed admiring how slim and fit he was. He had stood up and slowly and unselfconsciously draped his clothes over the chair. Just a little bit vain about his body perhaps?

She let him lie down beside her and then stood up

herself, taking her own clothes off even more slowly than he had, turning as she did so to allow him to look, pleased to see him admiring her, pleased to see that his cock was still full and half erect.

'You can lick me,' she'd said, 'while I get him ready again. Lie flat on your back.' He'd smiled and slid a little down the bed. She straddled his chest and lowered herself slowly on to his face, positioning her clit on his mouth. His arms circled her waist, pulling her firmly on to him.

'That's wonderful,' she had told him, 'but go slowly with me.' She took hold of his cock as she felt his arms loosen their grip. He was already stiffening again. She took time to study it. It was an exquisite thrill to feel her pussy tingling while she studied his rising cock, still shiny with its own and her juices. She bent down to lick its head, hearing him moan as her tongue circled it, feeling him pulling her more firmly again on to his mouth. She had pulled back, saying, 'Easy, easy.' She'd paused a little to let herself be amazed by herself – this was sixty-nine, wasn't it? And hadn't she started it? – and then she gave herself to it. He wouldn't come quickly again, she was sure, however stiff he was again already – and big, she thought, as she sat up again to study it – he really was a very attractive young man – and she was going to find out more about playing with and sucking cock – and if she came while she was doing it then she would just carry on.

She held him firmly, he was beginning to thrust his cock again. 'Easy baby, leave it to me,' she'd said, 'let's see what I can do with him.' She wanted to find how deeply she could take him, she pushed her mouth slowly down, feeling him reach the roof of her mouth, the back of her throat. Then she would lean back a while to breathe freely and to admire his cock again. Now she was thrusting. He felt her need and pulled her on to his mouth. Now was her time, she was holding him but finding her rhythm on his mouth, feeling his tongue exciting her, pushing into her, then licking her again. She felt her orgasm coming from a long way off, and she could savour the thrill of its oncoming arrival. She'd screamed loudly, still holding him firmly – maybe too firmly? She tried, even in her excitement, to avoid hurting him, but when her feelings flooded over her, she was able to hold him gently and keep him happily on the edge. She sat up a little, lifting herself off his face. His arms released her but then she felt a light slap on her arse. 'I was enjoying that very much,' he'd said, 'and I don't think she really wants to leave.' He'd pulled her on to his face again, licking her more gently this time.

'I think you're just happy with the attention your friend is getting,' she said, rubbing his cock a little more firmly.

She felt his face move – 'It's true I love what you're

doing with him, but I love kissing this gorgeous pussy.' – and his tongue pressed on her clit again.

She felt slightly amazed, she wanted him to carry on like that – even though she'd just come. It kept her pussy gently happy while she focused again on his cock. 'I'm impressed,' she'd told him, 'and I don't want you holding back.' But his build-up was slow, she loved the time, alternately studying it and sucking it, feeling it respond to how she licked or gently bit, feeling her jaws slowly start to ache – yes, he really was quite big – until she felt him slowly start to thrust again. This time she would allow the build-up, holding him firmly to control him in her mouth. 'I want you,' she'd said, 'I want to swallow you.' Had she really said that? Yes, she had, and she smiled at the memory – what a slut! And then she'd felt the pulses and tasted the warm blobs in her mouth.

She'd leant back to look. 'Please, no, don't leave him,' he'd called, and she took him in her mouth again to take the last drops.

She'd moved quickly to cuddle him and let him kiss her, what a strange taste with all their flavours, and as their breathing slowed, they let their hands run over each other's bodies. They'd talked, each finding ways of letting the other know that there were no expectations beyond the night.

'But I did want another work meeting,' he'd protested.

She'd taken his cock in her hand. 'Yes, so does he.'

'No really. I honestly learned so much earlier on.'

'And this is my reward, is it?' And they'd both laughed.

Later, he'd gone to the bathroom, and she'd gone to the living area to get water from the fridge, they stood together in a naked embrace, he kisses her deeply again. She felt his cock rising again against her hip. His fingers moved to her pussy. She was still very wet. Her hand moved to his cock, she felt it stiffen fully again. Why not? she'd thought to herself, and she'd turned to face the big window, she put her hands on the back of the sofa and bent forward. 'You know what you've got to do,' she'd said, amazing herself again, but one hand was already on her hip, the other guiding his cock into her again. This time they could both move more slowly, the intense excitement was on the horizon again, but it was a long way away. She felt his hands wandering over her, over her back, over her hips, over her cheeks. She'd felt him stretching them apart. Visual, she'd thought, but she liked him admiring her, just as she'd loved examining every detail of his cock earlier. She'd stretched her hand between her legs to touch his balls gently, she felt him stiffen and grow. She pulled them carefully against her and felt her clit tingle. And as she'd rubbed him gently, she'd felt his rhythm speed up. Now he'd gripped her hips and was thrusting very deeply, he was big, she'd thought again, almost uncomfortable she'd thought with a small triumphant smile. He was coming again, she knew, and she loved being held like a doll as he pushed and pushed his cum into her again. He'd embraced her and kissed her again and then moved her to the bed, making her lie on her back while he lay between her legs, slowly licking her again. She knew she would come again, but he could take his time – and he'd moved and licked slowly, letting her enjoy it all. But when she felt his fingers moving, pushing slowly and easily into her holes, she'd felt her excitement mount. She'd begun to enjoy these sensations, especially these new and unexpected ones and as his fingers pushed deeper while his tongue pressed harder, she was coming and screaming again.

But this time when he slid up to embrace her, she'd fallen asleep almost instantly.

And now it was morning, she was sore, she ached, she was alone – and she was curiously very happy.

18

She floated through the day. It had its little emergencies, like all conferences, but her team dealt with most things, few people got lost and keeping everyone to the timetable proved relatively easy – she had a mental list of the usual suspects, so she watched their groups closely for the smokers and the telephone diseased.

She checked the dining room preparations in the afternoon and welcomed some of the partners when they arrived. It would be a festive evening. It barely crossed her mind that she'd be missing the usual Friday phone call. She had felt relieved as she showered that morning that she wouldn't have to talk to Jack straightaway. She would be open, of course, but to discuss it in the immediate aftermath didn't appeal.

A text came at three:

Know you're very busy. Hope it's going brilliantly, I'm sure it is, you're a star at those things. Missing you. Jack xxx.

She smiled, she felt like a star today and when the previous night came into her head again, she was amazed at how warm and good she felt. Maybe when she got home it would hit her, that gut-wrenching mix of guilt and angst. But she knew she might only feel a little guilt about Jack, never about Dave. And Jack hardly merited feeling guilty about.

She checked the main conference again, confirmed with the crew that everything was still more or less on schedule. The groups were reporting back and keeping their presentations crisp, there seemed to be some good-natured but nevertheless penetrating discussion so she felt she could head back to reception and continue the welcoming duties. The partners loved coming. She recognized many of them and they spoke to her like old friends, so she got back to her room, as usual, with barely any time to change. The large bouquet looked splendid – there was always one to take home. But it was usually given to her at the dinner, amongst the speeches and thank-yous. Puzzled, she picked up the envelope, why were they changing things?

I really did learn so much, my heartfelt thanks, Alan XXXXX

Wow, how lovely, and five big kisses, not Jack's three small ones. She reassured herself, it was one night only, they'd been very clear about it. He was just being lovely. And what would happen next time? she thought before realizing that she now had to move quickly to be at the reception first.

The evening was wonderful, full of smiles, warmth and laughter; the usual complainers drowned out by the bonhomie around them. She drank one glass of wine and then stuck to water, the only way to manage the occasional incident which often threatened to spoil the later stages of the evening but tonight there was nothing just many hugs, some, of course, too familiar, and smiles and good feelings.

The morning sessions were always contentious, delegates not at their brightest while their partners had lie-ins and leisurely breakfasts. But they had found that good work came out and gave worthwhile direction for the tasks to come and the buffet lunch let everyone mingle again. Some couples would stay the extra night, many said their goodbyes in the afternoon. It was tea time when she got home. Dave came into the kitchen when she was putting her flowers into vases. He looked at the bouquets.

'One of them from the boyfriend?' He was surlier even than usual.

'No, one's from the conference and one's from the hotel.'

'With fucking roses?' And he walked back out before she even had to think of a reply. But his question had been too pointed. He'd got something in his head. And she had a knotted feeling in her stomach.

On a Saturday the kids stayed up late and trying to get them to bed would only have meant resistance and delays and anyway, she wanted to put off any confrontation even more than she wanted to be rid of the sick feeling in her stomach. Even when they went to bed, she stayed in front of the television, rather than seeking Dave out. She could have gone to bed, but if he chose to hammer on her door, as happened sometimes when he was drunk and angry, that would only alert the kids. She dozed but became aware after a while that he was sat in the armchair opposite her. He looked altogether dishevelled and his eyes were bleary. He'd obviously fallen asleep, drunk, and woken with his surliness and anger still fresh but unfocused. He was staring at her.

There was a long silence.

'What's up, Dave?'

'What's up? What's up?' His speech was slurry, he was very drunk. Another silence fell. She was not going to break this one. He would have to say what was on his mind.

'Lovely photos on your computer.'

Now her stomach turned over.

'That's the boyfriend's cock, I suppose, in front of your smiling face.'

'How did…' she stopped, that would be pointless.

'You think I'm just a stupid cunt that can't open a computer. You're such an arrogant bitch.' His voice was rising.

'Say what you want, Dave, but don't wake them. If we're going to talk, let's talk.'

'Talk? Talk?' He was screaming.

'Dave, shhh.'

'Shhh? You don't keep your mouth shut when he gets his cock out, do you? Oh no, wide open, get it all in and then bend over for him. You fucking slut! You fucking slut!' He was trying to stand but was too drunk to manage his limbs. She was standing by now and easily dodged the punch he aimed at her. She kicked his leg and made him fall over.

'Don't you try that again, Dave, I'll have the police here in no time. We'll talk if you want but don't ever try throwing punches again.'

He scrambled to his feet and took one step towards her. She was pressing buttons on her phone. 'I mean it, Dave. One more step and I call them.'

'Fuck you. I'm not talking. Where the fuck did that ever get us? I've said my last word to you.'

He slammed the door on his way out. The kids were probably awake by now, but they had learnt to stay in their rooms when there was shouting and let Mum come and explain later. But when she heard the front door slam and the car start, she was alarmed. He would be a real danger on the roads, but she was frozen about what to do. Her only hope that at one in the morning he'd make it unscathed to his parents' house only a mile away. Should she ring them? It wouldn't be the first time. She got a bleary response, 'Hello, Claudie, love.

What's he done this time?'

'He's drunk, Pat, and driving. I hope to God he's only coming to you.'

'Had a row?'

'Yes.'

'Well, he'll get here, give him a couple of days. I'll sober him up and talk some sense.'

'I don't think it'll be that easy this time. I'll tell you about it tomorrow.'

'OK, love, I'll talk to you then, but I'll let you know if he gets here.' She paused. 'Oh, I can hear a car now.'

'Thank God.'

Pat laughed. 'Don't know about that, love, it sounds like he's hit the gatepost on the way in. Let's hope no-one saw it. You see the kids are OK now. We'll talk tomorrow.'

'Yes, Pat, and thank you.' And floods of relief swept through her. It wouldn't be this easy, would it? And a little voice said no, it never is.

The girl was awake, plainly relieved to see mum without a bruise on her face and to hear that Dave had gone to his mum's. Claudia offered no explanations. It wasn't a first. Maybe she'd have to say more when he didn't reappear the following evening – and this time he probably wouldn't.

She felt surer of that when she spoke to Pat the next afternoon. That was very awkward. Pat had come around. They sat in the kitchen while the kids watched television in the other room. Pat was normally on her side, she knew Dave could be wild and had many times said how grateful she was that Claudia had helped him settle and given him a family life. But her questions had a different tone now.

'You've got somebody else, have you?'

'No, I haven't. I've seen someone else, that's true, and Dave's found out. He's told you?'

'He's said he's found some photos. That's all.'

'It's someone I worked with. He's moved away now.'

'You still speak to him?'

'Yes.'

'So, it's still going on?'

'He's six thousand miles away.'

Pat poured some more tea. 'It's still going on, is what I'm hearing.'

'Look, Pat, it's a long time since I had any feelings for Dave. I'm sorry. I thought we were getting through things for the kids.'

'So, what happens now?'

'I don't know. That depends on Dave.'

'He says he never wants to see you again.' She sipped her tea and smiled.

'He says that every time, doesn't he?'

Pat laughed and nodded. 'Yes, he does.' She paused.

'But this time' – she shook her head – 'this time you've got something else to think about. Is he married, this new man?'

'Divorcing – but that was before he had anything going with me.'

'Well your heart's somewhere else, isn't it? And bless him, he's my son and I think he tries to be a good dad, but I think he's a deadbeat husband. You might be happier apart, Claudie, just don't take the kids anywhere.'

'No. You know they always come first, and they're happy here mostly.'

'I know, love, and you know I think you're wonderful. I wish this hadn't happened, but I understand it, I think. But we love the kids too, and you might need our help.'

'Oh, Pat.' The tears welled as they stood up and held each other.

'I know, I know, it's very hard – but we'll get through it.'

When they sat down again, they poured more tea and talked about other things, just as they usually did, and it began to seem ridiculously normal again, just without Dave. Maybe the little voice was wrong. Maybe it would be easier.

19

Malcs' message came out of the blue:

Sylvie wants to meet you. Come to dinner? Malcs

That was intriguing in a few different ways. Even the name, was it a pet name or was she French? Was she the host or would that be Malcs?

Love to. Just the three of us? C

Your husband want to meet me? Malcs

Absolutely not! Haven't told him anyway. C

Then it's just the three of us. Thursday? Malcs

And Pat was happy to babysit. Claudia didn't know if the reassurance that the date was not with the new man was necessary, but she felt Pat would be an ally if she remained open about everything.

The flat, Sylvie's home, was small but elegant and immaculate, like Sylvie herself. She'd been greeted with a warm smile and a hug, and she felt instantly underdressed – Sylvie's Mawi necklace could have looked ostentatious but she carried it off superbly. Malcs handed her a glass of champagne. He too looked very good and she had to quickly recompute. This was not the schoolboy from Fife. This was a trim, handsome man in his thirties, looking entirely at home in an elegant London flat with an elegant French partner – the accent had been very light but unmistakable.

The small talk covered a lot of ground very quickly. Malcs had a house in a small village in Berkshire – that was easier for his work. She worked in the city so her flat suited her and moving between the two gave them both pleasant options. She had no children and no contact with either of her exes, the first French, the second English and there would be no third. She had looked at Malcs at this point and they had both laughed easily. It was obviously a position they shared.

Claudia said nothing about Dave's departure – she'd heard only from Pat in the five days since he'd left – but hadn't shrunk from describing her relationship as difficult. She only hesitated when Sylvie asked, 'Do you have anyone else?'

'Er, yes, but he's six thousand miles away.' She wasn't going to say anything but then she thought that, warm and welcoming as Sylvie evidently appeared, entertaining a strange and unhappy ex-girlfriend of your partner's in your own home might be seen as threatening. The discussion moved on then to jobs and travel as the food appeared, seemingly magically, the courses served alternately by her two hosts. Sylvie was by far the most well-travelled of the three of them, both with her job and from the lives she'd led in her marriages and, it became clear, on her own.

'We go every year to Carcassonne and stay with my parents, so Malcs knows a lot about my childhood. He's even met my first boyfriend. But he won't take me to Scotland.'

'It's so dreary. Claudia will tell you.'

'I wouldn't call it dreary, but you got away as soon as you could.'

'And you were his only regret, my dear.'

Claudia laughed loudly. 'Is that what he's told you? Malcs, you're still outrageous. You left dozens of broken hearts. He hasn't told you about those?'

'Oh, he's told me about them, but you were the only one who didn't fall for him.' She took Malcs' hand and they smiled at each other. 'I'm afraid my poor little devil is not very used to that. I think he's only with me because I turned him down at first.'

'Three times,' said Malcs, still smiling.

'Three times, but I already wanted you after the second. I just wanted to see how serious you were. Anyway, I hope you'll forgive me, but I thought if I met you, I would at least find out more about his childhood.'

'And his misspent youth?'

They laughed. 'Oh, definitely about his misspent youth. But I can see why he fell in love with you, my dear, you are very beautiful.'

Claudia gulped and blushed and quickly grabbed her wine glass. That was something she'd never been called before.

'So why don't we sit down and chat some more while Malcs clears away?'

They sat together on the sofa. The talk at the table had been animated, Malcs had always been talkative, it had been part of his charm, but Sylvie was even more so. Now Claudia could study her more closely. The dark bob had flecks of grey. The hazel eyes were large and bright and had plenty of laughter lines. Her lips were full, and she had kept them immaculate, always returning from any brief absence with them retouched. She was petite and slender with breasts that had probably had attention, the cleavage demure but, Claudia assumed, tantalizing for any man.

'What about this man of yours, so far away? Do you love him?'

Claudia laughed. 'I suppose I do. I haven't felt this way for a very long time' – she paused – 'well, if ever.'

'And he will stay away?'

'At least three years, I would think.'

'That is difficult, yes?'

'Oh, that would be impossible if I never saw him, but I'll go there in September, and I may see him in October in the US.'

'And that will be enough?'

Claudia laughed gently again. 'No, probably not, but it's the best I'm going to get.'

'And he is happy with that?' Sylvie's eyes had narrowed.

'I think he is, unfortunately, he has his amusements where he is, but at least we talk openly about them.'

Sylvie smiled and nodded. Malcs wandered in from the kitchen. 'They do like their amusements, don't they?'

'What are you talking about?' asked Malcs.

'Claudia's new man has his amusements.'

'Of course, he does.'

'That's his answer,' said Sylvie but she was still smiling. 'I knew it would be, that's why I made him wait before I let him take me out.'

Malcs smiled at her. 'You're not being open with Claudia, my angel, you have your own amusements too.'

Claudia felt a little shocked, but more than a little intrigued. 'You....' And she stopped, aware that her mouth was moving like a fish.

Sylvie laughed as Malcs left the room. 'It was the only way, and anyway, I like men. That was a problem in my marriages, well, with the second one, which got very boring, and I was enjoying living on my own. I knew I wouldn't get Malcs to settle down, I just decided to find out if he could live with me having the same life that he would have.'

'And he's happy?'

'He seems to be, what do you think?'

'I think he seems very happy. He glowed when he

spoke about you when we met. I was expecting to meet up with an unhappily married man…'

'Who would try to take you to the woods again?'

And they both laughed. 'Exactly, but he didn't try to talk to me in that way at all.' She lowered her voice. 'It seemed like he wanted to spend more time with you and that you were the one who wanted to keep your lives a little separate.'

Sylvie nodded and sipped wine and spoke more quietly. 'Yes, he needs to think that way. But if we were together more often, he would just wander more. I love being with him, but I think this way works.'

'But you have other relationships?'

Sylvie paused and closed her eyes, then spoke in a whisper, 'He thinks I do, but I don't.' She paused again, clearly thinking about what to say. 'I do have other men, I like them, but he knows all about that.'

'You tell him everything?'

Sylvie laughed. 'I don't have to, my dear, he sees almost everything.'

This time Claudia couldn't stop herself looking surprised. 'I'm sorry, I didn't mean to shock you. Should I explain?'

'I wish you would. I'm sorry if I looked shocked. It's entirely your business, but I admit I'm a little intrigued.'

'Well, Malcs may have his little affairs, I don't really know.' She was talking more freely now; they could hear a television in the neighbouring room, Malcs had clearly decided to let them talk alone for a while. 'I thought he might try to start one with you again, but I was so keen to meet you that I thought the risk was worth it.' She laughed gently. 'If he hadn't persuaded you to come, I would have assumed he had started something but here you are and you're lovely.'

Claudia smiled. 'Thank you, it's a real compliment from such a beautiful woman. It's not one I hear very often, I admit.' She paused, uncertain about how to continue. 'But you were saying he knows everything.'

'Yes, he knows everything – but he doesn't know he knows everything. He makes assumptions about what I do when I'm on my own. I could be offended that he thinks I conceal or tell fibs, but I'm not. It just seems to keep him more attentive if he thinks I'm seeing other people.'

'But you do see other men. You just said.'

Sylvie sipped her wine again, pausing to think about how much to say, 'Maybe now I shock you a little...'

'Go on.' Claudia was enjoying the little mystery.

'Well, we have parties we go to sometimes.' She paused to let the thought sink in. 'We think they're fun, some people call them sophisticated, some people call them bad things. But we enjoy them and then we enjoy each other a little bit more. Have you ever been to a party like that?'

Claudia spluttered. 'If I'm understanding this right, no, I definitely haven't. I've now got some wild pictures in my head about what's going. Are you saying people are having sex?'

Sylvie's little laugh chimed. 'Yes of course. Have I shocked you too much?'

'Well, surprised. I'd hate to admit I was shocked. I mean, I don't have anything against it, not that it's any of my business anyway. And you two seem to be thriving on it.'

'Oh, I think we are. But it's not good for everyone. It was my first husband who first took me, it started in Paris and then, when we moved to London, he found a new group of people and we just carried on, but I was much too jealous, really. I was trying to watch him, and I wasn't very good to the men who wanted me. Occasionally someone would interest me, and I would get some enjoyment but mostly I was worried about what Phillipe was doing – and it turned out he was doing quite a lot and not just at the parties, so I left him. It was easier than I thought. I found I'd stopped loving him anyway. But it did make me look for a boring Englishman and that was also a big mistake. I discovered I was missing the parties, I'd always enjoyed sex since I was quite young, but I'd spoiled the parties by worrying about Phillipe. So, after I was married again and I was quite sure my husband would not like that sort of thing, I just started going again on my own. Well, some friends took me, if a girl comes alone everyone gets suspicious of her, so people arrive in couples or in small groups. And you never have sex with anyone you come with. Men can't come alone either. Some of them try to come with prostitutes, of course, but that's usually obvious, and they're asked to leave.'

'Gosh, who manages all that?' Then Claudia laughed and blushed. 'Listen to me. You're telling me about extraordinary parties, and I'm just thinking like I do at work. Who runs the show? Who manages the event?'

Sylvie laughed. 'It all seems to run very informally. There are one or two places we go to. They're owned by rich people who have men attending who are very discreet at dealing with the undesirables. I know it happens, but I've never actually noticed. You just see people chatting, drinking, moving around and occasionally having sex, sometimes in quiet rooms sometimes very openly with others watching – and sometimes more people join in. It can be a little awkward, but most people can sense when to join and when to just watch or to stay away. I wouldn't say there's no pressure, if a man wants you it's pretty obvious.' She laughed again. 'Especially if he's naked.'

Claudia laughed too, almost despite herself. 'I think I've only ever seen people having sex once.'

'Ah,' Sylvie was smiling, 'that would be Malcs, yes? When you were younger?'

'He's told you more about me than I really want anyone to know.' But she was aware she didn't mean it. She had warmed to Sylvie's openness, it was utterly disarming. 'I don't know why I'm worried, I've seen my friend making Malcs happy once. You must have seen it lots of times.'

'Sometimes, yes, but not lots. It's not like my first husband, my eyes don't follow him. Of course, if I can't see him, I know what he's doing, and I'm usually busy myself.'

'Chatting and drinking?' Claudia wanted it spelled out.

Sylvie laughed again. 'Chatting and drinking, yes, but also having sex. If I like the man, I usually like the sex. Then we can chat and drink again.'

Claudia was silent, Sylvie watched her. 'I'm sorry, I feel like such an innocent. I'm so curious, but I shall say or ask something silly.'

'That's all right, my dear, everyone feels that way at first. You should perhaps come with us. That would answer your questions.'

'Oh, I couldn't possibly, no.'

'You disapprove? Have I said too much?'

'Oh, no, no, please. No, I find it an exciting idea, honestly but I don't think it's a step I can take.'

'Most people don't do anything the first time. They just come along to see if they feel comfortable. We could take you; you could see what happens.'

'Well, I admit I'm very intrigued,' said Claudia, amazed at herself, and wondered whether, despite trying to restrain herself with wine, she hadn't drunk rather too much.

The conversation moved on – to the apartment, to Sylvie's dress – until Malcs wandered in again.

'More coffee?'

The ladies both nodded.

'Cognac?'

'Not for me,' said Claudia quickly, 'I'm driving. My God look at the time. It's gone one. I've got to get home, I'm working tomorrow.' She paused. 'Gosh, I'm sorry, that's very ungracious of me. I'd love a coffee please Malcs. I've been having such a wonderful time it's just flown by.'

'Claudia's coming to a party with us,' announced Sylvie when Malcs put the cups in front of them.

Malcs stopped, his eyes met Claudia's. 'She's told you all about them?'

'Yes,' she turned to Sylvie, 'and I thank you for the invitation, but I still want to think it over.'

'You don't have to do anything,' said Malcs, moving to the sideboard to pour two cognacs.

'I know, Sylvie's told me, but I'd be watching

people, wouldn't I?'

'Well, you're mostly just talking to people there, but it is going on around you. You can tell the newcomers, they're the one with a white ribbon round their wrists and they're staring rather a lot.' He and Sylvie chuckled.

'Well, I could cope with a lot, I think, but I'd have to look at you two.' The thought had suddenly made her nervous.

'Oh, you probably wouldn't see me,' said Malcs, 'I'm a creature of the shadows, but Sylvie's the exhibitionist.'

'Malcs!' exclaimed Sylvie with mock indignation, but they smiled at each other. Claudia was suddenly a little disturbed by a mental picture of this elegant woman being in the middle of a group of naked men. Disturbed, but somehow slightly fascinated.

Sylvie turned her big, hazel eyes to Claudia. 'We're absolutely not pushing you, my dear, but it does sound like you could do with some life while your lover is so far away.' She paused, Claudia lowered her head and said nothing. 'We're going to a party on Friday next week. You could think about it. You can stay with us afterwards, yes?'

'Wow, OK, I will think about it – and thank you. I have to say it's very nice to be asked.'

And her mind was a whirl on the way home as

strange pictures came into her head of what the party might be like – and what Malcs and Sylvie would be doing. She gave no thought to herself being any more than an observer. But she started to wonder why a woman she'd only just met, warm and sincere as she seemed, had been so keen to invite her to a party like that.

20

She had so much to talk to Jack about, and she was nervous about all of it. She was desperate for him to call, but worried about what to say. How could she approach her night with Alan, it was so out of character for her – or was it, really? It would certainly not correspond to Jack's expectations, his idea of her with other men was probably just a dirty fantasy of his and the reality of her enjoying another partner – and she had enjoyed Alan and had, until now, no regrets – might be something that turned him away.

And Dave leaving. How might he react to that? Would he suddenly feel a little trapped now that she was no longer securely married?

All in all, it would be easier to talk first about Malcs and Sylvie. He would want to know about their lifestyle, maybe that was a lifestyle Jack wanted, and he would certainly encourage her to go along to the party, but would he really mean that?

Sylvie's question – did she love him? – had caught her off guard. She knew it was a question best avoided and when the afternoon passed with no text or call, she knew why it was best avoided. And when she realized she had the right to contact him and she was being merely reluctant, she was even more sure.

It was after five, already late for her to be leaving – Pat was with the kids, but she didn't want to take advantage of that – she'd already been very late last night – when the text came:

Sorry, flight delay, expect you've gone home already. Any chance of catching up tomorrow? Missing you xxxxx.

And warm feelings flooded through her (five x's, the number was increasing!). She stopped the car and texted back:

Wonderful idea. Dave out all day. Call when you want XXXXXX

And she drove on home happy, apart from the little worm burrowing in her brain – that was a misleading thing to say about Dave. But she could hardly have put anything in a text. She would be open with him tomorrow: about Malcs and Sylvie; about Alan; about Dave. It might be a long conversation, and a difficult one.

And Jack himself might have some interesting or difficult things for her to listen to. It had been two weeks since they'd spoken.

Is now a good time? xxxxx

He was being unusually considerate, texting first was a new thing. It was ten thirty, and she had the house to herself, the kids were with friends.

Call when you want. No, call soon! XXXX

'I've missed you. You're too busy!'

'I'm listening to Mr International Traveller. Do you want me to talk about your availability?'

'Ah, have I got this off to a bad start? I've missed you, that's what I meant to say first.'

'I've missed too, Jack. I've been busy but I have been missing you. I keep telling myself it's only seven weeks now. I've made it more than halfway through. You've been gone nine weeks.'

'I know. It's racing by, but it seems so long since I saw you.'

'That's because it bloody well is.'

'I know, I know but you've been busy, you said. Are you going to tell me about it?'

'Of course, but I want to hear about you first. I didn't think you were travelling this week.'

'I hadn't planned to, but things came to a head with the general manager in the Philippines business. I had to go there with HR and fire him. We always do those things on a Friday, I'm not sure it's best. The victim needs to get on with his life and there's not much he can do on the weekend except mope and take it out on his family. And we need to talk to his team and explain things and make sure they're all right, but mostly they just want to get home. Although the truth is that bit was easy because most of them expected it and wanted it –

apart from a couple of cronies of his who we'll probably also get rid of soon anyway.'

'What was wrong with him?'

'Well, we're often told that relationships are all important in business in Asia, you need to be close to your business partners and I can see that. But when you give some of them overly favourable terms and lock out others who are potentially, or even actually, more important, then you're getting it wrong. When we investigated the numbers some of the smaller retail chains were getting much bigger discounts than the larger ones. It had been pointed out to him two years ago and he'd done nothing about it, so our stuff is underrepresented in the biggest stores. I'm glad it was obvious, we didn't have to delve into the, how shall I put this, the soft discounts he added to their rebates.'

'What do you mean?'

'I think he entertained them, or got young ladies to entertain them, in ways inconsistent with our corporate philosophy. Have I put that tactfully enough?'

She laughed. 'I'm getting the picture.'

'Fortunately, we didn't have to make that point, much less prove it, because the rebate problem was so obvious. But I did have to be very clear with the guy taking over that we don't do business that way.' He laughed. 'Well, not any more, we don't.'

'So, no-one gets young ladies to entertain you?'

'No,' he said very firmly, 'I've had offers, of course, but I think you undermine yourself completely if you go down that route.' That sounded surprisingly pompous for Jack, but he could get that way about business sometimes. Serious, he would call it.

'And you have your own entertainment anyway. How are the ladies?'

'They're fine,' he said slowly, 'well, I have only seen Martha in passing since the last time I told you about.'

'And, how was she?'

'She just said she was looking forward to the next time but that she wasn't ready yet.'

'Not got over the last time?'

'Something like that, I guess. I don't know that I'd want to be confronted with the evidence of my handiwork and I doubt whether the marks disappeared that quickly.'

'And Joanna?'

He answered more slowly, which made her suddenly feel nervous, 'Well that's sorting itself out, I think.'

'Go on.'

'Well, they now have an end date for Rick's contract here and it looks like she'll go back ahead of him – before you come out here, in fact.'

'Oh, such a shame, I was looking forward to meeting her.'

He laughed. 'Yes, I suppose that was a stupid point to make. You do a very edgy line in sarcasm, by the way. Anyway, she leaves next month.'

'What aren't you telling me?'

'Openness?'

'Openness!'

'She had been getting more attached; I could feel that, so it's good that she's going. I like her a lot and I thought her being married made it safe. I mean I thought the whole non-vaginal thing was more funny than hypocritical and it didn't bother me, although it would trouble me to get close to anyone who thought that way.'

'And she wanted to get closer?'

'Yes, she did.'

'How did that come about? Was she offering you the forbidden fruit?'

'Yes and no.'

'You're being unusually coy, good sir, where's openness in this?'

'She wanted me inside her, Claudie, but not in the adulterous channel.'

'She had you in her mouth, you said.'

'Yes, but I like being behind you, Claudie.'

There was a silence.

'Are you being deliberately thick to make me say this? Up your bum, my dearest, up your bum. And you seem to like it. My God, I'm not sure about this openness thing.'

Claudia hesitated. 'So that's what she wanted?'

'Yes, for her it was a new level, but she still wasn't in conflict with her strange view of her marriage vows. I think maybe she wanted to offer me more and she was also a bit curious.'

'So, did you?'

'We tried it, yes.'

'You tried it?'

'Yes, it doesn't work for everybody,' he paused, before adding, 'apparently,' too hastily. 'She was very tight and nervous. She hadn't tried it before.'

'Look, Jack, I was a virgin there too,' she said quite crossly.

'I know,' he said slowly, 'but you relaxed so beautifully. You did like it, didn't you?'

'As you've worked out by now, I loved it. I amazed myself, but I did. I do get turned on by your dirty ways, unfortunately.'

'Unfortunately?'

'Oh, Jack, this is a funny life. I wouldn't try to change any of it while I can't. I even accept your Singapore life, you can't say I don't. But that doesn't mean I wouldn't like to try living in a different way.'

'I know, Claudie, that goes for me too.' He paused. 'You know that, don't you?'

'No, I don't, Jack, but it doesn't matter. I'm thrilled with what I have. It's not easy but I'm not going to risk losing it.'

'Neither am I. But now I really do think you should be telling me something about what you've been up to. How did the conference go?'

'It went well, and I've lots to tell you, why don't you fix yourself a drink while I get some coffee? Do you have time?'

'I've all the time you want. Shall we say fifteen minutes? I'll call again.'

Typical Jack, ask a question and assume an answer. But she needed the time, she thought, to compose herself. He'd been very open again and that set her a challenge. As she went to the kitchen, she realized the break wasn't helping. It would have been better to have ploughed on.

'So, what have you been up to?'

'I met Malcs and his partner.' That was the easiest way to start, and Sylvie's story would appeal, she knew, to Jack.

'How did that happen? I thought he was lining you up for another trip to the woods.'

'She wanted to meet me. She's French. They travel there quite often but he's never taken her to Scotland, and she wanted to know about his past. Well, his childhood. I think they both have adult pasts, but they are aware of those. He'd talked about me, apparently, so she got him to make contact.'

'You'd obviously made a bigger impression on him than you thought.'

'So, it seems. I was surprised. But anyway, I spent most of my time talking to her. You'd love her.'

'I'd love her? So, what embodies my tastes if it's not you?'

'She's French, she's beautiful, she's elegant…'

'And?'

'And they go to parties, apparently. Parties you'd probably like.'

'Don't let me make any embarrassing assumptions. Are you going to tell me what goes on at these parties?'

'Sex. Lots of it apparently, but lots of chatting and drinking as well, they say.'

'And you think that's my scene?'

'I could see you fitting in well – although I don't know if they cater for all your more exotic tastes.'

'I don't know that it's quite me anyway. It's the sort of thing I'd like to imagine you at.'

'Me?'

'Yes, I know you think I'm kinky, but I like to think of you being fucked by someone else.'

'So, you think I should go? They've invited me to one next week.'

'Oh, wow, then you should definitely go.'

'You really want me to go?'

'Yes, I do, on two conditions.'

'And they are?'

'Well, you have to tell me all about it of course. I mean, I don't know that it's what I'd be into, but I want to hear all about it.'

'And the other condition?'

'You have to fuck somebody – and tell me. This openness goes two ways.'

'I know it does, Jack, and I'm the one who was pushing for it, the openness, I mean, but when I hear about Joanna and what she wants I'm no longer so sure.' And Claudia couldn't quite suppress a smile that the silly bitch had obviously found the attempt quite painful. She'd read it could be like that and had been very surprised that she had found it so easy, and so exciting, with Jack. 'But Sylvie says that first-timers usually just watch and get used to it and make up their minds about whether they come again, or not.'

'Well, you will go anyway, won't you?'

'I don't know, Jack, I'm not really minded to.'

'But I'd like you to. I think you should.'

It was Jack; he was being warm and funny – but also a little too pushy. He should be more sensitive to her reluctance – just because his behaviour had no apparent boundaries didn't mean that she should follow.

'I'm going to think about it some more and I'll

make my own mind up. And if you're trying to push me to fuck someone, then it's time I told you.'

She froze suddenly. This was not the way to do it. He always approached his stories with a little care, allowed her to build a little cushion of suspicion to soften the blow of information – and here she was just blurting something out provocatively. And there was an ominous silence on the phone.

'Jack?'

'Soooo, you do have something to tell me.'

'Yes, Jack, I do.' Best get through this quickly, she thought, delaying would make it seem worse. 'I met a guy called Alan at the hotel. The manager introduced us; he's got to run a conference and the manager told him what I do, and he wanted me to have dinner with him and talk about it and after dinner, he came to my room and things just sort of happened.'

There was another silence. She didn't know what to say next.

'When it's me talking, this is where I normally have to tell you all the details.'

'I'm finding this hard, Jack.'

'Openness, Claudie, openness.'

'It's difficult.'

'Do you have any regrets?'

'Well, I didn't, until now.'

'This being open is new for me and it's honestly

helped me. I know what I get up to is hard for you to listen to but telling you means I'm not going around with a knot of guilt in my stomach all the time. We have something special and I think it's growing, and I don't think it would if we start keeping secrets. Are you worried you've fallen for this guy and you're trying to work out how to tell me?'

'Oh, Lord, Jack, no, not that. I mean, he was lovely, but it was one night.'

'And you enjoyed it?'

'I had a lovely time; you've kind of taught me to enjoy myself.'

'Ah, so you led him on.'

It sounded like he was teasing, she hoped he was. 'No, I didn't really. He came to my room.'

'But you didn't stop him.'

'At first – but then I thought, what the hell. He was young, handsome and charming and he'd been very nice to me. But a few months ago, I wouldn't have dreamed of letting anything happen but suddenly I found myself taking the lead.'

Another pause.

'Doing what?'

'Well, sixty-nine, I suppose you'd say. I sat on his face and sucked him while he ate me. There, I've said it, are you happy now?'

He laughed. Relief! 'Congratulations, even we haven't done that.'

'You haven't caned my arse yet, Jack, but that doesn't stop you with Martha.'

'Oh, that will come, my dear, I promise you. I already have your cane, and it will hurt much more than that silly paddle. Are you ready for that?'

'Yes, I'm ready for that,' she said slowly.

'Excellent, just like I'm ready to hear more about sixty-nine. Did you enjoy it, or were you just curious?'

'I was curious but then I started to enjoy it and yes, damn you, I started to think about how I could make it exciting for you. Are you happy now?'

'Yes, I'm happy now. I'm a little anxious that it might mean more to you than one night, but that's the danger we live with. I miss you and I'm desperate for you to be here, but I enjoy what I get up to without thinking my feelings are threatened.'

'I just want you, Jack. I admit my night was enjoyable, but it just makes me want you more.' Was she saying too much now? Was she pinning him down?

Now she couldn't tell him about Dave.

'That's even more reason to go to the party, then. What will you wear?'

And reluctant as she was to return to that topic, at least it meant they didn't have to talk about Dave. She would tell him, of course, but that would be too much in one conversation. And anyway, what would she wear to an orgy?

21

The thought nagged at her the following week – and when she caught herself giving in to it, she would laugh, attracting more than one odd glance in the office. Worrying about what to wear when she was contemplating being in a strange house watching couples shagging, and maybe more than couples, maybe more than shagging. As the week wore on, she became slightly more terrified – and slightly more curious – but by Friday she had still not convinced herself she would go. After all, she still had nothing to wear! But she had lined up Pat to babysit for the night.

She had texted Malcs. Curiously his text:

Are you with us? XXX

Had crossed with hers on the Tuesday:

I'm coming Friday, that OK? And what time? X

Come to us around 8.30, we'll have a snack and head off later. XXX

But she knew the text didn't commit her. What finally made up her mind was a text from Jack on Friday afternoon:

Have fun tonight. Tell me all about it. xxx

She was irritated. He should have rung. She knew

his schedule, he was in the office all day. She wasn't spying, she told herself, it was in the corporate diary. Why couldn't he have called her? But she would have kept him on the phone, used him, maybe, as an excuse not to go.

She spent a long time getting ready, dithering over the dress, dithering over the underwear. Would she really be showing that off? No! But best be prepared anyway.

'You're looking very glam, dear,' said Pat when she finally came down, 'new man?'

'No, Pat, no. It's a couple I know but she's very chic, very French, and I don't want to be too outshone.'

'Well you'd outshine anyone, I think Dave's realizing that.'

She was a little alarmed. 'Has he said anything?'

'No dear, he just mopes and drinks,' she sighed, 'but I think that's all he was doing anyway, wasn't it?'

It seemed like Pat wanted to talk. 'It had got like that, I'm afraid. Listen, could we talk a bit more about that tomorrow? Can you hang on a bit when I get back?'

'Yes, yes, of course. You get on, don't mind me. I know Dave hasn't given you too many nights out in the past couple of years. You get off now.'

They hugged warmly and she kissed the kids. The girl at least said, 'You look nice, Mum.' The boy didn't look up from the screen.

It was nearer nine when she got to the apartment. 'I'm sorry I'm late. The traffic…'

Malcs ushered her in. 'Hey, it's no problem. We don't want to get there before eleven.'

'Gosh, that sounds so late. I'm sorry, I'm babbling, I'm nervous, you can guess.'

Malcs put his arms around her and pulled her to him. 'Of course, you are, but you must only watch, remember.'

Sylvie came into the small hallway. 'Ah, how lovely to see you and you look so beautiful.' Sylvie held her hands and touched cheeks.

'But you look stunning, Sylvie.' And she did, she glittered. There was some jewellery, and the black dress had some shiny beading, but somehow her face shone, and her eyes sparkled, she was dazzling.

'Thank you, my dear, but you really do look very elegant. We shall have to watch you if you want to be protected. But that's much later, let's have a drink and relax.'

Claudia felt a million miles from relaxed as she followed Sylvie into the sitting room that felt strangely familiar to her. She'd only been there once but that evening, that conversation, had been so surprising it had left an indelible imprint. She settled on the sofa. She heard the champagne pop in the kitchen.

'Have you heard from Jack?' was Sylvie's first

question when they sat down.

Claudia was flustered, had she mentioned Jack's name? She didn't think so, she had tried to be so discreet but then she thought, why bother, it wouldn't matter.

'Yes, yes. We had a long conversation last weekend, but he travels a lot in the week, all around Asia.'

Sylvie's eyes narrowed a little. 'And you told him about our little party?'

Claudia laughed. 'Yes, I did. I had to. I make such a big thing about him being open with me that I had no choice, really.'

Sylvie took her glass from Malcs. 'And here you are, so he obviously liked the idea.'

Claudia felt on edge – was this pressure too? 'Why do you say that? I might be coming to spite him.'

'Ah, but you love him, my dear, don't you?'

'Yes, yes I do,' she said slowly.

'So, you want to make him happy and not angry.'

'Well, that's true, but does it matter?'

'It does, my dear, it does because what you should be thinking about most of all is making yourself happy.'

They raised glasses and sipped champagne. The thought hit Claudia quite hard, she tried to clear her thoughts.

'You're right, actually – and you saying it like that makes me realize I almost never do that. I'm always running around for other people.' But she settled back and smiled to herself, thinking about the night with Alan – OK, she'd responded to him pushing into the room but after that everything was as she had wanted and maybe that was why there had been no guilty aftermath. She had finally done something just for herself, and it would hurt nobody – she had a happy memory, and she felt sure Alan had felt the same. Was she now starting to worry about his feelings? She laughed silently at herself, she was doing it again, worrying about other people.

'You're miles away.'

'Er, yes, you're right, I'm sorry. It was what you said. It made me think, and you are dead right.'

'I think so. It's what I've learnt. I can only make Malcs happy if I'm happy myself. Happy in myself and happy with myself, so I think your Jack might be happier if you're happy.'

'Ha, well maybe, but I think he also has a kinky fascination with the idea of me being with someone else.' And they both laughed.

'That may be more common than you think. Even my second husband, when it all came out in the open, got quite attentive and romantic for a while and wanted to know more about what I had been doing. But, of course, he'd been insanely angry at first and said some unforgivable things. Well, nothing's unforgivable if you love someone but I didn't love him any more.'

'I suppose that's how I feel about Dave now. I can't see him trying to come back but at least I'm prepared. What do you think, Malcs?'

Malcs had been sitting in the armchair, looking relaxed but clearly following their conversation.

'Ha, what about? Forgiving everything – or having kinky feelings about Sylvie with other men?'

Claudia suddenly felt embarrassed that she might have asked a difficult question.

'Well, I was asking about forgiving things, but I suppose the other question bothers me too.'

Malcs pondered, Sylvie leant back and turned towards him. 'Hey,' he said, 'your eyes are on me. I'm not comfortable with women's questions.' But he laughed and still seemed relaxed. 'I think if you're open and you know what you've agreed to, then there's not so much to forgive – but if there were, I'd certainly try. If we hit any bumps in the road, I'd want to sort them out. I'm happier with her than I've ever been in my life.'

'Oh, sweet,' said both the girls simultaneously and laughed, which made him laugh too.

'But on the second part, yes, I think she looks beautiful with another man's cock in her mouth.'

Claudia gasped. Sylvie laughed.

'So yes, you can call me kinky.' And they both seemed very relaxed still.

'Mmm, well Jack gets up to things in Asia. I'm glad

he tells me about them but I'm not sure I get a kinky thrill out of them.' She tried not to sound disapproving.

'I think you're right,' said Sylvie supportively, 'I don't think too much about it when Malcs slopes off to a quiet room. It doesn't bother me. It's part of him. I wanted him because he likes sex – and he's very good at it, as you know.'

'That was years ago,' protested Malcs – Claudia wondered why.

'But she's right,' said Claudia, smiling and pleased to get back on to the wavelength of the conversation, 'you were very good.'

'I'm going to beat a retreat in embarrassment and get some food ready. We've just got canapes and light bites, is that OK? We find it makes the best preparation for the evening.'

'Yes, that's perfect. I'm too nervous to be hungry.'

'Come with me,' said Sylvie as Malcs disappeared. They stood, Sylvie took her hand and led her through the hall to the main bedroom and closed the door behind them.

'I hope you'll forgive me, but I thought, as it's your first time, that you might want to talk about what you're wearing.'

'Oh,' Claudia spluttered, 'I hadn't... I thought... actually, you're right. Is my dress OK?'

'Your dress is perfect. Simple, elegant – and easy

to slip off, I think?'

'Well, it is, but I hadn't thought I'd be doing that tonight necessarily.'

'Well maybe you won't, but I think you probably thought about it when you chose your underwear.'

Claudia smiled and nodded slowly. 'Yes, I did, a bit – and I admit, I had absolutely no idea. So, any advice you…'

But Sylvie was already slipping out of her dress – a simple unzipping manoeuvre and she was stepping completely free of it. She picked it up and draped it carefully on the bed.

Claudia was open-mouthed. It was a cliché in front of her, but a stunning and exotic one. Sylvie did have a petite body, but a very feminine one. The waist was slim enough to make the hips look curvy and they were accentuated by the garter belt that held the black stockings up. The tiny knickers were diaphanous and made it obvious that Sylvie waxed completely – Claudia found herself staring reluctantly and reflecting on her own now pathetic-seeming attempts to shave herself. Then she found herself staring at Sylvie's breasts. She still couldn't decide if they'd been enhanced, but they did look wonderful. With delightful dark nipples peeking over the top of the black lacy platform.

Sylvie turned unselfconsciously around slowly. She has a peachy arse, thought Claudia, made to look curvier and more prominent by being framed by the belt, straps and thong. 'Wow, amazing,' gasped Claudia.

'I'm afraid it's impossible to be too obvious. Very few men appreciate style and subtlety in this area.'

Claudia found herself stripping out of her dress. 'I'm afraid I've gone rather demure.' She looked down – black lacy bra, showing cleavage but no nipples, black lacy thong, one of her purchases for Jack, and black holdups.

'No, no, you look wonderful. You have a wonderful body. Turn around.'

Claudia turned around. 'Oh, la, you do have a perfect arse. No wonder he still dreams about the woods.'

'Will I do? I mean, if I decide to take my dress off.'

'You will look fabulous.'

'Really?'

'Really.'

'But you look sensationally sexy.'

'Ha, I have been working at this for years. My first husband gave me so much advice. He wanted other men to surround me so he could go and do what he wanted. And it worked. I usually get attention.'

'I'm not surprised. It's the garter belt that does it, isn't it? Well, and your breasts, I suppose.'

'But you can have a garter belt if you want. I do feel sexier, it's true, maybe it works for you.'

'I don't possess one. I thought about it for Jack, but…'

Sylvie was pulling two packs from a drawer.

'Here, try these, I'm sure they're your size.'

'Sylvie, I can't.'

'Of course, you can, try them, see how you look, see how you feel.'

Claudia began slowly unwrapping the belt and stockings. 'Sylvie, forgive me, but I'd like to ask a difficult question.'

'You can ask any question, my dear.'

'Well, I'm worried about seeming stupid or ungrateful.'

Sylvie sat on the bed, being careful to avoid her dress – that made Claudia retrieve her own from the floor and drape it over the chair.

'You're being lovely to me. You've been so welcoming and warm, but you've only just met me. I'm just a wee girl from Malcs' distant past.'

'Try those things on, I will tell you something.'

But Claudia stopped and sat on the chair. They looked in each other's eyes.

'I was honest. I wanted to know more about Malcs and his youth, and you were the one he talked about most often, so it was logical to ask him to find you. But what I didn't say was, and here I will be a little more honest, he talks about you because he still has a little dream about this wonderful girl he left behind. I wanted him to meet a real person, living a real life, maybe enjoying the things he and I enjoy but mostly showing him that his dream girl had become a real woman by now and had probably left her dreams behind.'

'Well, she's certainly done that.'

'I don't know, I think you still have a dream, but the dream is in Asia.'

Claudia nodded slowly.

'So, there you are, the whole story. Well, not quite the whole story.'

Claudia raised her eyebrows.

'I know why he kept his dream, you are very lovely, but also, I think you are gorgeous too, and I think you and I will have fun together. Now give me a hug.' And they stood and embraced, too quickly for Claudia to worry about holding another woman's semi-naked body, but it lingered long enough for her to begin to feel uncomfortable.

'Now come on dear,' said Sylvie as she pulled away, 'let's see how stunning you look in a garter belt.'

Malcs had the table laid when they returned.

'What conspiracies have you two been contriving?'

'Just a wardrobe check,' said Sylvie.

'Sounds interesting.'

'You'll find out soon enough.'

'Well maybe,' said Claudia quickly.

'Oh, I hope he will, I hope they all will. She is very beautiful, Malcs. I know why you still cherish your little woodland fantasy. But we should eat something now.' And she gestured for Claudia to sit.

Malcs poured the rest of the champagne and filled the water glasses.

'Would you like some wine?'

'I'd rather make sure I keep my wits about me.'

'Very wise,' said Sylvie. 'Sometimes the young girls drink too much and then get silly. That can end in tears but Peter's guys sort that out very quickly.'

Then the conversation moved on to other things. Claudia was relieved. She didn't want to think or plan any more. She would just go along with things and see how she felt.

They were still chatting animatedly when Malcs' phone rang. 'OK, we'll be right out. Car's here ladies.'

'Oh, I haven't even shown you your room. Never mind, we can sort that out later and don't worry, we'll come away as soon as you want to.'

''I'm not that timid. I'm sure I'll find it interesting.'

'Yes, my dear, I think you will,' said Sylvie with a knowing smile.

22

'Are we going far?' Claudia suddenly felt an attack of nerves.

'Barnes, near the common, it won't take fifteen minutes,' said Malcs from the front of the Mercedes. The driver clearly knew the address, Malcs had said nothing to him. They were soon going over Putney Bridge, the traffic still quite heavy even at eleven, but it eased once they'd turned right to go along the side of the river.

The large white house was set well back, and the car had plenty of room to turn and let them out, even though there were many cars on the gravelled area. Claudia looked around when she got out, lots of expensive machinery, some of it exotic. The Rolls, a Bentley and two Ferraris were easy to identify, but a couple of supercars less so. Large Mercedes mopped up the remaining spaces. At least we aren't the first, she thought.

The front door took a few seconds to open. Claudia looked up to see the cameras, they were clearly being checked. The door was opened by a tall, slim man, dressed all in black with a shaved head. He had a warm smile but, nevertheless, a menacing presence. 'Lovely to see you here again Malcs, Sylvie.' The dark brown eyes turned to Claudia.

'This is Claudia, Andreas; she hasn't been here before.'

'Ah.' His eyebrows rose, and his face formed what passed for a smile. 'Then we must make her very welcome. Would you like to take one of these, Claudia?' And he plucked a white ribbon from a bowl on the console table. 'Let me tie it for you, your left hand, please.' And he tied an elegant, delicate bow, perfectly symmetrically and quite tightly around her wrist.

'Peter's back in the dining area, why don't you go and introduce your new guest?'

Claudia was trying not to be overwhelmed by the house. The hall was all marbled, as was the grand staircase that swept up in a graceful shallow curve beside them to the first floor. Double doors opened on to reception rooms on either side of the hall. Directly ahead of them was another double door opening on to where most people seemed to be. Claudia looked straight ahead, frightened of being confronted by scenes in the front rooms that she was not yet ready to face. Ahead the chattering people looked very sociable and fully, if sometimes exotically, dressed.

'Sylvie!' called a tall, elegant, silver-haired man as soon as they entered the room. He left the group where he had seemed to be holding court and moved directly towards them. He embraced Sylvie warmly and kissed her cheeks.

'You look absolutely enchanting,' he said, leaning back as if trying to take her all in, while not letting go of her hands. 'And Malcs, it's wonderful you could make it.' There was a very manly handshake before he turned to look directly into Claudia's eyes. Even in heels, and she was wearing the killers, she had to look up to his pale blue eyes. They were set in a tanned and very handsome face. A man in his fifties, probably, but looking much fitter and younger than would be typical. 'And this is Claudia,' he said smiling. She was taken aback that he knew her name. He put his hands on her shoulders and moved her gently towards him as he kissed her too on each cheek. 'Sylvie,' he turned to her, 'you told me she was beautiful.' He looked back at Claudia. 'She's much more than that!' He smiled, it was a warm, friendly smile but Claudia was instantly on her guard. It was a dangerous smile.

'Let me organize you something to drink. Champagne?'

'Of course,' said Sylvie.

'Of course.' He smiled at her and left them to move off into the kitchen.

Claudia looked around. A very large room led on to a terrace and a large garden beyond. There was a pond beyond the terrace, subtly lit, as were the surrounding trees. A few couples were outside sitting and talking in the still warm summer night. There were a few groups dotted around the room they were in, in the centre of which was the largest, and probably the most ornate, dining table that Claudia had ever seen. She quickly counted fourteen dining chairs, well-spaced around it but there was still ample room for the talking groups. The men, in the main, looked older but mostly in good shape, the women were almost all slim and beautiful. About a half looked in their twenties but Claudia was aware that they had probably paid a great deal to retain that youthful sheen. All were dressed expensively and a few quite provocatively, split skirts and deep cleavage were common, but no-one looked cheap, only seriously sexy.

'Hannes, thank you,' called Sylvie to the man who brought the tray with three glasses. He could have been the twin of Andreas the doorman – although Claudia was sure that their roles entailed a great deal more than answering doors and serving drinks.

Two men soon detached themselves from a group and came to introduce themselves, although they clearly knew Sylvie very well. My God thought Claudia suddenly, she's probably had them, and the thought, catching her off guard, made her miss their names. One left his arm draped around Sylvie's shoulder but stared very purposefully at Claudia.

'I'm sorry, I just didn't catch the names.'

'This is Alphonse,' said Sylvie, gesturing with her glass to the taller, darker one, 'and he's bad. And this' – she dug her elbow into the ribs of the man embracing her – 'is Graham, and he's very bad.'

The men smiled.

'Alphonse, are you French?'

'On my mother's side,' he said, with no accent, 'and I was born there but I grew up here.'

Claudia noticed that Malcs had quietly moved. He was still in the room but had attached himself to another group, one with more women than men.

Peter returned. 'Ah, the bad boys have already approached the new beauty, I see. I'll let you have them later if you wish, my dear, but it would be remiss of me not to show you around and frankly,' he was now talking in a mock conspiratorial stage whisper, 'I'll be astonished if you can't do much better than them.'

He put his arm around Claudia's shoulder and guided her towards the hall.

'You know what goes on, don't you?'

'Oh, yes, Sylvie's told me,' she said, trying to sound as nonchalant as she could.

'Good, well, the two reception rooms here tend to see introductions and conversations.' They moved left through the doors under the stairway into a dimly lit room, book-lined, with button-back leather sofas and armchairs. There were a few couples sitting and talking, but on the sofa in the window, a young woman was bent over the crotch of an older man, plainly fellating him. She looked up at Peter and he smiled at her. 'Some people like to get started here before they move upstairs.' No-one else was paying any attention to the couple on the sofa. Peter's arm came around her shoulder again and he guided her out. She felt she'd passed some sort of test, but she wasn't quite ready for the larger reception room on the other side of the hall. It was more brightly lit, although the immense main chandelier had plainly been dimmed. The room had an elegant pale colour scheme with immense, thick silk drapes covering the windows. She was taking in the pictures, the overly ornate side tables, the crystal wall lights, the large, deep sofas, very aware that she was trying to avoid looking at the sofa, again in front of the window, which was attracting a few people's attention.

'Ah,' said Peter, drawing her gently towards it, 'I see Alice has started already.' Claudia looked at the slim blonde woman, wearing only a garter belt and high heels, bent over the arm, her mouth dealing with a half-naked man seated on the sofa while another stood behind her fucking her very vigorously. 'They'll be there some time. Come, I'll show you upstairs.'

They picked their way past couples sitting on the stairs. There was plenty of space in the rooms, but some seemed to find it easier, or more private, to begin conversations, or negotiations, on the stairs – the fragments that Claudia picked up seemed to be about particular preferences the couples would indulge in or, in one case, who else they wanted to join them.

The bedroom doors around the spacious landing were all open but the rooms were dimly lit. Peter guided her into the first, in which there was only one couple. They were naked, and the woman was straddling the man and energetically bouncing on him. His hands were groping her arse and they were both clearly close to orgasm.

Peter's arm tightened around her shoulder and he leaned towards her and whispered. 'A little bit vanilla, darling, don't you think?'

She nodded but was nevertheless strangely fascinated by the scene.

'We'll look in on the main bedroom; people gravitate to that.'

And they had! There were more than a dozen people in the large room, at least half of them active and even the spectators, naked or nearly so, were in couples, all stroking or stimulating each other. On the huge bed, one couple were enjoying sixty-nine, and Claudia remembered her night with Alan and smiled. Peter noticed. The other activity on the bed was a threesome with a strikingly beautiful blonde woman sandwiched between two men. The upper one was black, and not small. She thought of the odd clip she'd discovered on Dave's computer – and found repellent – but then remembered Jack's vibrator and how she had taken that easily while he fucked her. The black man, however, was much bigger than a vibrator, but the woman's cries as he pushed into her were much more like ecstasy than pain. And once the three had settled into a rhythm – and the black man seemed to be very deep inside her – she was able to pay attention to the man standing at the foot of the bed holding his cock to her mouth.

Peter squeezed Claudia's shoulder and she looked up at him, he smiled, apparently pleased to see that she was clearly fascinated.

She leaned up to his ear and whispered, chuckling. 'Do you have to sleep in here later?'

He laughed. 'Oh no, on nights like this we keep the top floor to ourselves.'

'Your wife is here?'

'Yes, of course, that's her in the middle.'

Claudia was shocked but hoped she concealed it. Would Jack be like Peter? Is that what turned him on? But Peter showed no real interest in his wife's activities, they didn't appear to be stimulating any kinky reaction on his part.

'You're coping with this very well for a first-timer,' he said, 'let's see what your tastes run to. You might find the cellar interesting.'

They walked carefully down past the changing population of couples on the stairs.

'Yes, but not with him!' was one snippet she picked up from an indignant young woman – far from the prettiest and, Claudia thought, probably not given so many choices or options as others. She suddenly found herself shocked by her own thought – how strange to be judgemental like that, here, of all places.

They got to the far corner of the hall where a single door opened on to a dark stairway with loud music coming up at them.

'We keep it fairly dark, so let your eyes adapt a moment.'

'And very noisy,' she shout-whispered into his ear.

'You'll see why we do that in a minute. The BDSM people get a bit noisy and it's best to drown them out a little. Are you OK with BDSM? Not everyone comes down here.'

'I'm intrigued.'

'Have you tried it?'

'Just heavy spanking, paddles, you know...' Claudia felt a little ashamed of not wanting to appear naïve.

'Dom or sub?'

'Oh, sub,' she said quickly – and then worried about what that might lead to.

Peter was looking into her eyes, smiling again, embracing her gently.

'Well, this might interest you then. It sometimes goes on down here. Shall I lead the way?'

She nodded, having no real idea of what to expect and even less about how she would react.

They went down the stone stairs. The walls were rough red brick. They reached the bottom and turned. They were in a large space with chambers off to the side, two on the long side and one at the far end. Most people were milling in the middle, along the long wall there was a bench on which an array of drinks was available. There were also bowls which Claudia first thought were filled with snacks until she saw a man take one, tear at the edge with his teeth and begin to roll its contents down his erect cock as he turned to the first chamber. It was crowded, and she couldn't see clearly what was going on in the chambers. In any event, she was interested in the people and their costumes. The majority still in clothes or variations of the underwear she and Sylvie had selected, but there were a number in leather with chain decorations and a few with full-head masks. Peter was smiling broadly. He put his mouth to her ear. 'I love it when they live it fully,' he shouted, barely audibly. 'Come,' he said and took her hand and pushed to the front of people watching the activity in the first chamber.

A girl was lying on a small leather table with a rest to support her head. Her mouth was filled with a ball gag attached behind her head, something Claudia had only ever seen in Dave's videos. Her wrists and ankles were tied and strung to two vertical poles either side of her head, making her completely open now to her audience, one lover having just left her and her next, the man from the snack bowl, still in the process of fitting his condom securely. He moved to her, grabbed her breasts fiercely, and pushed himself violently into her. She shook her head, as if in protest, and he slapped her face. She stopped making the guttural screams that had escaped from around the gag and began to move her hips to accommodate him. He pushed harder and squeezed her breasts even more, seeming to dig his fingernails in as he grabbed them. He then kept thrusting for a while, and she seemed calmer, pushing herself on to him, making the pre-orgasm noises as he ground his pelvis on to her clit. She was suddenly silent as he withdrew. 'Wait!' he said roughly to her and went to the side of the chamber to pick up a tube. He squeezed something from it and smeared it thickly on to her anus, pushing his fingers in deeply. Claudia watched, entranced but found herself being tugged away by Peter, who was talking loudly into her ear.

'Nice, I know, but I think the next one will be more to your tastes.'

Claudia made an 'Oh!' disappointment noise but smiled at him and let him pull her away.

'I think they're just about to start something. Let's get a drink first.'

He poured two glasses of champagne and eased his way through, with her following, to the front of the crowd. A woman wearing a cape stood to one side of the chamber, looking strangely calm. At its centre was a trestle with a padded leather top. Its legs had lined leather cuffs, plainly to act as restraints. The wall at the back held a row of canes, whips and paddles. Claudia's stomach flipped. Curiously she thought of Martha and whether she would want to subject herself to this. A bare-chested man wearing black tights and a mask went up to the woman and undid the cape's clasp at her neck and cast the cape to one side. The woman's white body had small breasts and full hips, but she was smooth-skinned and quite well toned. Her buttocks when she turned were well-rounded and smooth, and not hidden at all by the small thong she was wearing. The man took her hand gracefully and led her to the trestle, she followed obediently. He took a ball gag from the wall and offered it to her, but she shook her head. Claudia heard Peter mutter, 'Big mistake,' barely audibly. She looked up at him, he smiled and shook his head. The masked man gestured to the trestle and the woman bent slowly over it, allowing her arms to drop down the far side to the waiting cuffs. The posture made her bottom look even more prominent as she patiently waited for him to tie the cuffs.

The man buckled the cuffs on to her wrists unhurriedly. He moved behind her and stroked her cheeks sensuously, then slid her thong down past her ankles.

'NO,' said the woman, 'I didn't…'

The man looked up at Peter, who nodded slowly. The man took a cane from the wall and slashed viciously at the woman's bottom. She screamed and her legs flailed wildly. The masked man waited for her to calm down before buckling the cuffs, much more roughly this time, around her ankles.

Peter had positioned them to one side of the chamber, and they had a perfect view of the large bottom, now with one very deep red stripe across it. The stripe was changing colour even as Claudia stared at it.

The man stood up, stroked her cheeks again and said loudly, but barely audibly above the music and noise, 'You are here to learn to be obedient, Clare. You have no code yellow.'

Peter leaned towards Claudia's ear again. 'Normally you can call yellow when you want someone to stop but this is a little different. But don't worry, Artur won't go too far. He knows what people can stand. That's why people ask for him again when they come back. He takes them beyond their boundaries, but they feel a little pride in that.'

Artur had fetched a tube from the rack. He squeezed a huge dollop into the crack between the woman's cheeks.

'NO, NO,' she was almost screaming.

Artur merely shook his head impassively and began paying closer attention to her bottom. He stretched her cheeks wide and began smearing the lube around her anus. Her cries abated a little, only to be renewed when he pushed a finger inside her bottom. Her head was shaking, but her hair was obscuring her face so Claudia could discern no expression. She seemed to calm slightly as Artur removed one finger only to push two into her again and when he introduced a third, she seemed to sigh and almost welcome it. He squirted more lube onto her anus and his fingers. Claudia wondered why but that soon became obvious when he turned to the rack and returned with the largest plug Claudia had ever seen. She had assumed they were only joke items when she'd seen them in Ann Summers but no, here was Artur with this improbable object, inserting it slowly into the woman's bottom. She sighed at first, but the sighs turned to sounds of consternation as she could obviously feel him beginning to push, carefully but very insistently, and ended with an outright scream as he finally pushed the whole plug home.

Claudia looked up at Peter, concerned. 'Are you sure?'

'Shh, just wait. She'll be fine. She'll want to be taken further next time.'

'Further? Not possible. Did you really see that thing?'

'Of course, don't worry, there are bigger ones.'

'What?'

'Yes, really, but it's the gays that tend to use those – or the odd male sub who wants it. Anyway, he hasn't really started yet, watch.'

Claudia turned, bizarrely fascinated by this woman with the large, white, smooth and curvy bottom, the cheeks now split by the protruding end of the large black plug, waiting for what was, presumably, the high point of her evening.

Artur had taken up his cane. He smoothed it over her buttocks and thighs, gently tapping occasionally.

Finally, he asked, 'Are you ready, Clare?'

The woman mumbled something.

'I can't hear you, Clare. Are you ready?'

'Yes, I'm ready, do it!' shouted the woman.

Artur brought the cane down. A white line appeared instantly parallel to the first and then slowly changed colour to match it.

'Arggh!' the woman screamed.

'There, there,' said Artur soothingly, rubbing his

hand gently across the two livid marks. 'Only eleven more.'

'Ten,' said the woman.

Artur lashed even more severely with the cane. The woman screamed more loudly.

'The first did not count, of course, that was for disobedience, just like that one. There are still eleven more.'

The woman merely whimpered.

Eleven more, Claudia thought, and the three already seemed to have raised ridges on the skin.

Artur brought the cane down not quite so heavily, as far as Claudia could judge. The first and third swipes, the punishment ones, had clearly been more vicious. The woman whimpered each time as the cane fell and her body twitched but there were no more screams. What there was, was a large bottom, formerly white, which was now a quilt of deep red ridges merging into two almost perfect rectangles on each of her cheeks. Artur was clearly a craftsman and, not for the first time that evening, Claudia found herself marvelling at her own strange reactions.

Artur carefully removed the plug, but the woman groaned very loudly as it came out and then he draped the cape over her before he unbuckled the cuffs. He helped her up and clipped the clasp together for her. Her eyes were wet and dark where the makeup had run. She put her arms around Artur's waist and buried her face in the hair of his chest as he gently put his arms around her.

Peter put his arm around Claudia's shoulder, his hand came to her chin which he lifted gently to look into her eyes. She didn't want to look at him. She knew he would realize that she had felt extraordinarily excited, but she knew, as she put her face to his chest and her arm around his waist, that he had already guessed.

'I must get you back to Sylvie. They'll be wondering where you are.' He turned towards the stairs. Claudia took his hands, she leaned up and kissed his cheek. 'It's OK, I'll find them. You have all your guests to look after.'

'Thank you, my dear, I hope you're enjoying it.'

She looked up at his shining eyes. 'Mmm, much more, I'll admit, than I expected to. But you guessed that, I think.'

Peter smiled but shook his head noncommittally. 'Well, I'm not sure yet. I'll look for you later and see how you feel. Off you go.'

The place was fuller as she made her way into the hall and most people were in stages of undress. She wasn't uncomfortable fully clothed, but the idea of taking her dress off had crossed her mind, she could probably be slightly more anonymous. The dining room, when she got there, still had groups of people talking although one man was leaning back on a chair pushed away from the table being serviced by the bobbing head of a brunette between his knees. There was no sign of Sylvie or Malcs. She went to the doors of the kitchen, not there either. Alphonse appeared at her elbow.

'You're looking for your friends?'

'Yes, but it doesn't matter.'

'I think they are both upstairs.'

'Together?' asked Claudia, slightly surprised.

Alphonse laughed. 'No, no, of course not, but maybe you should see what they're up to.'

'Oh, I'm not sure of that.'

'It's OK,' he said, 'half the fun is watching.'

'I don't know about that either. I've just seen a woman on the trestle. I admit I enjoyed watching it, but I'm not sure she really had too much fun.'

'Ah, that's a strange thing about that. People come back. You think they hate it at the time, they scream quite wildly, some of them, although most are quite stoical.'

'Well, this one screamed.'

'No gag?'

'No gag. Peter said that was a mistake. And she had no code yellow. What was that about?'

'I don't know in her case. Sometimes, if guests misbehave, Peter will only let them return if they submit to Artur and Artur never really hurts people.'

'Oh, this woman's agony sounded pretty genuine.'

'She'll want to be caned again in a month, I assure you.'

'It's funny you say that. My boyfriend – he's in Asia at the moment so I seldom see him – has visits from a woman who likes him to cane her, and I think he only sees her once every three or four weeks. I'd assumed they like to wait until the marks fade.'

'It's partly that, I think, but it's also something they have to miss and start longing for again. They'll tell you that the memory of the pain fades and they need to refresh it again. But it's not just about pain.'

'No?'

'No, a lot of it is the humiliation. They have a feeling that they want to be treated like that for having been naughty. They want to be controlled. I think that was part of it tonight, if it's who I think was.'

'Her name was Clare.'

'Yes, that's it. She got drunk last time. There was a man she wanted, and she made a scene when she found him screwing someone else. Andreas had to take her home. She wrote to Peter, apologising profusely and begging to be allowed to come again. He made her wait three months and then told her the conditions.'

'Had she been caned before?'

'Not here, I don't think, but Peter is very astute

about reading what people want, deep down and when she replied so quickly, he was sure.'

'Hmm, I had the feeling he was looking a little deeply into me.'

'You have something to hide?'

'No, I don't think so, but it was a little uncomfortable, being read like that.'

'And a little exciting?'

'Yes, a little exciting. But you seem very knowledgeable about what these people want.'

'Oh, not really. I've had girlfriends who like it but it's not such a big thing for me. I bring them here and let them spend time with Peter.'

'Oh,' Claudia spluttered. 'Oh, so he likes to…'

'It's his main pleasure, I think. I don't want to give his secrets away, but he'll have looked at you, admired your beautiful arse, and worked out quite quickly that you might be intrigued by subbing.'

'No, no, not at all…'

'But your boyfriend?'

'I know, I know. OK' – she looked into Alphonse's eyes, he was smiling – 'I admit it's crossed my mind – and I did tell Peter we'd done a little of that.'

Alphonse laughed gently. 'I wasn't prying, honestly. But it helps to discuss these things to make sure you get what you want out of these evenings.'

'Well, not that, certainly.' She paused. 'I don't

think. Not yet.'

'Come on, let's at least have a look round and see what interests you. Are you comfortable, in your dress?'

She looked at him and laughed. 'You're fairly astute yourself. No, I'm not. I was beginning to feel out of place.'

She reached for her zip.

'Let me,' he said, moved behind her, unzipped her easily and slid the dress to the floor. She stepped out of it. He looked at her but, before it became a stare, he picked up the dress, draped it over a chair, put his arm around her shoulder and said, 'This way, come with me. You are very beautiful, by the way.'

She looked up. His somewhat saturnine looks were softened by gentle brown eyes and an easy smile. His voice was deep and warm.

He guided her towards the library, as she had christened the room with the brown leather sofas. It was quieter than before, only two couples, a woman over the back of a sofa being taken from behind by an older, slightly portly man and a blonde girl leaning back in an armchair very volubly enjoying the attentions of the man between her knees who was licking her passionately.

'You're smiling,' said Alphonse.

'Was I?' She laughed lightly. 'It's nice to see that the attention isn't all one way.'

He laughed. 'OK, I get your point. But your friends,

they're not in here, are they?'

Claudia shook her head and allowed herself to be guided to the large room. The sofa in the window was still occupied, but by a different pair of men now entertaining the indefatigable and apparently insatiable Alice. The other people in the room were chatting in small groups, paying the trio no attention.

Claudia stared for a while at Alice but allowed herself to be guided out of the room and up the stairs, which were emptier now, the couples from earlier having evidently concluded their negotiations and become, she assumed, active.

The quiet bedroom from before still had only one couple. The woman was kneeling on the bed, bending deeply, the man stood behind, his hands clenched firmly on her hips, sustaining a steady rhythm and moaning softly as her hand reached back between her legs to caress his balls. Claudia focused on their movements, the woman's tanned, taut skin looking wonderful, the man had a pale northern skin colouring but an athletic shape.

She looked more closely at the woman; it was the blonde from the bedroom threesome, Peter's wife. She looked at the man's face, his eyes closed, a picture of ecstatic excitement. It was Malcs; and when he pulled the woman off the bed to make her stand and bend deeper, she realized just how much that moment in the woods had meant to him. She turned away, strangely happy, but slightly betrayed – and nervous about what feelings he might still hold for her.

The main bedroom was even busier than before, the bed similarly occupied but the couples around now more actively engaged with each other, using the two armchairs or the stool by the dressing table to help position themselves. The same black man was still on top of a couple, pushing his enormous object into the woman's arse while she straddled the man beneath her, whose face, eyes closed, had a beaming smile. She recognized Graham, Alphonse's friend. And the woman had changed, she was shorter than the blonde and had dark hair. The body looked newly familiar and when her faced turned, Claudia had already guessed that it was Sylvie, her lovely face slightly contorted, her breathing heavy, her hips seeming to push back to take even more of the huge man behind her.

Claudia was fascinated, but somehow appalled. She leaned close to Alphonse. 'Take me somewhere quiet.'

He took her in his arms and bent to kiss her. She wrapped her arms around him, giving herself voluptuously to the kiss, very aware of how wet she was becoming between her legs.

Alphonse led her to a smaller bedroom, not part of Peter's tour. They kissed again, she began undoing his shirt buttons. She had freed only two when he fell to his knees in front of her and pushed his face on to her pussy. She could feel his tongue on her clit through her knickers, but that lasted only seconds before she felt him sliding them down. Her hands went to the back of his head, pushing his face more firmly into her. She staggered back to the bed, lay back and spread her legs wide open for him. She wanted now to feel him inside her, but he gripped her and kept kissing her, running his tongue more gently now across her clitoris and down and into her vagina, then back to her clit again. It was driving her so close to the edge and, just as she felt the rush of coming getting close, he would ease away again, leaving her panting, waiting for the next wave.

'Please, that's absolutely wonderful, but please put him in me,' she heard herself gasping.

She felt him ease away, his tongue tip still flicking her cunt, he was obviously undressing, but his shirt was still on when she felt him move up her to kiss her lips and slide, with the minimum of fuss, his cock deep into her.

'Stay there a while please – but you do kiss fantastically well.'

He smiled, kissing her again, keeping his penetration gentle but deep.

'I think we've found one of the things you like.'

'Oh, you have most definitely done that, and I want more, more, more. But are you going to tell me what you like?'

'We have plenty of time for that. You must come first.'

'That's double entendre, I take it.'

'Most definitely,' he said, and she saw his smile disappearing down her belly to bury itself once more in her cunt.

She was a little more relaxed now. She had had him inside her. Now she could let him make her happy. His tongue slid around her again, she was wildest when he just used the tip on her clit, pinning her with his hands firmly on her hips, keeping her wide with his shoulders between her thighs, but warmer, deeper feelings came when he slid lower and licked inside her.

Then she felt him free one hand to slide under her and lift her, letting him poke his tongue deeper and then letting it slide lower to lick her anus. This had astonished her when Jack started just a few weeks ago and now she found it thrilling. She tried to lift her hips higher to let him lick where he wanted, but he moved back to touching her clit with his tongue tip while he gently slid fingers into her. Now she couldn't wait, now she could feel it coming, unstoppably. She knew she was moving violently, he was using shoulders and arms to pin her, to make sure his tongue stayed exactly on her clit even as her arms and legs shuddered, and she began screaming, screaming, screaming at the top of her voice.

She was still breathing heavily when his face appeared smiling on the pillow beside hers. He kissed her, gently but sensually.

'Now we must do what you want.'

He leaned up on one elbow. 'We have plenty of time, relax.'

'I'm sure you're trying to sound more patient than he is,' she said and reached for his still hard cock, slightly shocked to find it clothed in a condom. She hesitated with her touch.

'You're surprised at that?'

'No, no, of course not.' Although she was. 'No, I was just amazed at your skill at putting him on. I mean, I was sure you had' – although she hadn't actually thought about it and cursed herself – 'but I didn't notice it at all.'

He smiled. 'I'm flattered I could distract you.'

'Oh, you certainly did that, your kissing's amazing.' Now she held his cock firmly, pleased to feel it growing very stiff once more. 'Do you want to keep this on? I could take it off and kiss you. Can I make you come in my mouth?'

'I would love that…'

'There's a but, isn't there? Come on, Alphonse, I want to make you happy.'

'You are a beautiful woman, Claudia, and you also have an absolutely fabulous arse.' He looked deep into her eyes. 'I've been lusting after it. I want it. Can you handle that?'

She smiled slowly at him, 'I would love you to have me like that. Make me wet first, though.'

'Of course.' He was reaching into the bedside table from which he pulled a tube. 'Now turn around and let me admire you.'

She turned around pulled up her knees and held her arse as high as she could. He moved behind her, positioned his cock in her vagina and pushed slowly and deeply into her. She felt his flat belly on her bum as his cock found a tight place deep inside her. They moved slowly together. She moved her hand between her legs and began stroking him.

'That feels wonderful,' he gasped, 'but you'll make me lose control too soon.'

She continued stroking, then felt a very sharp slap on her arse.

'That won't stop me, you know, I actually like that – very much.'

'I know you do but you can have much more of that later.'

'Promises!' she muttered into the pillow as she buried her face. She felt his hands on her cheeks, smoothing over them, clearly enjoying them, and then she felt a large, cold dollop of lube land between them.

'You're sure you're OK with this?'

'Alphonse, just take me. I like being told. I like you doing absolutely what you want. Order me! Make me! Do anything with me!'

He slid from her and moved to her side. His arm clamped her waist. She felt his fingers smoothing the lube around her, then slowly, sensually, inside her. She sighed heavily and pushed her arse higher to take more – it felt gorgeous – and to show him how much she was enjoying it. She felt herself being stretched by more fingers and the thrilling sensation increased, especially as he was managing to keep her clit stimulated all the while. She was gasping loudly, 'Yes… yes… more… more…'

His hand left her. More lube was applied, and the fingers returned.

'I love it… I love it…' she cried, unsure how far she was being stretched but finding it ever more thrilling – but she was still even more excited when she felt him position herself behind him again. One hand held her hip, the other was plainly positioning his cock by her anus and then he pushed, slowly and deeply and, a fleeting thought, embarrassingly easily, until she felt his belly again on her cheeks. His hands held her hips tightly, he found a lovely slow rhythm. She heard him breathing, 'Oh… oh…' on every push. She felt completely full – and completely comfortable – and tuned in to his rhythm. It felt exquisite. She knew she would touch herself and make herself come, but that could wait. For now, she wanted to feel his cock push deep into her belly, to feel him stretching her, radiating a thrill from his cock's touch out to every nerve in her body.

His hands moved over her cheeks, letting him push even deeper, changing the feelings in her, pushing her ever nearer her edge.

'Oh, you feel even lovelier than you look,' he gasped, 'I would like this forever, but I can feel my control deserting me. Are you ready?'

'Oh yes, oh yes, I can't wait myself.' And she put her fingers to her clit as she felt him pushing harder and harder and getting noisier and noisier until finally, he came very deep within her just as her own feelings overwhelmed her.

He was still deep inside her when the blur of her climax had passed, he was still firm, just moving more slowly, more gently. She still felt full and, as he slowly pulled away, reluctant to release him.

But then happy to feel his arms around her as she nestled into him.

'The sex was wonderful,' she said, 'absolutely amazing. But am I allowed a little bit of affection now? I know it's make-believe, but I'd like to snuggle into your skin for a while.'

He laughed gently. 'Of course it's OK. I don't want

to let go of you either.'

'Good,' she said, held him more tightly and closed her eyes.

He was gone when she woke. She was seized by a panic. She had no watch; her phone was in her bag. Where was her bag? She looked around, desperate, but knowing she'd left it downstairs. But she did find a note by the bedside.

You looked too lovely to wake. I won't let you sleep too long. A xxxxx

She immediately felt calmer. He hadn't woken her, she can't have been sleeping long.

As she stepped down the stairs, the party had noticeably thinned and some couples, fully clothed, were saying their goodbyes at the front door. She headed for the large dining room where she found Sylvie and Malcs, dressed again, talking to Peter and Alphonse and the tall blonde woman from the threesome on the bed earlier – Peter's wife. The conversation seemed to change as she got there – had they been talking about her?

'Claudia,' Peter boomed loudly, 'I hear you've been having a lovely time, our poor Alphonse is terribly stricken.' Alphonse smiled warmly at her, but it was Peter's arm that encircled her – so they had been talking about her.

'Well, I'm stricken too, he's a lovely lover,' she

said, thinking to brazen her way through, not wanting to seem stupidly demure. 'But we're leaving, I think,' she added, looking at Sylvie and Malcs.

'Oh, you most definitely are not,' said Peter, tightening his arm around her waist, 'this is your first time, you have more to learn. We're going to let these old people go,' he smiled at Sylvie and Malcs, 'they have no stamina. Andreas is going to drive you home later.'

'We've given him the spare key,' explained Sylvie. 'I'll put your things in your room, we'll probably be asleep when you get back.'

Claudia felt slightly awkward but curious about staying. Peter was clearly orchestrating things for her but Sylvie and Malcs looked relaxed, although she was a little cautious about regarding Sylvie as her new best friend. She was having an extraordinary but thrilling evening, but things happened, she thought, to suit Sylvie.

'Anyway, terribly remiss of me. I haven't introduced Yvonne. Darling, this is Claudia, the young lady Alphonse has fallen in love with.'

Claudia was dazzled by the woman's smile and wondered how she still looked so perfect after so energetic an evening. The woman offered her hand. 'I'd rather thought of him as mine, so you and I are off to a very bad start.' But the smile was unwavering, and the remarks seemed to be made in good spirits.

'I'm going to see Sylvie and Malcs off, darling. Will you look after Claudia?'

'Of course.' Yvonne turned her back on Malcs as if she didn't know him.

Peter's hand moved from Claudia's waist to her shoulder, which he pressed gently to turn her and make her look at him. His hitherto unceasing smile left him for a moment. 'You and I have one or two little pleasures to explore, my dear, I'm keeping you captive.' Something twisted in Claudia's stomach, as Peter's smile flashed back on, he turned to Sylvie and Malcs. 'Come, good gentles, I know you will away. Your chariot awaits.' He led them into the hall.

Claudia looked from Alphonse to Yvonne and back. 'I don't want to look like little girl lost, but what's this about?'

Alphonse looked to Yvonne to explain. Yvonne was laughing lightly. 'It's absolutely nothing to worry about. Peter likes to play these games. He thinks he can assess people's deeper, darker desires and he likes to free them. I live out mine as I want to now, but it took Peter to make me open up.'

Claudia's mind flashed back to the main bedroom earlier and Yvonne's place between the two men. No, it had become three when the third man held his cock to her mouth! 'But what about the woman in the cellar earlier?' She looked at Alphonse. 'Wasn't that just a sort of punishment?'

'Oh, assuredly not,' said Yvonne. 'No,' Alphonse joined in, 'the fact that she made a scene on an earlier visit just gave a pretext. Some people feel happier if they can feel they're being justifiably punished, they don't want to confront that side of themselves directly. Peter had guessed that's what she wanted and told her when he replied to her letter.'

'Peter never gets it wrong,' said Yvonne, looking directly into Claudia's eyes, 'and no-one ever, ever does anything they don't, deep down, truly want to do.'

Claudia's eyes narrowed, she had a mistrust of that level of conviction, and wondered what assessments Peter was making of her. 'Well, I've already gone way beyond what I expected.' She put her arm around Alphonse's waist, and he put his warmly around her shoulder. 'I'm just not aware of anything else I want.'

'Then Peter won't do anything,' said Yvonne, but her smile had gone a little colder. 'But I'm being a bad hostess. Is there anything I can get you?'

'I know it sounds terrible after all the champagne, but I would love a cup of tea. Is that bad?'

Yvonne laughed and now the smile seemed warm again, perhaps she just didn't like Peter's magical insights being questioned. 'I think that's a lovely idea. I feel the same way myself. Alphonse?'

He shook his head. 'I'll catch up with you later.'

Yvonne led Claudia into the enormous kitchen. A small group was sat chatting at the breakfast table, the main kitchen area looked astonishingly tidy and sparkling for the late stage of a party but then Claudia noticed Hannes busying himself putting things away and moving some trays into what she assumed was a utility room which would plainly be, she thought, much larger than her kitchen.

'Hannes, my darling,' said Yvonne, 'could we possibly have two cups of tea?'

'Of course, my angel. Earl Grey?' Claudia caught the slight campness in his speech.

'For me of course but, Claudia, what would you like?'

'Oh, Earl Grey would be great, thanks.'

'Why don't you go through to the library, darlings, I'll bring it to you.'

'Thank you, Hannes. Come, Claudia.'

And Claudia followed her, unable to avoid looking at the perfect, tall body with its tan of exotic holidays probably but maybe also sunbeds, and the figure with the slender waist and the peach-perfect bottom – was Alphonse so taken with hers, she thought, when he plainly occasionally had Yvonne's to enjoy? She felt slightly elated about the company she was obviously being evaluated in.

The library was empty. Yvonne went to a sofa in the middle of the room and beckoned Claudia to join her.

'It's your first time?'

'Yes. Do you have these parties often?'

'About once a month or so when we're in the country.'

'And how much is that? Oops, sorry, I can't help being a little nosy.'

Yvonne smiled. 'About eight months of the year. We're in the Caribbean most of the winter. I love it and Peter can still manage his business from there.'

Claudia was intrigued by what business might generate this much wealth, but she knew that would be a question too far. And she guessed that Yvonne might not have a very clear idea anyway.

'You've been married long?' Claudia let the absurdity pass her by of two women, at least one of whom was beautiful, dressed only in exotic underwear, just making small talk. But now Hannes brought the tea in bone china cups on a silver tray and Claudia found it hard not to giggle.

'Seven years.' Yes, that was probably obvious. It couldn't have been much more. Yvonne was at most early thirties, although she looked younger, and there was plainly at least a twenty-year age gap.

'I'm his third.'

'He seems very happy.' Was she really saying something so inane? But Yvonne seemed unflustered by it.

'I think so, I hope so. He's just such a free spirit. He loves people to open and to enjoy themselves. I was so inhibited when I met him.' Claudia found that astonishingly hard to believe – or maybe the woman had a different view of what inhibition was. 'But now I find it very easy to enjoy what I like.'

'But what does he like?'

'Oh, he has his preferences, of course, but his main thrill, honestly, is working out what people want and putting them in a position to enjoy it.'

'Like the woman in the cellar?'

'Yes, like the woman in the cellar. He's very clever like that. He says that's how he makes his money. He can read people so well.'

'There you are!' Peter's voice boomed again from the doorway. 'I've been looking for you.' He moved towards them and sat on the armchair opposite.

'I had to ask Hannes,' he turned to Claudia, 'he knows everything. And tea is a wonderful idea. Champagne is, of course, also wonderful, but at this time of night…'

Hannes re-entered and placed a cup in front of Peter. Claudia was momentarily dumbstruck. Peter was still fully clothed but black tights, like Artur's, had replaced his elegantly cut trousers.

Yvonne stood. 'I'll go and see how people are doing, darling. It's been lovely to meet you, Claudia, enjoy the rest of your evening if I don't see you later.'

'Thank you, thank you, er, lovely to meet you too,' Claudia stuttered, still unnerved by Peter's change.

Peter watched her leave.

'Beautiful woman,' he said, as usual quite loudly, and Yvonne wiggled her hips when she heard him. He turned back, smiling, to Claudia.

'More beautiful than the others?' asked Claudia, not willing to be less than bold. If she wished to be submissive in some areas, it wasn't going to apply to conversations with intimidating men – and Peter was certainly that, however charming he also appeared.

He was laughing. 'Ah, leave girls alone and secrets will out. No, not more beautiful, but more… well, relaxed with herself, I suppose. The others… the others had everything' – he laughed again – 'and walked away with a lot of it. But they wanted to impose constraints upon me, constraints I would never have imposed on them. I mean, as you've seen, Yvonne does exactly what she wants, and I love it that she does that.'

'It never makes you jealous?'

'Good Lord no. I love seeing her happy.'

'Does it excite you?'

'Not particularly.' His eyes narrowed. 'I think

301

maybe you're asking with your own situation in mind.'

'Ah, is this Peter the psychologist?'

He laughed again. 'That's an exaggeration.'

'But people say you love working things out.'

'It's true, I do, but I don't claim any special powers or gifts. I just listen to people carefully.'

'And what have I told you?'

'I have to say that I have other inputs but most of my guesses, and that's what these are, come out of what you've said – and not said.'

'Go on. Or am I keeping you from the others?'

'Oh, they'll entertain themselves, my dear. You are my project for the evening, you intrigue me. You're more complex than most.'

'Me?' Claudia spluttered, genuinely surprised.

'Yes, you. You wreak more havoc than you know. Poor Alphonse is quite obviously smitten, and now I finally understand Sylvie and Malcs' problem.'

'Sylvie and Malcs' problem?' Claudia was open-mouthed.

'Yes, they love each other, and they make each other happy but she's always aware that he carries an old dream with him. And now I've met the dream and I understand why he's still captivated, but I think Sylvie wanted him to see that his old dream wasn't a beautiful young nymph in the woods but a grown, real-life woman. The problem she now has is that the real woman is a person vastly more attractive and interesting than any young girl, so he was looking quite dejected when Alphonse was talking, ever so discreetly, I assure you, but talking with glowing eyes about the beautiful woman he'd just made love to.'

Claudia was shaking her head.

'I'm right so far, my dear, I promise you – and Yvonne was quite serious about resenting you winning Alphonse. She still must learn that she can't monopolise people's feelings. At least she doesn't try with mine. But we're talking about you – and the man who loves you but is excited by you being with other men. He knows you're here, doesn't he?'

'Yes, how did you…'

'You love him. You wouldn't do things behind his back, that wouldn't be your way at all. Have you been lovers for long?'

'Only weeks' – she hesitated – 'well, I've loved him for a long, long time but it suddenly happened a few weeks ago, just before he went to live in Singapore.'

'Oh, he lives there, it's not just travelling. That makes it tough, and curiously more intense, I think, am I right?'

'Of course, you are.'

'And in the short time you've had together, you've discovered more of the real Claudia.'

'Yes, I suppose I have.'

'The Claudia with richer, darker desires than she ever suspected.'

'Yes.'

'You'd not slept freely with men before.' It wasn't a question.

'No, absolutely not. Alphonse was…' – and she stopped herself saying unique – 'a rarity – but a lovely one, I have to admit.'

'And you will tell your lover about him.' Again, not a question.

'Yes, he tells me everything. Well, I insist, I thought it was the only way to survive a long-distance relationship.'

'You're very wise. But you've learnt things you're not sure you wanted to know.'

'Yes, he seems quite busy in Singapore, and not just with work.'

'Well, he's a man of exquisite taste, you're lovely, and clearly of wider ranging interests. He introduced the paddle to you.'

'Yes, he did.'

'And you found you enjoyed it. You are normally in control and you like life that way but sometimes you like to be taken, to be told what to do. He gave you no choice with the paddle, did he?' It was phrased as a question, but it wasn't really meant as one, Peter clearly knew. She nodded. 'And he wants to go further?'

'He does go further.'

'Ah.' Peter leant back. 'I see, but with someone else.'

Claudia lowered her eyes towards her lap. 'Her name is Martha, she's American. She's head of a bank in Singapore. A powerful, dominant woman, apparently, but she likes Jack to cane her sometimes. It sounds quite serious. The caning, I mean, not the relationship.'

'No, that's not uncommon, people with quite a narrow focus in their sexual lives. You needn't worry, no relationship will develop.'

'Was that Clare's problem earlier?'

'Oh no. She has the problem of loving people who aren't going to love her back. She's too focused on herself for that, but it does make her a little more interesting.'

'Why is she interesting?'

'Because she could form a loving relationship, but she gets in her own way, first you must give, and then you can hope to receive, only then can you hope at all. You may well be disappointed, many are, but you at least give yourself a chance. I don't think this Martha will, I can admire her, but she wouldn't interest me – we'd never ask her here, for instance. But Clare could, if she could just trust herself to put someone else first. You do, I know, you've done it more than once in your life.'

'That's true, I think. But Clare, the caning, the humiliation?'

'She would need to build that into a relationship because she needs it. She could learn to enjoy it even more. That's why you're here.' He looked very directly at her, she felt challenged but met his gaze with her own. 'I don't think you need it in the way that Clare does, but your lover wants a deep relationship with you in which you enrich each other's lives in many ways, where you explore each other's personalities and sexuality and you want to go on the journey with him. He's a little older than you?'

She nodded.

'And he's taken you past your boundaries?'

'Yes. Definitely. We do things I'd never dreamt of.'

'I think you probably had dreamt of them, but suppressed them, maybe.'

She nodded, more slowly, more thoughtfully this time.

'Well, we're going to take you past one more boundary – and then you'll have a gift for him.' Claudia's brow furrowed and she shook her head. Peter's gaze was unwavering. 'He wants to cane you. You want him to cane you, but you don't know what your boundaries are. He will be careful, he won't want to hurt you, he will pull back and be frustrated.' He left a pause to allow her to fill in the unspoken: and then he will visit Martha again. 'And you will be frustrated because you know he will be holding back, and you will miss two important things.'

She was still looking puzzled, but her head had stopped shaking.

'You will be aware that he is not fully happy – and you will not have found where your own boundaries are – and they are further, possibly much further, than you think.'

He paused again. Now she was still, just looking at him.

'So, we are going, with your permission, to help you explore.'

'You don't look like you're expecting me to give permission.'

'No, you won't,' he said slowly, 'it would break the spell if you did, you must not ask, you must not even speak. Andreas will come in shortly with your dress and a black cape. You may choose. If you choose the dress, he will take you home. If you choose the cape, he will bring you to me in the cellar. It's quiet now but there may be some people there. I shall be waiting. You will say nothing. You will be buckled on the trestle. There will be some preparations, but you needn't fear the enormous plug. And then I will spank you, first with the paddle. I want you to remember that because the cane will feel different. It will sting much more, I promise you that, and even after the first you will intensely regret putting yourself in that position.'

'Will I have code yellow?'

'Not until after six, I'm telling you that now. But I'm also telling you that after six you will want the next twelve because you will want to know what you can bring to your lover, what you can challenge him to do, and you will also know what your own boundaries are.'

She nodded slowly.

'I will leave you now. If I don't see you in fifteen minutes then you should know that it has been a rare pleasure meeting you and I certainly want you to come again – Alphonse will bring you, it may be complicated for Sylvie and Malcs – but' – his blue eyes stared at her, he was smiling gently – 'I do expect to see you downstairs soon.'

Claudia sat in the sudden silence. There were only distant murmurs of conversation. The music from below had softened. She sat, resisting the temptation to fetch her dress straight away and ask Andreas to take her back. She was sure she would choose the dress. She wanted to talk to Jack, he seemed further away than ever. He had drifted in and out of her thoughts all evening. When she'd woken up after Alphonse had left, she'd thought of Jack wandering around the flat with her still in bed. When she'd watched Malcs and Yvonne fucking, she thought about the moment with Jack in the window. And whenever champagne had been brought to her, she thought of Jack opening Taittinger and clinking glasses with her. But then she thought of Clare in the cellar, and she wondered how Jack was with Martha. Did she just want to substitute for Martha, to replace her in that part of Jack's life? It wasn't that, she was sure. There was something else, deep down – she did want to be told, she did want to be mastered, she did wonder how many ways they could excite each other, she did wonder where she could be taken to.

Jack had pinned her in positions, it was true, but only with his hands. How would it be if he bound her before he did whatever he wanted with her? Would he bind Martha, she wondered, when she wanted more? Would Martha want that? Where would that stop? Would she want that herself?

And by the time Andreas came in, she knew she wanted to find out. She took the cape from his arm.

She draped it around her shoulders. Andreas watched as her nervous fingers tried to fix the clasp.

'Let me help,' he said, 'it's an awkward thing.' He fastened it, then drew the cape open and took her hands in his. 'In a week, maybe two, you will want this again.' She could not look at him. 'Not here, not like this, but you will want to explore with your lover just what you can be for each other, what secrets you can share, but if you don't prepare yourself like this, if you don't find out here what you can do, you will never fully lose yourself with the man you love, nor will he with you unless you can show him how far you really want to go.' She nodded slowly. 'And don't worry, there will be other people around, but you will only be aware of yourself and Peter and, somewhere inside you, Jack.'

He let one hand drop and, holding the other, led her slowly to the door.

She looked straight ahead as she walked, conscious of a few people around her but deliberately avoiding their gaze, if indeed they were looking. Knowing what she now knew, she would see anyone in a black cape and know instantly where they were going. But what did that matter, this was between her and Peter and, ultimately, Jack.

She stepped down the dark stairs behind Andreas. The music had changed, classical now, not the metal of before. The crowd was much smaller but there was still a girl in the first chamber. A different girl but tied in the same way, this time surrounded by a small group. She was holding the cocks of men on either side, and a woman was kneeling between her legs, evidently kissing her. Claudia glanced only quickly at them. In the next chamber was Peter, his shirt abandoned and the mask obscuring his face but not hiding his identity. Beside him stood Artur. The composure she had gathered on the short walk down now tried to abandon her. Did she need them both? She wanted Peter, with his tall, tanned handsomeness and his piercing insights. Andreas led her to them and then left her. If there were any people watching the little trio, she was completely unaware of them.

Peter stepped forward, he undid the clasp of the cape and cast it elegantly to one side.

'Artur will prepare you then hand over to me. We will not gag you since it's your first time and you will want to feel free to say yellow but, as I have told you, that will be ignored until the sixth stroke. Nod if you understand.'

She nodded. His tone was no longer the sympathetic psychologist; now he was the stern headmaster.

He turned away to the rack. Artur stepped forward, took her hand and led her to the trestle. She settled herself against it and felt the soft padded leather against her thighs. She took hold of the legs on the far side and lowered herself down. As her weight was taken by the leather padding and her arms dropped free, she felt that a bridge had been crossed, there was no turning back. She would find out now what this was like. Now she was Martha, now she was Clare, and now she was Claudia, and this was what she wanted, the feeling came over her powerfully as Artur's strong, gentle hands pulled the clasps round her wrists into place.

He moved behind and slowly slid her pants off; she

felt freed, released and enjoyed the moment of unencumbered nakedness. Her nervousness had not retreated, but she felt a tingle of excitement in her loins.

Artur wrapped the clasps around her ankles, now she was spread, and her sex was fully open.

She heard Peter's voice. 'This next part will not hurt at all, you should find it very pleasant. We will adjust it until we judge it to be optimal for you.' Artur was behind her, she felt a strange small device being inserted into her vagina and clamping over her clitoris and on to her pelvis. Artur stepped back. She began to feel vibrations from the device running all the way through her, radiating out from her clit. She was gasping almost involuntarily. As the vibrations became more intense, she began to feel she might come; she couldn't let that happen. They couldn't let that happen, surely? And then the vibrations eased, now just sending gentle waves of pleasure all through her, keeping her orgasm on a distant but, for her, clearly visible horizon.

Artur was behind her again, she felt cold lube between her cheeks, she tried to relax but remembered Clare and the huge plug. But she had no need to fear the huge plug, Peter had said. She felt reassured as Artur pressed at her anus with some simple smooth device that entered her easily. 'Mmm,' she heard herself sighing, had Jack changed her so much?

'I think perhaps a larger one,' she heard Peter say

and the smooth plug was pulled slowly from her, feelings again radiating through her but now from behind. The idea of being stretched a little further wasn't scaring her, it was exciting her. She had come to love Jack stretching her, especially while he was playing with her, but she did not want Artur to go that far. She felt more lube being squeezed on to her, they were considering her feelings and her comfort, and the insistent vibrations around her clit were relaxing her. She felt Artur begin to push the tip of a new plug into her. It soon began to feel uncomfortable, and she gasped loudly, 'Oh, oh, no, careful!'

She felt relieved as Artur pulled back and removed the thing, but then shocked as a moment later she heard and then felt a very loud thwack and a searing pain across her buttocks. She screamed and tensed against the clasps. When she relaxed again a while later, the pain softening to a strange warmth, she heard Peter, speaking softly, 'We are your guardians in this situation. You will feel pain from the paddle, and later, from the cane, that pain might even seem considerable, but we take great care not to harm you, but we also make sure that you do go beyond your previous boundaries – or how will you know what you and your lover can enjoy? Now Artur will begin again, it will not be pain you feel from him, merely, at first, great discomfort, but you will certainly come to no harm. Now, no further words from you.'

She wasn't sure about Peter's judgement. That had been pain she had been feeling when Artur was pushing but, after he had applied more lube, she felt him pushing again, and it was truly, as he pushed harder, truly a ring of pain she was feeling and was crying out against until suddenly it was gone, and she felt intensely full but intensely warm and satisfied. Her orgasm had moved closer, it would be wonderful when it came with the huge object inside her and the insistent tingling from the small vibrator in her clitoris.

'Thank you, Artur, you may leave us.'

She now felt very alone. There may have been people nearby, but she was here now as Peter's willing victim, clamped in a position that exposed her completely, waiting for pain to overwhelm her, pain that she knew from the blow from the paddle already would be considerable, intolerable even.

But she wanted to know.

'The first ten you will find hard,' said Peter's soft but matter of fact voice. 'The second ten you to your surprise, you will find increasingly pleasurable.'

As the first blow crashed down across the exact centre of her buttocks, she jolted fiercely against the trestle. She cried out. Yes, he was right, that was hard. The second, slightly lower, was just as hard, just as painful and the pain radiated out and seemed to amplify the effect of the following strokes until Peter paused. Her whole arse was on fire.

'That's ten. I would normally insist that you count, but this is new for you. You can begin counting when I cane you, but for now, it's just the second ten with the paddle.'

And the noise began again but this time the feelings were different, the new strokes radiated into a heat that was going all through her body. Her arse was still on fire, but the sensation was becoming almost pleasant, and she could differentiate the sensations, the fullness of the plug in her behind, the delicious tingling of the small vibrator and the fierce increasing warmth across her buttocks until she felt almost disappointed to hear him say, 'That's twenty, you've done well.'

She exhaled heavily and became suddenly aware of how much she had been holding her breath.

'We will pause for a moment while you enjoy feeling the vibrator and the plug acting on your body.'

He was right. She had been aware of them while he was thrashing her, but now she could focus on them for a while. She began to relax, but then she felt the vibrator's intensity increase. She found herself gasping, being thrilled by it, but very aware that her orgasm was moving closer until, just as she was beginning to feel she couldn't stop it, the vibrations decreased, leaving her panting heavily and feeling lifeless.

'I think we're ready now. Remember, you must count, and I will not stop before you have taken six.'

She felt the cane being stroked down across her buttocks and thighs. It was pleasant to be touched, but it felt ominous.

And then the noise came, the swish and the thwack, followed by the most intense pain she had ever felt. She screamed and found herself sobbing, but quickly tried to check herself; this was something she'd wanted. At least wanted to find out about. And she knew, clamped as she was, that it would now continue. She tried to relax again. The time stretched out.

'I'm waiting,' said Peter.

'Oh, one,' she muttered.

That swish again. This time it felt worse because she knew what to expect and she screamed again, and again some sobs, but this time she said 'Two,' more quickly.

The third came and it was searing agony, and she had a brief flash that she would hate Jack. She was already beginning to hate Peter. 'Three.'

The fourth came, lower than the previous three and nearer her thighs and, if anything, still more painful. But, as the pain subsided slightly, she began to wonder how her arse would look in the morning. 'Four.'

Was this getting easier, she asked herself, but the fifth when it came seemed to land on an earlier one and made her scream. She breathed heavily and quickly, trying to master herself. Gradually she got control again, enough to wonder why she was waiting. Then she remembered. 'Five.'

The swish for six sounded different, louder, faster, and the pain, when it came was incredible. She screamed again and it brought tears to her eyes.

'Six.'

She waited, the vibrator still stimulated her gently, the plug still gave her a satisfying fullness, and the searing pain in her arse was slowly turning itself into a heat that she was almost beginning to enjoy.

'Do you have anything you want to say to me?'

The strangest feelings ran through her. Here she was trapped in the most undignified imaginable position, her sex, her arse fully exposed to a man she had only met that evening and to anyone else who happened to move towards them, waiting to be brutally caned again – but she felt curiously liberated, curiously in control. She shook her head.

The cane came down again, just as sharply, just as painfully as before but she felt now that she was guiding it, that it was somehow responding to her wishes and it astonished her to think, even as new strokes brought new impacts of pain, that she was controlling Peter, just as surely as she would be controlling Jack.

'Eighteen.' And she had a level of awareness, of

sensitivity to her body and her feelings that was altogether new. But she still had an ache, a sense of a being on a ledge that she wanted to leap from. And she located the ache as the vibrator on her clitoris began to increase its intensity. Peter was turning its control and watching her excitement build. Only let him be right, she thought, only let him be right, as slowly but certainly she felt the waves coming, and she began screaming in the most sublime ecstasy. It was a long slow slide down from that immeasurable high. She could feel Peter gently pulling the plug from her, almost sending her back to those heights she had just scaled but, with it and the vibrator gone, her body could relax completely into an exquisite peace. She was barely conscious of Peter undoing the clasps, of him draping the cape over her, even as she stayed slumped over the trestle. He waited. Slowly she stirred herself. He took her hand to help her and, as he embraced her, she wrapped her arms around his waist, buried her face in his chest hair and began weeping.

He kissed her head and they stood there a long while.

When she began to detach herself, he said, 'There's a bathroom in the corner. You'll find your things in there, your dress, your bag and anything else you need, towels for a shower. You can even have a bath if you want one.'

She laughed. 'That seems like the ultimate absurdity. But thank you, I will have a quick shower.'

He smiled at her. 'There are also creams you might like to use. You'll be surprised how quickly you can recover.'

'Oh, but not from the mental scars.'

He looked momentarily alarmed, but he was already beginning to relax when she smiled at him.

'That was… well, I feel so many things I don't think I'm going to even begin to try to describe, but Peter…'

'Yes?'

'Thank you.'

'You are very, very welcome. You have done extraordinarily well. Your Jack is a very lucky man. I'll be waiting for you upstairs.' He leaned down and kissed her very tenderly.

When she came out of the bathroom the cellar was deserted, but the music was still playing quietly. She walked up the stairs to an empty hallway, and through the dining room to the kitchen where Peter was talking to Hannes and Andreas.

'Where's everybody gone?'

'The guests treat four a.m. as Cinderella's midnight,' said Peter, 'it's, shall we say, an expectation I impose. If they stay later the magic goes missing and we end up shovelling comatose drunks out on to the street.'

Andreas smiled slowly. 'It's a very long time since that happened.'

Peter smiled and nodded. 'That's true. You do a wonderful job of managing the atmosphere.'

'I'm sorry,' said Claudia, 'I truly didn't know. Can I ask you to take me, Andreas?'

'He'll give us five minutes,' said Peter, 'we'll have a little chat in the library. Would you like another tea?'

'No, no thank you. I don't want to keep you all up.'

'You are our only concern, my dear.' He smiled warmly at her, put his arm around her and guided her through the dining room. She felt curiously relieved that the elegant trousers were back.

She went to the same sofa. She sat, positioning herself to put weight on her hip, still very aware of the fire burning her cheeks. He sat beside her.

'You are a wonderful woman and a lovely person,' he said, smiling again, 'and I for one would love to see you here again. But I think you will not come.'

'Oh, I... you may be right, but I'd hate you to feel that I'd just exploited this.'

'Oh, my dear, don't be silly. You've brought joy to people here tonight. I'll admit Alphonse falls in love more often than he should, but he did seem especially struck tonight – and I understand why. And Malcs and Sylvie, well, you've helped them more than you can possibly judge. You will probably feel when you look back, if you don't already, that Sylvie has somehow exploited you.' Claudia nodded slowly. 'Well, it's true, she has. But you will have helped her and Malcs move on and put his silly dream behind him. So, you probably won't see them again, either.'

'No, I think you're right. But I am very grateful they brought me here.'

'And I'm very grateful that they brought you here. Most people who come here are richer for the experience, but few are or become truly whole and healthy. But you are, I think, or will be when you have absorbed and reflected on this experience – and it's good, I think, that you won't see Jack for a while – you'll find your way to a much richer relationship with him and you'll probably find everything you want in each other.'

'It's strange to hear you say that.'

'Strange?'

'Well, these parties, they're the opposite of a monogamous lifestyle.'

'These parties are for people who need them and enjoy them, and I don't mind what they need. I only ask, well, actually I insist, that they genuinely enjoy themselves.'

'And you?'

'Me?' He guffawed and looked at the ceiling. When he looked back at her, he was no longer smiling. It seemed as if a mask had dropped. He breathed in deeply.

'I will say something. I wouldn't, I don't, to anyone else. But I trust you and, as I said, we probably won't meet again. That distresses me, but I do feel I'm setting a beautiful bird free from a cage.'

Claudia felt her eyes prickle.

'I love the process of people exploring themselves, of making themselves richer, of making themselves more whole, even if few of them get there. I certainly won't. My first wife was a little like you, just not as in touch with herself, or not so prepared to find out. Well, maybe she was, but I had already lost her trust before she could make any headway. I love doing what I do, especially when it can help someone like you discover themselves, but I will be honest, and I hope you don't feel debased, I do enjoy the dark side of people like Clare undergoing the process, whether I'm watching or giving. Clare will be back, and I will thoroughly enjoy caning her. You will not be back. You will find a way, I think, if Jack is as good a man as you deserve to fall in love with, of integrating these darker facets of yourself into a very rich relationship. You will stand with him at the water's edge, you must decide together whether you will swim.'

Claudia looked down at her clasped hands in her lap. She felt a tear drop on to them. 'Peter, you're amazing – and lovely. May I kiss you?' They stood and embraced, their lips came together in a long soft slow kiss. Finally, he pulled away, smiling.

'You really are very beautiful, my dear, I wish you a very happy life.'

'Thank you.'

'I just have one final word of warning.'

'Oh.'

'Probably Malcs will call you. I think you will all be much happier if you make it plain that that won't work.'

She nodded. 'I feel very sure you're right.'

'Oh, you'd probably have come to that conclusion on your own. I just wanted to reassure you that being straightforward, even blunt, is much better for everyone than trying to be kind or polite.'

She laughed.

He nodded. 'Yes, that's a mistake you make too often, isn't it? Come on, let's get Andreas to take you home.'

He stood on the steps waving as the car pulled away. An extraordinary man, she thought, but turned her face to the future.

23

It was past five when she got to bed, but she still woke before eight. She showered quickly and tiptoed out of the room. There was no sound of movement from Sylvie and Malcs. The door to their workroom was open, she took a blank sheet of paper from the printer and an envelope from the desk and went to the dining table to write the note:

Sylvie and Malcs,

I apologise profusely for sneaking off like this, but I really do have to get back for the children. I just can't thank you enough for taking me last night. Despite my reservations, and you know all about those, I had a wonderful and very enlightening time and met some intensely memorable people. So many, many thanks for taking me and for your wonderful hospitality. I very much hope to see you both again soon.

Many kisses,

Claudia.

OK, she thought, this new era of honesty and openness still doesn't extend to thank you letters. Even without Peter's conversation, she knew Sylvie and Malcs were not part of her future. She propped the letter against the vase on the table.

She tried to close the front door in absolute silence. There was a loud click, but at least she didn't need to slam it. Even if it woke them, she would be well away before they could see she was gone. Her sense of relief easily overcame her inhibition about parting without a proper goodbye and within a few minutes she was driving down the Kings Road, heading for Putney Bridge. There would be no right turn this time.

She was home soon after nine, the kids still in their pyjamas.

'Look at you.' Pat called to them, 'I told you she'd be home soon, and you've not even washed.'

'It's OK, Pat. I can never get them to do anything before ten on a Saturday anyway, unless they have their own plans to go out.'

'Did you have a nice time?'

'It was wonderful. They took me to a party. My God, the place was like a palace and there were some very interesting people there.'

'Were you up late?'

'Very. I'll try to get through the morning but I'm definitely planning a siesta. Have they been good?'

'I think they conned me about bedtime,' said Pat loudly, the kids turned and smiled sheepishly, 'but they were very good. He even showed me how to play Super Mario.'

'She's actually not bad,' said the boy.

'She? Who's she?' called Pat with mock indignation, 'it's Gran to you!'

The boy smiled and turned back to the television.

'Come on. I'll make you a cup of tea. Have you had breakfast?'

'No, I left them sleeping and just sneaked out.'

'Let's go into the kitchen and have some toast then.'

Dave was moping and had been drinking even more but, when she found two empty bottles of scotch in his room, Pat had decided to tackle him. She'd waited until the evening and she had George as back up, but before she made tea, she'd made them sit down to tell him it couldn't go on like that. There was always a room for him, of course there was, but she wasn't going to have him just getting drunk every night, especially not sad drunk. Even George, who hated confrontations, had been supportive. Dave was still insisting that he wasn't going back, but Pat was guessing that Claudia didn't want that anyway.

'I've got to admit, this suits me much better,' said Claudia, 'but it's quite a burden for you. He doesn't do a lot around the house.'

Pat guffawed. 'Well, that's my fault, isn't it? It's mothers who spoil boys. But your little one's a gem, tidied all his tea things away last night without being asked. No, don't worry dear, I've got George trained to do more these days, so it's not much extra work. But what are you doing about money?'

'Well, that's not easy, I admit. He'll have to give me something for them, but the rent was coming out of my money anyway. I don't know how I'll tackle him on that.'

'I'll have a word, leave it to me.'

'Would you? Thanks ever so much. It's going to be difficult whenever we talk but that wouldn't be a good first topic.'

'Well, if it comes to it, I'll make him pay me for his lodging and I'll give it straight to you.'

'That's ever so good of you.'

'Nonsense. I'm afraid you deserve better than my son's been giving you.'

When Pat had gone, Claudia went to the bathroom to check the damage. She gasped when she looked in the mirror. She hadn't known what to expect but the vivid purple rectangles astonished her, all the stripes seemed to have merged into one colour. She applied more of the gel that she'd taken from Peter's bathroom, very doubtful that the marks would fade for ages. Not the time to get hit by a bus, she thought.

Jack's text came in the afternoon. She picked it up when she woke:

How did it go? Can you talk? Xxx

Out with the kids, going to the cinema. How's tomorrow? Xxxxx

Openness? She had just sent him an outrageous lie but, love him as she did, she just could not manage that conversation now – and even tomorrow would be much sooner than she wanted.

Taking the kids to the new Bond movie, about which they were quite enthusiastic, was a spontaneous response to the fib she'd just told but it salved her conscience about Jack and about the kids. She hadn't been doing enough with them lately anyway. And at least she would be able to start tomorrow's conversation, if it couldn't be avoided, with an authentic story. Although when she sat down in the cinema seat, her arse told her that a three-hour commitment was a bad idea. It felt like very bad sunburn being baked again with no shade for relief.

By the next day it was a little easier, but she was still positioning herself carefully on chairs. She had a tumult of topics she would need to talk to Jack about and absolutely no idea about how she could approach them. Would she be selective again? She had still said nothing about Dave, and she had no idea whether her dominant feeling was of embarrassment about all the things that had happened or a dread that Jack might not respond in the way he should.

But she knew that appearing bold would be the best way to start so she texted him:

Your Sunday buffet finished yet? Xxxxx

Hoping to catch him occupied – but then worried about what he might be occupied with.

It's nine here, of course it's finished. Shall I call? Xxxxx

Please xxxxx

'I knew you'd have finished eating,' she said when he rang, 'but sometimes you have to socialize afterwards.'

'Not today. I'm avoiding that at the moment.'

'Recovering from a hard week?'

'You could say that. I've had a couple of days in Bangkok.'

'I saw that on your schedule. Was that just your business?'

'No, I had one day in our office but there was a conference of business leaders in Asia that I wanted to attend.'

'Worthwhile?'

'Oh, yes, I still feel very at sea here.'

'Did you know anybody?'

'A couple of Singapore people I knew and a couple of my own GMs. I need to groom them and make sure they see a bigger picture. Sorry, cliché! But it was a good conference.'

'And Bangkok?'

'I don't like it.' He hesitated, that was becoming a signal for him to admit to something new. 'But I did see a different side of it.'

'I think I'm going to learn something.'

'Yes,' he said slowly, 'Martha was there.'

'At the conference?'

'Yes, at the conference, she a business leader in Asia, what were you thinking?'

'No, that's what I'd assumed but she could have been travelling to see you.'

'No, she has a big job in the region and several clients at the conference.' He sounded tetchy and again there was a pause. 'She did manage to organize some pleasure with the business.'

'This is going to be an interesting story, isn't it?'

'I hope that's all it is.'

'So, what's interesting?'

'There are hotels in Bangkok that cater for people with special tastes. The rooms are themed, and you can use them as couples or groups or, if you want to pick a theme and you're on your own, the hotel arranges the appropriate company. Some of the rooms are like seraglios and the hotel will provide your harem for you. It's not just the middle-eastern visitors who like that apparently.'

'So, you wanted to be a sultan.'

'Oh no. I didn't know anything about these places,

but Martha had heard of them.'

Claudia went a little cold as she began to imagine what might have happened. 'So, they have rooms for Martha's special tastes.'

'Exactly. I did kind of guess when we got there but the room was still something of a surprise.'

Claudia kept very quiet, her mind very much on the second chamber at Peter's. 'Go on.'

'Well, it was set up like a torture chamber. Two walls were bare stone, with manacles and chains hanging from them and a rack with all sorts of whips and crops and canes dangling and on the other walls, the usual hotel furniture, including a cupboard with an ice bucket and champagne.'

'So, you tied her to the wall?'

'No, no. In the middle of the room was a trestle with a padded leather top and clamps for ankles and wrists.'

Claudia's stomach knotted.

'Had she been there before?'

'I don't think so, she seemed as surprised as I was. OK, we'd specified a punishment room, but it looked more authentic than we'd imagined.'

'We? How did you select the room?'

'We'd googled it the night before.'

Claudia's turmoil was caused, she knew, by a jealous reaction to Martha and Jack seeking the room out together but also by what she would have to tell Jack later. She took a deep breath. Jack was hesitating again.

'Claudie, I'm just going to say what happened, then I'm going to tell you how I feel about it later.'

'OK Jack, I'm listening – and I'm absolutely not judging.' No, she thought, I'm absolutely hoping it makes it easier for me to talk later.

'Well, we opened the champagne. We'd been drinking at the conference dinner, so we weren't entirely sober anyway, but I think we both thought we needed to get the rules straight. She'd always had this as a fantasy, apparently.'

'And you?'

'Not really. I admit I find stories about that a turn on, but my fantasies haven't run beyond slapping you with a paddle and fucking you when you get excited.'

'But she wanted more?'

'Well, she'd already had more when I'd caned her at my place. That was as much as she wanted, apparently, as far as the caning itself was concerned. This was more about being mastered and bound and being unable to resist. Can you understand that?'

'You know I can.' There was another long pause. 'And I know that in some way it appeals to you to do it. I learnt that in our hotel room.'

'It's true. I admit I was getting excited. I wanted to find out how it would feel. So, I began to describe to her exactly what I planned to do to her. Well, I didn't have a plan, I was making it up, but that was getting her excited. I made her undress slowly. That was a little strange. She had her usual black business suit but was wearing very exotic underwear.'

'Well, she would. I know I would.'

Jack seemed to hesitate.

'Sorry, that's put a different picture in my head. I'll come back to that. But I was glad of the alcohol, it was easier to go slowly, and when I'd strapped her wrists and ankles, I made her wait a while. I spent a while abusing her, telling her how dirty she was and how she needed to be punished. I must be honest and say I wasn't really into that, but it was what she'd dreamed about. She really is just into this caning and punishment scenario.'

'I've heard there are people like that,' said Claudia, remembering Peter's words.

'I'd read that too, but she's the first person I've met who's so focused on it. Anyway, we'd agreed I would cane no harder than I had at my place and that I would give her twenty-four strokes.'

'And if she'd wanted you to stop?'

'She would call out "yellow".' Was this universal? thought Claudia.

'Didn't she ask you to paddle her first?'

'That's funny, yes, she did.' He hesitated, apparently unnerved by the question. 'So that's how I started, twelve with a paddle, quite hard too, she was very red afterwards. Then I stopped and took a drink and abused her some more, telling her how much she deserved what I was about to give her and then I made her wait again until I was ready. I'm not finding this easy, I need to talk to you afterwards, but let me get through this.' He paused, she guessed he was taking a drink. 'Anyway, then I started with the cane and even though the paddle had made her very red, the cane marks were very clear, and she was shouting quite loudly every time – but she wasn't saying yellow, she was just screaming and then counting.'

'You made her count?'

'No, she just started that herself. I began to worry and eased off a bit after ten but instead of screaming she just shouted "harder", so I did. I admit I was enjoying it, but it wasn't an unmixed pleasure. I did finish with a very hard twenty-fourth, I knew she'd want that, and she did, but it left her screaming and wriggling. Normally she'd have been touching herself and making herself come, but her wrists were still bound.'

'You forgot the vibrator.'

'I did what?'

'You should have clamped a vibrator on her clitoris and wound it up at the end.'

'Claudie!'

'So, what did you do?'

'Well…' Jack was clearly completely unnerved.

'Well, I played with her. I played with my fingers. I couldn't do anything with him, anyway, I mean, I found it exciting but, somehow, he just wasn't responding like he normally would, so I stood beside her and touched her. She was incredibly wet, and in a matter of seconds her orgasm flooded through her and left her slumped on the trestle. Her arse was a mess of red and purple, but she seemed quite transported by it all and she just lay there for a long time, even after I'd undone the clamps.' He paused. 'But what's this vibrator thing?'

'Are you ready for my story?'

'Yes, I think so,' he said very slowly.

And she felt calm, and she felt surprisingly bold, and she told him all about Peter.

She left out Alphonse but only because she didn't feel she should complicate the story. She described watching Clare being punished and how she'd found that intriguing, exciting. She told him about the vibrator, but not about the plug. She told him about Peter's offer and her own conscious decision to be taken to the cellar, her own reaction to the cane, her own orgasm when the vibrator's intensity was increased, her own feelings of fulfilment after the orgasm, her sense that she had somehow gained control because, towards the end, what was happening was what she wanted, not something being imposed on her. 'And I wanted it to be you, Jack, I wanted it to be us. I know that now. You've excited me with the crazy things you've done to me. I've felt strange about them, so much is new, but I knew I wanted more, and I knew you would want more, but I didn't know how much further I could go. I do now.'

There was a long silence. She expected that. She had to give him time. She liked time herself when he told her anything newly outrageous. He had to speak next.

'I don't have a simple reaction to this.'

'I don't suppose you do. I never do when you tell me about Martha or Joanna.'

'I wasn't convinced about all this openness, and I have to say, maybe I'm still not. The idea itself, of you being naked and tied up and someone caning you, I can get excited about that. It may be an unhealthy fantasy but somehow it stirs me. I admit to that as a fantasy, but the idea of you actually being like that at a party with people around… I'm having a hard time with that.'

'It was just Peter and me, Jack, if there was anybody else, I was oblivious. And I used him, not the other way around, because I wanted to find out more about me. I won't ever do it again unless it's with you.'

'So, you're saying I shouldn't see Martha again?'

'No, I'm not. This is a very hard relationship anyway, but if I expect you to live like a monk as well, it's doomed. Just as it would be if we start keeping secrets.'

Another long pause. 'I know you're right, but

somehow I'm struggling.'

'I admit I struggle too. I find looking ahead helps me.'

'I know you're right. Don't worry, I'll get through this.' He paused. 'And you've given me a new favourite fantasy. I'm picturing you tied up for me now. Do you really want us to try this?'

'I want us to try everything together that excites us. It's weird to be saying it. I used to think of myself as being so staid. Well, let's face it, I was. But I've already done things with you that I never ever imagined doing and now I want us to try going further.'

'I'm sorry, I feel bad, I haven't reacted as I should have done.'

'It's OK, it takes me a day or two to get over some of your stories. I just think we're special and I keep looking ahead.'

'That's what I have to do, I know.' A pause. 'Thank you for being so open. I'll ring again soon in case I've worried you; I should have reacted better. I know you're right, being open is the only way.' But it wasn't conviction she heard in his voice.

And when she put the phone down, she was immediately seized with guilt. She should have told him about Dave.

But why? It was irrelevant. That was just her domestic arrangements. It had no bearing on Jack and her. It was just a benefit, she was freer to organize her life.

But she knew Jack might see it differently.

Jack,

I was so happy we spoke yesterday, but I wasn't surprised you were taken aback. I hope now you've had time to reflect that I am seeing all of this just in terms of where it can take us.

But it overshadowed something else I should have said. Dave isn't here, he is now living with his parents. He walked out two weeks ago when he found some photos on my computer (you know which ones). I am not trying to get him back.

His mother is being very supportive of me, so my life is much easier to organize.

I don't see it as a big thing, but it is something I should have told you about, and I didn't want to wait until your next call before I told you.

Call soon, please.

Claudie xxxxx

It didn't surprise her that he didn't.

24

It didn't surprise her, but she had to admit to herself after two weeks that she was disappointed.

Very disappointed.

And when an email came from the head of the China business, effectively Jack's number two in the region, that he was immensely looking forward to introducing the conference and how honoured he was that Jack had asked him, she was angry.

She was angry for the whole day in the office, numb when she was giving the kids their tea, and then weepy sad when they'd gone to bed and she was alone with the gin bottle.

She retained enough wisdom not to reply to the email from Alan that had come through earlier. His was not her favourite gender that day.

Dave was being difficult about money. She'd had no direct dealings with him, but she knew from Pat's reaction that there was a problem and she suspected that the money Pat was giving her was not being taken from Dave but simply being taken from Pat's own savings. She knew she would have to tackle Dave herself – but maybe after she'd spoken to a solicitor.

She'd had a difficult conversation with Malcs. She had been very effusive in her email, thanking them for what they had done for her and saying what a wonderful time she'd had but had also tried to hint, as strongly as was polite, that she didn't see a future in a threesome. Malcs had rung subsequently and made it plain that he was not thinking of a threesome either. She could have talked about her family commitments or about seeing Jack soon and her feelings for him, but she had found it surprisingly easy to be straightforward and blunt – 'A little affair just doesn't fit in my life, Malcs, and I honestly doubt whether it should fit in yours'. It was only later, feeling a little used and dirty, that she remembered Peter's advice and realized how exactly right he had been.

And Jack! She wanted to challenge him. He had expectations of her that he wasn't fulfilling himself. She had idealized, almost idolized, him for years it seemed. She had seen him deal with business pressures and sensed him dealing with domestic pressures and she had admired him in every situation and had delighted in the conversations they had had, surprised by his insights and his sensitivity and yet, and yet, here he was behaving apparently like a jealous boy. OK, she had pushed for her cherished openness. She'd had to cope with much more than she'd truly expected to from him, but she had always dealt with it, always bounced back.

Yet here he was – failing at the first difficult situation. Would he have preferred to tell lies? Were they all liars and cowards? As she struggled to pour the gin – 'Fuck!' as some spilt on the papers beside her glass – she had enough self-awareness to stop pursuing that line of thought.

She looked again at Alan's email – 'Fuck!' again as she almost deleted it in trying to open it.

....you were so amazingly helpful and a lot of people here have been so complimentary about my preparations – all the ideas are ones I got from you – but if I could persuade you to let me talk you through everything it would help me approach the event (it's only two weeks away!!!) with so much more confidence. Could you find an hour or two? I could come to your office. Or could you (my strong preference) let me take you to dinner to give us more time on the topic?

'Or could you let me get your knickers off and fuck your brains out?' She stopped sharply. She realized she was slurring and that she was talking loudly – and that the girl, whose bedroom was next to hers, didn't go to sleep that early. She took a deep breath, the music in the headphones would drown everything – most nights she had to go in and physically remove them.

Maybe that was a little unfair to Alan – but probably not, she thought. But she at least stopped herself sending a reply.

25

Having Alan come to the office was much the most sensible idea. Most of what he wanted to show and discuss was on his laptop and the conversation would have been impossible in a restaurant over dinner. She was quite thrilled with what he'd done; she could see her own influence in many of the ideas and in the structure of the programme he was planning.

She was impressed.

As were, for different reasons, other ladies in the office.

'Who's the dish?' was only one of several similar questions and comments she'd got when fetching drinks or attending to her own business.

And there were several winks and expressions as people uttered, entirely unusually, their goodbyes on leaving for the day.

That made her realize how late it was getting.

'Alan, I'm so impressed, it's kept me talking far longer than I meant to. I really do have to be getting home. Have you got all you wanted?'

He smiled. 'No. Definitely not! Seriously, I'm so grateful for everything, you've been immensely helpful.'

'But I've done nothing today – except tell you you're in very good shape.'

'But that means so much to me. I admit I'm feeling nervous about it.'

'You'll be fine.'

'I'm beginning to feel that now, thank you. But I'll admit I was hoping you might have time for one small drink on your way home.'

'Alan, I can't, I'm late as it is.'

'Just one, please?'

Pat had been getting the tea anyway: 'That's fine, love, you take your time. Their homework's done anyway. Well, his is, I'm not convinced about hers.'

'I'm done,' Claudia heard the indignant dry voice in the background. 'Anyway, who's her? We have to say Gran.'

'Cheeky! Lay the table!'

It all sounded, as usual, very good natured.

She put the phone down and looked at Alan. 'I have an hour.'

He smiled again. 'Thank you. I'd like more but I'll take what I can get.'

They were soon in the garden of a nearby pub. It was a warm, sunny evening and they'd got the last free table. They didn't escape being noticed by some of Alan's new admirers from the office. There would have to be several conversations in the morning explaining the mysterious stranger.

'I loved your office,' he said when he sat down with the drinks, 'so colourful, so open. I could never see our guys abandoning their little cells.'

'It helps to keep people communicating but that's a mixed blessing when you look at them.' She nodded to the table where the office girls were, and he looked over his shoulder in time to catch them giggling. 'They're in their forties, some of them and it's like teenage gossip.' But she was more amused than irritated. 'You've made quite an impression.'

He smiled and nodded. He didn't need to tell her that that happened quite often.

'You have a girlfriend?'

'No-one special. I was engaged for a while, but it didn't survive me moving jobs.'

She smiled at him. 'But you do OK for ladies' company.'

He laughed gently. 'OK, yes, but the night in the hotel was an absolute rarity for me.'

'Well, what do you think it was for me, young man?' She tried to sound frosty.

And he looked a little alarmed until he saw her smiling again. 'Gotcha! You're very sweet. I love your mix of boyish enthusiasm and your Mr Cool suavity. It's very attractive, especially for a married mother of two who has one night out on her own in a very blue moon and has the deep misfortune to be pounced on by a priapic lothario.' He laughed. 'Seriously, I had a lovely night, but I did manage my re-entry without too much emotional damage.'

He looked slightly troubled. 'Well, I accept your point and I'm glad about that, but I didn't just get over it like that.'

'Alan, sweet boy, it's very lovely of you to say that but let's just agree it'll be a lovely memory for both of us.'

'I know you're right, of course you are. And I really was desperate to talk to you about the conference again, that's the main reason why I came. But I hope you don't mind me saying that I really wanted to see you again.'

'Of course, I don't mind, I'm very flattered – and I almost don't want to admit just how rare a treat for me it was. But now we've cleared the air we can just talk about work in the future, yes?'

He had a lovely, slow smile and she became aware of how noble she was feeling. It would be mad to be tempted. But she did admit to herself that she was. Jack, she thought, where the fuck are you?

26

Talk? Xxxxx

    On a Wednesday?

She was surprised, angry and excited in the turmoil of reaction. She was stalling, not sure how to respond. Cool was the best start, she thought.

    Of course. Give me half an hour? Xx

    Half an hour then xx

She hadn't given up on him, but her great lake of hope was decidedly muddy these days. She had tried to work out his itinerary. Where would he be in two weeks when she was in Singapore? Or would he really nominate a deputy for the conference and just stay in the office himself. She would be travelling in ten days and what had been the trip of a lifetime when she first planned it had begun to feel like a descent into a nightmare.

Making him wait half an hour would help her gain some composure and ensure that the office was nearer empty. The tactic once again failed to work, she had no clear idea of what she wanted to say to him and was more worried than ever about what she might blurt out and regret. And nothing she tried to fill the half hour made the clock go any faster. But he would ring on time, she told herself, it was nearing midnight for him and he wouldn't be going anywhere, surely. Surely? And new doubts crept into her head.

'I've been an arsehole, Claudie, I'm sorry.'

'Well, that was my reluctant conclusion, I have to admit. I know I should have handled things differently, but I don't really know how...' She stopped herself, it would have been typical to talk and talk and just blame herself.

'Talk to me, Jack, please, what's happening?'

'You're coming to see me and I'm going to spend every one of your spare minutes making love to you.'

'Jack, I... I'm just not getting this.' She had taken the small glass office and most people had gone home, but it would still be obvious to those remaining that she was dabbing her eyes.

'No, I'm sorry. You're coming to Singapore to run an important conference and I'll be grateful if you can spare some time for me.' He sounded quite cheery, but she knew that, for all their intimacy, he was sometimes hard to read. But she hoped his last remark wasn't sarcastic. The conference was very important for her – but so was seeing him.

'I didn't think you were even going to be there.'

'Of course, I'm going to be there. It is important and I've got the senior guys on a three-line whip. I've even asked one of them to open the thing for you.'

'I know. He emailed me to thank me and say how honoured he was. I just assumed you were ducking out.'

'No way! I want to close the thing for you, give it a flourish at the end. I just thought it might help you if one of the locals introduced it – and he's very good, is Robert.'

'Robert? He's a local?'

'Robert Li. Some of them adopt English names; it's fair enough in a US corporation. Both his parents are Chinese though. I'm not sure how they got him to Harvard. But he's great, his English is perfect, and he's very enthusiastic about the programme. His business has been the most active in my region, so I think he deserves a higher profile.'

'I'm ever so proud of it, Jack, but I wouldn't call a regional event high profile.'

'Not high profile? You know you've got two board members here?'

She felt a chill.

'Two board members?'

'Yes, they come out every year for a few days, but they specifically arranged their timing to catch the conference. You didn't know?'

'No, I didn't, and I was nervous enough anyway.'

'Don't be. They'll be delighted with it and Robert's thrilled because he can get noticed – but he is genuinely committed to it and wants to kick the thing off.'

'I just thought you were trying to get out of it. You haven't called for over three weeks. All I've had is Robert's note saying he was taking your place.'

'I've been an arsehole about us, Claudie, not about my job. I think this way will work very well for you.'

'So, are you going to talk about us now?'

'Yes.' And she shifted in her seat, feeling suddenly cold. 'I admit I found your revelations harder than I should have done.'

'Which revelations, the party or Dave?'

'Well, I need to add the other guy to the list.'

'Alan?'

'Was that his name?' He sounded offhand; this wasn't a good start, she felt herself retreating into a shell.

'Did you want to talk about anything in particular?'

'I suppose I do, but first everything together did make quite an impact. It was all a bit unexpected.'

'It's been unexpected for me too. If you'd asked me a few months ago if I could see my life like this, I'd have found the idea ridiculous. The only bit that would have been imaginable would have been Dave moving out, but I'd never have dreamt of the pretext I apparently gave him.'

'Does he want to come back?'

'Who knows? He hasn't said anything to me, we communicate through his mother. I just know I don't want him but that was true even before you and I got together. I have a much better life without him there. The money's tough, I'll have to fight him for that, but otherwise I'm okay.'

'Is money a problem?'

'Jack,' she said sharply, 'don't go there. It's not easy but I manage. Dave just isn't important, he's irrelevant. I didn't say anything because I just didn't want you thinking I was waving a flag and jumping up and down shouting I'm free, I'm free, come and get me.'

'But you've made such a big thing about being open.'

'That's why I feel bad about it – and why I've been having second thoughts about whether it's such a good thing.'

'So, what would you have kept quiet about?'

'About me? Nothing,' she said quickly but then wondered if that was quite honest – but then realized it was. 'Nothing would have happened without us starting something and what's happened since, apart from Dave, has been part of that. And, well, Dave might still have been there if I hadn't made you take those photos. But the crazy point is, I've done things because I see them as part of what we do.'

'That's where I'm struggling, thinking of you at that party and thinking that's part of us.'

'I've told you, I just wanted to find out what I could

do so that we could explore each other without me putting up any artificial boundaries.'

'And did it work?'

'Yes, it did for me. I know I was looking forward even more to seeing you again. I'm desperate to see you anyway but I was getting really excited about how our relationship might evolve.'

'Was looking forward to?'

'Yes, I seem to have blown that chance. You're struggling, you said.'

'Yes, I'm struggling, but I told you at the start, I'm the arsehole. I expect things of you that I don't expect of myself. That's classic, isn't it?'

'I'm not going to say you're wrong. It probably is classic, but actually I don't expect it to be the same on both sides. What happened at the party was a one-off for me. It would only ever happen again if that's something we want to try. But I don't have any expectations about you and Martha. I'm not saying I like it. I'm not like you, I don't fantasise about you doing it. But if it stays at just that, I can live with it, it's safer really. I wouldn't want some pretty little Asian lady offering you everything and wanting the full romantic love package.' She paused. 'Jack?'

'Yes?'

'There's nothing like that is there?'

'No, of course not.'

'It's not an of course, Jack. You're a very attractive, powerful man and you're only a couple of legal steps away from being entirely free.'

'I'm not free, Claudie.' His pause made her nervous. 'I have you and all that means.'

'What does all that mean?'

'It means I miss you, very much actually, and it means, apparently, that I struggle with the idea of you finding other people in your life.'

'But you can have Martha and Joanna?'

'That's the thing. I know they're safe. I like their company. I'm ashamed to say I have fun with them, but I do, but I also know that a relationship isn't going to develop. Well, Joanna's left now anyway.'

'So, who'll give you blowjobs now?' she said sharply and then instantly regretted it. 'I'm sorry, Jack, I shouldn't have said that but my point is I'm doing everything preparing to meet you and to see what it means for us, and I'm accepting, sort of, that it's not quite the same for you and it won't be while you're out there, but it is a bit tough being judged by a different yardstick.'

'I know, I know, that's why I feel such an arsehole.'

'Well, you are, a little bit, but I suppose I should be a little flattered that you think men are queueing up to wine and dine and fuck me but it just ain't going to happen, Jack. I mean, I saw Alan the other day…'

'The guy from the hotel?' Oh, maybe she shouldn't have mentioned this, but she'd started now.

'Yes Alan, the guy from the hotel, he came to the office to talk work.'

'Just to talk work?'

'No, that's just the point. He wanted another date and I told him no. Even Malcs rang up wanting to see me again but I've told him no, and that he should make his relationship work. So I'm just not doing anything that isn't focused on you, and I've been worrying that I will seem too focused on you, that you'll think I'm trying to pin you down exclusively – and instead of you worrying about that – and that's the thing you really should worry about – you think I want to go off and bonk everybody at pervy sex parties.'

'You finished?'

'Yes.' She exhaled heavily. 'I'm glad I got that off my chest.'

'That was openness, was it?'

She laughed, not sure it was appropriate. 'Well, that's a good point. It was openness, yes, but it was more openness about feelings, not just about the facts about whose cock is going where or who's spanked whose bum.'

'I know you're right and it's feelings I'm trying to talk about. I'm struggling with mine – about what you've been doing, about what you might be feeling and about what I'd do if you do get fed up with seeing your lover at six-month intervals. I feel a bit vulnerable, Claudie, and that's never happened before.'

'Oh, Jack, you stupid, stupid man. You must know by now I adore you – and have done for much longer than I want to admit, and all I'm trying to do is to see what sort of a relationship we can have and I'm doing everything I can, some weird things I admit, to be able to make the most of us when we have time together. I'm trying to find out what pleases you – and what pleases me – and I've had some real surprises in that last category and that's why I'm excited about trying them with you.'

The long silence didn't worry her. She felt she'd said what she wanted to say. He would either accept it, embrace it and go on a journey with her – or he would somehow be less than she was hoping for, but at least she'd know.

'The funny thing is,' he said at last, 'we've been having wonderful sex where I've been playing at being in control and I suppose, when I think about it, I have been in control, but now we're talking about going further, and I think we are talking about going further, I feel much less in control than I've ever felt.'

She sighed heavily. 'I think I understand that but there were some when's and if's that make it a bit unclear.'

'I think we're going further, but I'm not in control.'

'Maybe this is becoming a real relationship.'

'I think maybe you're right.'

'But I still want you to play at being in control. I'm addicted to you, Jack, but you've also got me addicted to the things you do to me.'

'I think it's time I found out where your boundaries are for myself – and found my own, for that matter. I don't know whether what's been making my stomach churn these last few weeks has been simple jealousy, losing control of a situation, wondering exactly what I want to try, falling in love or a combination of all four.'

'Say that again,' she said sharply, then wished she hadn't. She'd heard very clearly and wanted to hear it again, but it would be best to let him deal with it in his own way. After all, he did seem to be getting there.

'I think you heard.'

'Yes,' she said, smiling, and picturing him smiling.

'Anyway, you're here in ten days. When do you get here?'

'On the Monday, around four.'

'For how long?'

'I thought I'd stay until the Sunday. I've got the kids sorted with their gran. They're all quite excited about me going and looking forward to the presents when I get back, I expect. Is that OK?'

'That's very OK. You're at the Ritz?'

'Of course, everyone is.' There was a pause. 'What's up?'

'Well, I feel a bit crummy, but it would be difficult if we're seen as an item. You know what the corporation's like.'

'Jack, Jack, stop. Of course, I understand. As long as we get some time to ourselves, I'll be very happy.'

'I don't just mean some time. I want to sleep with you every night, either here or at the Ritz.'

'I completely want to, but these conferences can get very busy, late nights etcetera.'

'I know, I know but now you also know my demands. I know I only get one evening to myself, the Saturday if I've understood you right, but midnight to seven a.m. your body's mine.'

'It's all yours anyway, Jack, but yes, I'll make it accessible at night.'

27

The flowers in the room were lovely. The larger bouquet, with some discreet red roses (six, she counted) was from Jack, the smaller from the hotel. But they barely distracted her from the views over the harbour. When she found that even the bath had a view, she couldn't suppress a laugh. She had seen the website but hadn't thought she would have a room (my God, it was a suite) like the pictures. And the huge, deep windows! She remembered Jack's flat and the London hotel. Wasn't Singapore a place where you could get arrested for doing that in a window?

She began to unpack – for six nights with three formal evenings it was worth getting properly organized and she wanted the room to stay pristine – when there was a ring at the door. She checked the spyhole. Jack!

She flung her arms around him, so new and fresh but so familiar, how easily their bodies fitted into the embrace, the kiss.

'How did you…'

'Easy. Well, easy to work out you'd be here from when your plane arrived. Not so easy to convince the front desk to give me your room number without ringing you first. Fortunately, the girl had remembered the flowers.'

'Oh, yes, they're lovely, thank you so much.'

'But you have another admirer, I see.' He was smiling, just teasing but she had been wondering what thoughts the last conversation had left.

'Oh, I've had to hide the larger ones in case you turned up and felt inadequate.'

'Well spanking you wasn't going to be the first item, but I can shuffle the plan.'

'No. I'll take your original plan, as long as it's fucking first!'

So much for pristine, she thought, as she surveyed the litter of bedclothes and clothing scattered all around them, but then she turned her attention back to his body, running her hand down through the chest fur and on to his cock.

'You want more?' he murmured sleepily.

'Of course. The second time is always lovelier, you can go slower.'

'I suppose it's ungentlemanly to point out that it will be the fourth time for you.'

'You're right.'

'That it's ungentlemanly?'

'No, that it will be the fourth time, I don't want a gentleman. So tough luck, mister, you don't get out of this bed until you've made me come again.'

'And how do you propose I do that?'

'I hate to seem too slutty, but you're going to find that surprisingly easy.' And she slid herself round easily to straddle his face, lowering her pussy slowly on to his mouth, happy to feel his hands on her cheeks, holding her, briefly, at a distance.

'Do you mind if I tell you that, also from this angle, you are a very beautiful woman?'

'No, but it's time you kissed her.'

'Again? That was orgasms one and three,' the last word was muffled as she pushed herself down on to him. She looked down at his cock, still small and recovering, glistening with their juices, surrounded by the late flecks of his cum that weren't inside her – he would be licking those now as his tongue went into her, distracting her momentarily, but now she held him gently and began to feel the life flooding back into his cock. She loved watching it, feeling it grow, seeing its shiny head emerge again. She massaged it slowly, delighted at how it soon rose to its accustomed height. She could feel her own excitement mounting again as his tongue circled her clitoris and pressed her, but she knew this would be slower and less frenzied than the hour they had enjoyed after he'd pushed her (or had she pulled him?) to the bed.

Now she bent down to take his cock head slowly into her mouth, thrilled to feel it grow so hard as her lips enclosed it. Now she could pull back a little and let her tongue play around it, delighted with the taste of their recent couplings. She could feel him eating her more greedily – it was exquisite, and she knew she would come again but for now, that edge was still distant.

Maybe not so for him, she thought, as she pushed her mouth as far down as she could, feeling him seem to grow even more as he filled her. She pulled back to admire him, feeling him pushing firmly into her hand.

She bent forward to touch his cock on her nipples and heard him moan appreciatively without interrupting his licking. She felt him adjust himself and pull her cheeks apart. His tongue tip squeezed into her anus, she sat down further on to him to help him get a little deeper but then eased her pussy on to his mouth again, it was time to concentrate on him, she could come again later.

She studied his firm shiny cock again, rubbing it gently to keep him completely stiff. Now she would become single-minded, she was going to take him completely in her mouth, she would control him coming. His tongue on her clit was a minor but very pleasant distraction but now she wanted this cock. She took it as deep as she could in her mouth, holding its base and cupping his balls as she moved her lips slowly up and down its shaft. She pulled back occasionally to tickle its head with her tongue before taking him deeply again, only easing back when she felt him getting too close to the edge. She was so thrilled to be having him again – and now even her pussy was threatening to betray her – and her jaw was beginning to ache as she stretched again to take as much as she could.

She sat up. 'Mister, you are going to come now. And I am staying on you until I have swallowed every drop you can give me.' She heard him moan loudly as she went down. She filled her mouth again but gripped the shaft more firmly now, trying to find his rhythm. They fell into harmony, she pulled back slightly, just keeping her lips around his head feeling his thrusts more firmly in her hand, now she could feel the pulsing begin, now she could hear his moans getting louder – and now the first warm blobs squirted into her mouth. She pressed harder and faster, swallowing some and sucking still more until his movements slowly began to subside. She kept sucking and swallowing as the blobs slowed to a trickle. She pulled back and watched, still holding him firmly, still large even though the stiffness was easing. She watched the later blobs emerging and bent to lick them as they did.

He was getting busier with her, she felt his tongue pressing harder on her clit, now she felt free to come too, she rubbed herself up and down on his mouth, loving the long slow build up. This fourth was going to be even bigger than the first three, she knew it. It wasn't creeping up, it was rushing at her, she could let it overwhelm her completely. She was aware of almost screaming, aware of pushing down on to his face, aware of his tongue on her and inside her and the thrill went on and on, unlike any before until she collapsed on to him, her face beside his only slowly softening cock. She felt completely limp, but the lovers' laugh caught them both at the same time, and their bellies rumbled against each other, making them laugh even louder.

He resumed licking her.

'No, you can't.' She laughed again. 'I'm not doing five, even for you.' She sat up on his chest, enjoying the feel of his fur on her tenderest parts.

They took room service. Some of her team for the week would be arriving, and they didn't want to be seen together and have the gossip distract people.

'You're feeling tired and not tired,' he said as they sat close together in armchairs looking out at the view.

'You're right. I slept quite a bit on the plane and it's only, what, early afternoon in the UK? But my body's telling me something's not right.'

'That might be the four orgasms.'

She slapped his arm gently. 'I may want more.'

'I'm happy to try but even my tongue is sore.'

'How on earth do you think my pussy feels?'

'Your arse might be feeling left out.'

'My arse is feeling left out but I'm sure you have plenty of plans for later.'

'Oh, yes.'

'That sounds ominous.'

'I have lots of plans for your arse, as you well know, but we'll leave most of that until the end of the week. I don't want you embarrassingly incapacitated for your big week.'

'Incapacitated?'

He looked straight at her. 'We'd said we wanted to find things out about ourselves. Is the kinky side something we want to integrate, or will you go to parties for that particular thrill while I keep caning Martha?'

'Jack, I am never going to another party, not one like that. Yes, it was a strange thrill, but it will only ever be with you. Just don't tell me about Martha any more. I think I've had it with openness. I just need to know that you want me.'

'Oh, I want you, and I wouldn't give up on openness quite so easily. I'm not seeing Martha any more, I wanted to tell you that.'

She was stunned. 'But, but don't you have to meet at work? How did that happen? What's she doing?' She had turned sideways to look at him directly, her hands gripped his wrist. Aware how agitated she must be looking she tried to relax, let one hand slip and held on to his hand with the other.

'It was a fairly business-like conversation, which you'd understand if you'd met her.'

'What did you say?'

'I said you were becoming more important to me.'

'And she said?'

'She just nodded, said she'd been having a wonderful time but hadn't expected a permanent arrangement.'

'What aren't you telling me?'

'She said she'd be happy to meet again if my situation changed. She thinks I'm quite a good dom, apparently.'

'Do you think you're a good dom?'

'No, I don't. I have loved what I do with her, but it's been very detached – and very much what she clearly wanted. I love your beautiful arse but I'm not sure how far I can go with us.'

Now she took his hand in both of hers. 'Jack, I want to find out. I've had all sorts of awakenings with you and found out strange and unexpected things about myself. I was thrilled to be taken like that at the party, but I know I wanted it to be you.'

'Well, I liked caning Martha, and I have to admit to you that I liked it more when it got really severe, but I can't say that I pictured that it was you.' He looked serious.

'No, her bum's too big apparently.' And they both laughed easily, aware of what they had agreed to try.

She slept fitfully, but each time she woke it

renewed her delight in finding him there and she snuggled in closer to him, sometimes rubbing her hand on his chest, sometimes kissing his ear. He slept soundly.

At around five when she woke for the sixth time, he was missing. She could hear him in the bathroom.

'Are you leaving me?'

He peered around the bathroom door. 'I have to go home and change. I'll see you in the office.'

'Is your place far?'

'No, it's walkable but I'd recommend you take a cab tonight.'

Her brain was a little scrambled. 'Jack, I've got to meet up with the team tonight.'

'Of course, you have. I even know where you're taking them. You'll love it, it's great food, not pretentious at all. But then you come to see me, OK?'

'Oh, definitely very OK. But come and cuddle me before you leave.'

He lay down beside her and pulled her into his arms. He kissed her softly. His hand slid to her arse. She felt his cock begin to stiffen against her belly. They both laughed.

'I think it's time I went.'

'I think it's time you went.'

She was sleeping deeply when the alarm went at seven. She was drifting off again when the phone rang five minutes later.

'Get up now!'

'Jack?'

'It's dangerous. You set the alarm for seven and then you go back to sleep. I don't want you coming in late for your first day in my office.' There was a pause. 'I'm not getting off the line until you tell me you're standing up.'

She unfurled herself slowly. 'OK, I'm standing up – and, Jack?'

'Yes?'

'You're lovely, thank you.'

'You're lovely, my angel, see you soon.'

28

The office seemed quite busy when she arrived at nine. It was strange to travel halfway around the world and find the office so familiar with its corporate template, all open plan and limited clutter, a row of glass-walled meeting rooms and a well-intentioned rest area around the coffee machines already under pressure from the expansion of headcount and desks. Mai showed her around, they had Skyped enough to feel they knew each other. The population was younger than she was used to and probably smarter. Yes, she thought, quite a lot smarter.

She could see Jack sat against the distant wall, talking to a couple of people, but she first sought out his head of HR, who she recognized from video conferences they'd shared. The woman was very engaged with the project and seemed very keen to help. She joined her when the team met later that morning. Claudia was using several volunteers from the region to help organize all the participants, so she had to explain how the sessions would be managed and how everyone would be controlled. There would be lots of quite junior people who would be presenting their ideas, and it would be important to make sure that the managers who would be evaluating the projects did so supportively and kept to schedules. They would be processing over fifty ideas, and although the main purpose was to pick winners in five categories, her principal objective was to make sure the participants felt respected and had an enjoyable time. In the combative way ideas were discussed, particularly in the western businesses, the younger people could sometimes feel crushed.

She would have her chance to talk to the managers on the Wednesday evening, but she knew that whatever she stressed to them before the dinner, they would need to be policed during the Thursday and Friday sessions and the team was vital for that. But she felt, after two hours with them, that they would be up to it.

She took them to the hotel in the afternoon. She'd had emails and conversations with the local manager going back months and felt confident he understood her needs – and recognized that the events would happen in sister hotels in several other cities and in DC in the autumn, so she knew he would be thinking of the feedback to his superiors.

The days had their inevitable share of panics, illnesses, missed flights, AV equipment incompatibility with some presentations but that was par for the course in this type of conference, she thought.

The managers she met on the Wednesday evening, prior to a reception for the participants. A few were missing, some apologies for late flights, some with no messages but, overall, a very good turn out and most of the questions were clearly supportive, just seeking clarity. She made a mental note of two of them whose questions implied scepticism, and she would speak to each of them later to try and make sure they were on side.

During the evening Jack had introduced two older men, Americans, who Claudia had seen at the back in the manager's meeting. One was smiley, the other rather dour.

'We like what you're doing,' said Smiley, 'I know you're very busy, but could you find some time for us tomorrow?'

The board members, thought Claudia, suddenly alarmed. 'Yes of course. If I could get the thing up and running, then I can make time any time after eleven.'

'Eleven suits us fine,' said Dour, 'we'll let you get back to your party.' And they nodded to each other and made their way out, shaking Jack's hand on the way.

'You could have warned me,' she said to Jack as he poured water for each of them. He'd pulled out the champagne, but she'd said no very quickly. She needed to be bright the next day. They settled in the armchairs and looked out of the window. She knew they'd be making love soon but, after the previous night at his place, she knew neither of them needed to rush.

'I'd told you they would be there.'

'But I didn't expect you to spring them on me.'

'But they only said hello.'

'They were at the back of the manager's meeting. You hadn't warned me about that.'

'I think they were impressed by how bossy you were. They're talking to you tomorrow anyway. You can say what you want to say then.'

'And what should I want to say?

'Whatever you want. It's a good programme. I think they want to see how the corporation will use it around the world.'

'I'm nervous.'

'Of course. But what are you smiling about now?'

'Oh, I'd moved on. I was just thinking, I know you're going to fuck me later but it's lovely feeling we don't have to rush. And I'm still a little sore from last night.'

He smirked. 'But I used loads of lube.'

'But loads more enthusiasm.' They both laughed. 'But don't get me wrong, I loved it all. But tonight, maybe, a lovely, long slow sixty-nine.'

'You are my lovely, kinky girl.'

'Well, you started that – and I believe there's more to come.'

His smile turned wicked. 'Definitely, but I love your idea about slow and gentle tonight. Shall we?' And he stood, pulled her up, wrapped his arms around her and kissed her slowly and tenderly.

29

The Americans surprised her. She'd found out a little more about them from Jack during the hurried room service breakfast but not enough to feel she was well briefed. What a board member did was still alien to her, but she knew they didn't devote large amounts of time to the corporation, so Dour's evident understanding of what she was trying to do had gratified her.

'We like to see the corporation trying to get its people focused and enthused, Claudia, it seemed to us that what you're trying to do is important for that.'

'And we liked that you're not going to take shit from managers who aren't on board,' added Smiley.

'Well, the guys with projects are quite junior people who are incredibly nervous.'

'Oh, we understand. It's not going to work if managers start pushing their egos into the room. We thought you did a good job of warning them. But tell us, how do you see this thing globally?'

And she talked about how the regions differed, as she saw it, but how important the basic elements were, how the programme needed grassroots publicity and how struck she'd been by the enthusiasm that had been generated in the regions she'd had direct contact with. And how glad she was that they had found time to attend. That was strange for her, neither showed any flicker of a response to her attempt at flattery.

It was a brief meeting. That was a little unsatisfactory for her. She hoped they were busy rather than bored, but she wasn't sure.

'They loved you,' said Jack, as he dashed from the office, 'see you at the party.'

She wasn't getting enough of him during the day, but she'd had three nights already and they had been wonderful. It wasn't by any means normal she told herself but last night, where they had been in each other's arms all night, cuddling mostly, fucking occasionally, then breakfasting together, had been, in its entirety, the most wonderful night of her life. Could she have more?

Tonight, would be different. She had wanted the big party on the Friday after the conference closed, but there were too many people who had too little time at home and who needed to travel thousands of miles when the day closed, so Thursday it was for the gala evening. She had organized entertainment and she had emphasized, principally to Jack, that any speeches should be short and warm. He had nodded tolerantly at her, evidently annoyed that she thought he might do anything else. But she knew she would see little of him before a bedtime that would be necessarily late. She was effectively the hostess and would be policing the bars to make sure that everyone would realize that the next day was still an important workday.

There were a few recidivists who had settled into a corner of the bar after most had gone to bed but the good-natured among them had dragged the two difficult ones away when she stood beside them and pointed to her watch.

She was delighted to find Jack fast asleep in her bed when she got to her room. She hadn't known whether she would see him at all. She showered and cuddled in beside him. His arms came around her. She turned her back and spooned herself into him, feeling his cock gently rising against her arse. She reached back and slapped his thigh. 'That's breakfast.'

'Too right,' he mumbled sleepily.

And it was. She heard the room service bell as he was down between her legs, kissing her ever more passionately. 'Jack, Jack, we have to let him in!'

She leapt up, wrapped her robe around her, signed the bill, took the trolley and said, 'No, no, please, we'll set that up,' keen to avoid the ritual of having the table prepared in the window, the juice and coffee poured, the simple courses explained. The man took the signed bill, smiled and nodded. She leapt back on to the bed with Jack.

'Where was I?'

'You know exactly where you were,' she said nestling on the pillows and waiting for him to resume. He didn't disappoint.

The final day moved relatively smoothly to a conclusion. She had organized a lunch for the participants while the judges conferred about the awards. She'd wanted to sit with lunch group, but she knew it was more important to get the judging completed on the right lines. It was easier than she had expected, most people seemed to have caught the atmosphere of enthusiasm and wanted to help reach a successful conclusion.

Jack led the final session for her, praising the winners, giving heartfelt thanks to all the participants and generally putting smiles on people's faces. Most seemed to be happy that they'd been there at all and the winners were clearly thrilled they'd be going to America for the corporate final.

She had planned to get the team together to thank them with another meal but had found that they too wanted to get home and were happy with a big group hug and the thank-yous they had received from everyone, particularly from Jack, who'd tried to single all of them out.

So, my dear, free evening for us, I think, or does your team need you? xxxxx

The text came while she was with her team. Jack was in the same large conference room but was being professional to the end. She looked over to him, he winked but then focused again on the group he was talking to.

Nope, they want to get home, does that mean I'm just stuck with you? xx

And I was just reconsidering your treatment! 6.00 my place. Be there!

She smiled but didn't look up.

30

He had the Taittinger ready when she arrived. They kissed. She had been so on edge for the past three days and now, with the work part over, she felt elated, almost shivery from the excitement.

He poured the champagne and handed her a glass.

'Are you happy with how it's gone?'

'I'm thrilled, I think, but I don't really know. Tell me. What was it like?'

'I think it was fantastic, I got a tremendous buzz from everyone I spoke to. Even the guys who were being a bit difficult.'

'What guys?'

He smiled. 'You know exactly who I mean, the ones who were a bit snotty in your briefing and who you had dragged from the bar. You got yourself some grudging admiration. Of course, having a perfect arse gets you attention, it doesn't get you respect but that's what you ended up winning.'

'And my arse?'

'Oh, that got you huge amounts of respect too. But you will have a bit of a problem now, I suspect.' He looked a little serious. She looked alarmed.

'No, no, don't worry. It's going to be a good problem for you, but you'll probably have some thinking to do.'

'What's happened?'

'Rod and Philip spoke to me before they left.'

'Rod and Philip?'

'You know exactly who I mean, but you are not going to trap me into calling them Dour and Smiley or I could make that mistake somewhere important.'

'What did they want?'

'They want the corporation to do more of this. They don't think it does enough to get its people engaged, so they complimented me on pioneering the programme. But at least I could put them straight on that.'

'Put them straight?'

'Yes, you must be very direct with these guys, so I told them I only ran it first, so I'd have a chance to fuck your brains out. They understood that completely, of course.'

'Obviously, you didn't.'

'Obviously, I didn't. But they were very impressed by you, and they wanted to know if I thought you should play a bigger role in rolling this thing out everywhere.'

She looked at him and raised her eyebrows.

'I said I thought you'd be brilliant, but I didn't know how your personal life could be managed. Neither of them regards that sort of thing as a hurdle. Anyway, you may be getting questions from the centre about a different role, especially as Johan seems to have abdicated – those guys didn't rate him at all. Just warning you.'

'Well.' She paused. 'I don't know what to think. I'm thrilled I suppose, but that's not something that happens to me.'

'It's been a year for new things.'

'It has that,' she said, watching him turn to the credenza behind him, open its wide top drawer, and pull a long, black-handled cane from it.

'Yes, some quite striking new things.'

CPSIA information can be obtained
at www.ICGtesting.com
Printed in the USA
LVHW031808310519
619761LV00002B/343/P

9 781903 136652